T0171641

Also by Bill Prickett: *Sow the Wind, Reap the Whirlwind*
For more information, visit ***www.BillPrickett.com***

THE MIND SET ON THE FLESH

Bill Prickett

iUniverse, Inc.
Bloomington

The Mind Set on the Flesh

iUniverse books may be ordered through booksellers or by contacting:

iUniverse
1663 Liberty Drive
Bloomington, IN 47403
www.iuniverse.com
1-800-Authors (1-800-288-4677)

ISBN: 978-1-4502-7814-0 (pbk)
ISBN: 978-1-4502-7815-7 (ebk)

Printed in the United States of America

iUniverse rev. date: 12/17/2010

"For the mind set on the flesh is death,
but the mind set on the Spirit is life and peace."
~ Romans 8:6 (The Bible; NASV)

~~Foreword~~ Forewarned

As I wrote on the back cover of my first novel, I repeat here: this is a story about religious people, but it is <u>not</u> a religious story. Yes, some of the characters are sincere Christians, but others are not. And even those who are Christians don't always act consistent with their faith. Also, there are gay people who maintain a strong Christian faith, in spite of the rejection and obstacles from mainstream churches and religious leaders. In addition, there's mild sexual content (nothing graphic), and some involves same-sex couples. So, I'm providing this word of caution up front for those who might find any of this offensive. But it's also to protect me from the angry reactions of those who thought they'd be reading a different kind of novel. (I got some of those after my first book.) If you do proceed, regardless of your response, I welcome your comments on my website: BillPrickett.com.

A Quick Explanation of "Flesh"

The title of my book is taken from a specific Bible passage, but more than that, it's a dominant theme in Christian theology. (Too much to cover here.) In its basic meaning, the word "flesh" connotes the physical aspect of our life, as in "we are flesh and blood." But it also refers to our basic desires, which are selfish and weak, in need of God's control. Many think *flesh* is only about (sexual) lust, but that's not true. According to the New Testament, *flesh* can also be exhibited as greed, arrogance, anger, dishonesty, malice, envy/jealously, gossip, in-fighting, appetite out of control, the "us" mentality, the need to control/manipulate and many other forms of expression which somehow are more socially and religiously acceptable. So, in this story, the person living the most obvious life of "fleshly" desire is not the only one whose mind is set on the flesh.

Dedication

This book is proudly dedicated to those who use enlightened faith and divine love to share the Gospel truly as a message of "good news." I especially want to thank the incredible men and women of *Evangelicals Concerned*. (www. ecwr.org) They are mentioned in the story and *yes*, they're real. I credit them with the health of my faith today. A portion of the proceeds from this book will be donated to this amazing organization.

Special thanks to my wonderful, diverse, always constructive (often brutal) editors: Robert Dirmeyer, Cherri Gann and Jennifer Jenson. Thanks to Nancy Crabb, who again designed the book cover. She's truly an artist!

And of course, to my loving, supportive and patient spouse. Even as a writer, there aren't words to express the love and gratitude I feel.

PART 1:

Indulging the desires of the flesh

ONE

NOT EVERYONE CAN WEAR A SKINTIGHT tank top. Indeed, most shouldn't try. But as he walked down the street, it was apparent he could. He wasn't a model, but that ribbed, white t-shirt could not ask for better marketing.

One of Kelly Clarkson's songs was blaring through the not-designed-to-be-subtle sound system when he ambled into the dimly-lit bar. Familiarity allowed him to maneuver without the aid of bright lights.

Almost everyone knew him, including the imposing sentry at the front door, who only nodded in his direction. His quick wit and outgoing personality—which could become outrageous after three or four drinks—made him likable and scored him more than a few one-night stands.

As he reached the bar, his drink was already being placed by the bartender. "Here ya' go, Thumper. I'll start your tab."

His real name was Barnabas Rivers, which was more than most casual acquaintances ever learned from him. He was barely five foot, seven inches tall and weighed one hundred and thirty-five pounds. His upper body didn't have the popular v-shape of broad chest and narrow waist that so many men wanted, but he was built solid and worked out religiously to maintain his low body-fat ratio. Tonight, because the late-March weather had graced the city with an unusual peek at summer temperatures, he'd dressed to accentuate his firm build.

His once stark red hair had darkened as he'd gotten older, which he felt made him look less like Opie Taylor. He did still have a hint of freckles, but people who looked at his face rarely found themselves noticing them. His eyes were a captivating shade of blue, with an expressiveness that would rival any silent film star, and could be just as alluring when he turned on the charm. Which was often.

"You're a darlin.'"

Thumper picked up the tumbler and tipped it toward the bartender with tight jeans, no shirt and a practiced smile. He brought the glass to his lips, glancing in the mirror that covered the wall behind the bar. An attractive young man sitting a few seats down was watching him.

Thumper leaned in and spoke again to the bartender, but didn't take his eyes off the reflected image of his prey. "And why don't you give him another one, and put it on my tab."

Once he placed the order, he moved the four-stool distance to sit next to the object of his attention.

"I'm Thumper. Why don't you tell me your name? I know before the night is over, I'll be screaming it out in ecstasy!"

The young man dropped his eyes toward the complimentary drink placed in front of him. "Is that a fact?" he asked casually. His disinterested tone was seasoned with enough flirt to keep Thumper's interest.

Thumper swiveled his bar stool and faced him, but didn't speak. Waited.

"Okay, my name is Jonah Caudle," he said with a sigh.

He had sandy blonde-almost-brown hair, cut short. He had a cute face and Thumper had wicked ideas of ways to use those full lips. He was wearing a light-weight sweater, which prevented knowing much about his physique.

I'll bet there's an equally cute body under that dreadfully large sweater, Thumper surmised.

"Jonah, prophet of Jehovah, who preached repentance to Nineveh. But only after running from the call of God and being swallowed by a large fish. Did you know the Bible never says it was a whale? That's the customary take on the story, but to be true to the Scriptures, it only tells us it was a big fish." Thumper leaned in close. "Not that size matters for a fish...except when it wants to swallow a man."

Jonah was listening to Thumper's discourse with a look of confusion, squirming on the stool as if the seat temperature had increased. "You some kind of uh, Bible student?" He finished by looking around the bar, as if to punctuate the incongruent context.

"Let's just say I know a little something about running from God." He lifted his drink and moved his seat closer to Jonah. "But much more about swallowing—"

"Your name is *Thumper*?" Jonah questioned, cutting off the statement. "It's a nickname, right?"

When Jonah talked, his voice had a deep, polished resonance, but with a shy softness. There was no hint of feminine affectation, nor was there the twang of a Southern accent.

"I made it up...just for you. It's the sound my heart made as soon as I saw you sittin' over here." He placed his hands over his heart and voiced the accompanying sounds. "Thump, thump, thump."

He saw that Jonah was enjoying the story, so he reached over, took the kid's hand and placed it in the same place on his chest. "Feel it? You make my heart beat faster, so Thumper will be *our* special name to always remember this special night."

"Thumper!"

The shout from behind them broke their gaze and they turned to see the person connected to the shrill greeting. Jonah jerked his hand away. "Imagine that! Someone else knows our *special* name."

Thumper waved at the guy rushing up to the bar. A hug and quick air kisses were exchanged.

"Is this your boyfriend?" Jonah asked with more than a little scorn in his tone.

"My roommate. He just got off work, didn't you?"

He put his arm around Jonah and pulled him close. "Matt, this is Jonah." Thumper rubbed his hand across Jonah's chest. "Adorable and delicious, isn't he?"

Thumper pointed to Matt. "And this is my old...oldest...ancient best friend, Matthew. Another of us queer-boys saddled with one of those cumbersome Bible names."

Matt was thin, and enough over six feet tall to be called lanky. He was twenty-four years old—barely a year older than Thumper—with dark hair and dark eyes to match. His olive complexion, combined with his slim body frame, gave him a look one might see on an Abercrombie and Fitch poster.

Matt took a step back and looked Jonah up and down. "Yep, I can see that."

He leaned in and whispered to Jonah, but still loud enough for Thumper to hear. "Hold out for dinner, dumplin.' Enjoy him, but don't fall for him. He's got a cute little body and a surprisingly big dick...for a munchkin, but he's got no heart for love."

Thumper slapped playfully at Matt. "Behave!"

Jonah looked up at Matt. "Can *you* tell me about his name. Thumper?"

"Hmm, which version do I tell him?" he asked in Thumper's direction. Looking back at Jonah, he answered. "Let's go with the animal analogy. It's because, in so many ways, he's like a horny little boy-bunny...without the fur." Matt reached over and patted Thumper on the chest.

"I'm gonna dance," Matt announced. "You two have fun."

Without waiting for a response, he skipped off into the crowd of gyrating bodies.

"You do know he has a huge crush on you?"

Thumper waved off the idea. "He just likes to be the center of attention."

Jonah took another drink. "I may be new to *this*." He made a sweeping motion with his hand, encompassing the entire room, but clearly signifying more. "I may not know much, but I can tell that he's crazy about you."

"And I'm crazy about you," he feigned. "Now, tell me everything I need to know to tell the wedding planner."

Jonah laughed nervously. "I need another drink."

As long as you're relaxed, Thumper thought.

"So, are you enjoying your first time in a gay bar?"

"Who told you that?" Jonah's face showed surprise.

"No need to. Like one of God's prophets, I see into the hearts of men. The fact is, I know *all* about you."

Jonah crossed his arms and waited, with a prove-it look on his face.

Thumper took the challenge, put down his drink and gazed at the young man. "You grew up in a fine Christian home. You were involved in Sunday School from the time you were a toddler."

He noticed that as he talked, Jonah would nod, grin or raise his eyebrows, giving assent to his assumptions.

"You did some mutual masturbation with one of the deacon's kids when you were thirteen or fourteen. You had a crush on your youth director when you were in high school. Everybody tells you that what you're feeling is wrong, but you've prayed and prayed and it won't go away. How am I doing?"

With wide eyes, Jonah asked: "How do you know...about me?"

Thumper gave him a knowing look as he leaned in close. "Because I *am* you. Or at least I was a few years ago."

While he was close, he kissed Jonah quickly on the lips.

Jonah jerked back, his face showing he'd been caught off guard. "Don't get too cocky, Kreskin. You missed a few minor facts: I *was* the deacon's kid and I masturbated with the Minister of Music's son."

"I once had sex with a Minister of Music," Thumper reminisced aloud. "He certainly knew how to play an...*organ.*"

"I wasn't sure about being here," Jonah confessed with a huge smile that utilized his full lips and spread over his entire face. "But I'm really glad I came."

This is going to be too easy, Thumper determined as he tossed some cash on the bar and took his conquest by the hand.

"Let's see if I can make you even more glad you *came.*"

The preacher was red-faced as he spoke with stern authority and equal volume. "God is calling out to this country, 'Come back to me and I will heal your land.' God is reaching out to our nation, 'Take my hand and I will lead you back into prosperity.'"

The two young men watched with raptured awe. They each had a Bible opened on their lap and followed along as the TV evangelist referenced various passages from the Scriptures, some only in passing. They would rapidly turn the pages of their Bible, rushing to the verses as if it were a contest. Often, they would pause the video-taped sermon and discuss a particularly salient point.

"The heart of our loving God is broken over the sin and immorality of this nation. If we refuse to repent, there can be no response beyond what is promised in Biblical prophecies. God is bound by His own promise to bring judgment if this country will not return to Him with our whole heart."

There were tears in Milton Andrew's eyes as he re-read aloud one of the passages the evangelist had mentioned. He closed the Bible and looked over at his friend, Earl.

"I can't believe how much I've missed, brother." Since his conversion experience nearly a year earlier, Milton called all his guy-friends by the family designation. "It saddens me that I've wasted so much of my life."

Milton was twenty-seven years old, and worked in construction, which he'd done since dropping out of junior college after two weeks. It paid well, and for years kept him in a lifestyle that had included an abundance of alcohol and plenty of women. The excess led to a couple of encounters with the law and a near-death experience a year ago. Now he was deeply ashamed of his past, and had committed himself to balancing the moral scale.

"But it's like Brother Jimmy says, Milt. God's grace is sufficient for all our sins." Earl spoke with a tenderness that always touched him.

He'd known Earl Sutton since childhood. Earl's genuine concern and compassion had been a source of support and comfort during his recovery from a serious accident, but he was especially grateful for Earl's role in the personal transformation going on in his life now.

They joined hands to thank God for the lesson, asking for greater insight into the Word and wisdom to make right decisions in life. Milton, as always, was crying and holding tightly to Earl's hands. He silently voiced his oft-repeated prayer that God would give him peace.

Heal my heart and cast out these demons of torment, he begged.

They joyfully and gratefully acknowledged the many wonderful gifts of God in their life. Within moments, they were both quietly praying in that mysterious and wonderful heavenly language God had bestowed on them when they were baptized in the Holy Ghost.

"Where's your new boy-toy?"

Thumper pulled his head from under the pillow and looked up at Matt, standing shirtless at the door. He had a tray with bagels, two mugs of coffee and a carafe.

"He was very cute and I was hoping to see him *nekkid*," Matt said as he took a seat on the bed beside him.

Thumper sat up in the bed, pulled the sheet over himself and took one of the mugs. He drank almost half the mug of coffee and allowed the warmth and the caffeine to do their intended work.

"He was cute, wasn't he? What was his name? John? Joshua? Something biblical."

"You are such a queer," Matt chastised. "His name was Jonah, though I doubt you know the names of most of your tricks."

"I wanted in his pants, not on his mailing list. Besides, I know as much as I need to know. He's a student…at CFNI."

CFNI—Christ for the Nations Institute—was a Pentecostal school for the training of ministers located south of Dallas' predominately gay district. The first time Thumper had attempted to visit the area, CFNI students were standing on a street corner, handing out religious materials. Several of the students had engaged him, quoting Scripture verses and offering dire predictions he knew all too well. He'd been so rattled, he turned and left the area. It had taken weeks before he summoned up the courage to return. And that was when he'd met Matt.

"You do have a sixth sense for that kind," Matt observed, taking a bite of a bagel. "Must be a homing device developed from your own religious past."

The past was something Thumper didn't talk about, so he concentrated on the coffee and bagel. Then he raised one hand in the air like those in his father's church. "The prophet Isaiah said the Spirit of the Lord is upon me to preach good news to the poor, to give sight to the blind and to proclaim release to the captives."

Thumper reached again for the coffee mug and let out a cynical grunt. "And I know of none who needs that more than those poor, blind religious prisoners. I am their…*redeemer*."

"So, when did he leave?"

"Oh, you know how it is for those in the stained-glass closet," Thumper sneered. "He *comes*…he goes. The holy guilt sets in quicker than the dick goes limp. Guess he needed to get back so he wouldn't be late for Sunday School this morning. I'm sure he's busy with full-on repentance, complete with tears of regret, fasting, weeping and gnashing of teeth, all wrapped in his finest Sunday-go-to-meetin' suit."

Thumper took a sip of coffee. "But, in a few weeks…or a few months, when the hormones overshadow the convictions again, he'll come back." He paused, then muttered. "They always come back."

"Can I get you anything?" Matt asked as he poured the last of the coffee.

"Well, since my young Pentecostal penitent ran off so quickly, I was left, as the prophet Daniel put it, 'found wanting.'" He placed his hand on Matt's bare shoulder, massaging softly.

Matt put his mug down and gently moved Thumper's hand. "I'm sure you can...*handle* it yourself. I have to get ready for church."

"But Mattie..." He said with a pseudo-whine. He reached over and gently glided his finger down Matt's chest, following the dark hair line down and across the top of his shorts. As expected, his body responded. His breathing rate changed in response to the attention of Thumper's hand, now sliding beneath the elastic band.

"Damn you," he uttered under his breath as he laid back and allowed the shorts to be removed.

I can always depend on Mattie when things get...hard.

Two

EARL LOOKED AT HIS WATCH AND resigned to another long night. Milton was still kneeling at the altar, with several others standing around him, laying their hands on him and praying fervently. Earl could hear them, but since most were praying in tongues, he knew it would be impossible to know the nature of their intercession on behalf of his friend.

They had been coming to the Wednesday night Bible Study at Eastmont Fellowship for several months now. Though it was a thirty-minute drive from his home in Garland, Earl enjoyed the topics and the discussions, which were often spirited.

There was a time when he rarely attended more than Sunday morning services at his home church. But Milton's passion had also brought an increase in Earl's church attendance—at a variety of congregations and Bible studies throughout the Dallas area. Earl attended as often as his work schedule allowed, and suspected that Milton went to even more gatherings alone.

Following the Bible study and discussions, the pastor would invite those with personal concerns and sickness to come to the altar for prayer. Milton was always the first, and the prayer-time would often stretch late into the evening. It made Earl's early morning shift at the hospital difficult, but he did want Milton to find the peace he so desperately sought.

"God promised to heal me," Milton declared through joyful tears when he returned to the pew where Earl was still sitting.

"Thank you, Jesus," a woman standing behind him added. "We speak it and it's done, in Jesus' name."

Earl stood and gave his friend a hug, then quickly picked up his belongings.

If we leave now, he figured, *I can still get at least six hours of sleep before the alarm goes off at five-thirty.*

Matt was sitting at the table when Thumper came into the kitchen. He leaned down and kissed Matt on the cheek, pushing aside the morning paper and stealing the cup of coffee.

"Hey," Matt scolded with a slap of the hand. "There's plenty in the pot."

"Ah, but don't you know that Jesus told us it's better to give than receive?"

Matt and Thumper lived in a two-bedroom apartment about five blocks from what was considered the gay section of Dallas. When they began looking for a place to share as roommates, they knew they wanted to be close to the bars and restaurants. In the weeks of searching, they toured many apartments in the area. Though they'd both listed 'pool' as a must-have, when they saw this one, they were captivated.

The building was built like a brownstone. Each of the four floors had only two apartments, one on each side of a small foyer. They lived on the second floor. There were beautiful hardwood floors, high ceilings, a floor-to-ceiling bay window in the living room and a working gas fireplace.

"I'll take sex in front of the fireplace over tanning by the pool," Thumper had said on their first visit.

Because it was an older building, the bedrooms were large, eliminating the discussion of who got the bigger room. Matt loved the kitchen, with an adjoining dining area. Thumper liked that his bedroom had one blank wall, which he used for bookcases to display his growing library.

Thumper did a long, slow stretch, with accompanying groans. "And that was certainly how it worked last night, with that new bartender from Razzles."

Matt folded the paper and looked up. "You nailed that gorgeous blonde surfer-boy?"

"Oh, yeah," he bragged, as he poured more coffee. He stretched again. "Every muscle in my body aches this morning. But I'm sure he's sore in very different places."

Matt rolled his eyes. "That's the third this week, isn't it? And it's only Thursday. Better save some strength...and bodily fluids...for the weekend."

Thumper grabbed his coffee and headed to his room. "Gotta shower and get to work. If I'm late again, Sharon will castrate me."

Thumper started working at Page Turner Bookstore at the end of his sophomore year. The store was located in an upscale shopping center in North Dallas, a short commute from school and home. Sharon, the owner, had allowed him to work part time during school and full time during the summer. Since graduating a year ago, he'd worked full time. Sharon had asked when he planned on leaving to pursue his career, but he told her that he had no definite plans and no clear career goals for now. She seemed pleased and he knew it was because he essentially functioned as her assistant manager and was her best sales person. His avid love of reading was an asset.

"Well, *that* would certainly put a crimp in your weekend activities, wouldn't it?" Matt mumbled as he turned his attention back to the newspaper.

"You got plans tonight?"

It was late on a Friday afternoon, and Matt knew what that question meant. He turned his eyes from the TV to Thumper, who'd just come in from work. "Do you wonder why I never ask *you* that question?"

"You wanna order pizza and rent a movie?"

Matt looked at his watch. "Won't you miss your whore nap?" It was Thumper's usual routine to take a nap after work on Friday, before going out for a long evening at the bars.

"I'm not going out tonight," he informed with a sigh.

"Friday night, and Thumper ain't gettin' no nookie?" To emphasize the mock surprise, Matt put his hand on both side of his face and manufactured a look of shock.

He walked over and sat beside Matt. "My folks are coming in town and they want to meet tomorrow for breakfast, so I have to get up early in the morning. I was thinking we rent a video, have a couple of beers and then maybe...who knows?" He raised a single eyebrow.

"Has the list dwindled to this?"

Thumper put his arm around Matt. "I *could* go out and spend the evening at the bars and eventually score, but—"

"But I'm easier. And convenient. Like a good fuck-buddy should be."

Thumper stared at Matt in confusion. "It's not like that. We're good together. And there's no complications, no head games. What's wrong with that?"

Matt pulled away enough to be able to turn and face him. "Don't you ever want more...hope for more, Thumper? Do you ever think about falling in love and settling down?"

The laugh was sarcastic and severe. "We're queers, brother Matthew. We don't fall in love, because our desire is unnatural. God created man and woman. We, dear boy, are an aberration. A testimony to the flesh out of control. Haven't you read the first chapter of Romans?"

Matt looked up at him with a sadness Thumper didn't understand. Or didn't want to understand.

"Well, I think you're wrong."

"Then you would be in a minority, my innocent Methodist friend." Thumper again pulled Matt closer and patted him affectionately on the head. "It's all there in the holy book. God condemns us to the damnation of hell fire."

"That's your father talking!?"

Thumper withdrew his arm and leaned back on the sofa. "He only preaches what Christians have believed for hundreds of years."

"So, do I finally get to meet your parents?" Matt was clearly changing the subject.

"I'm the only queer they know," he said, shaking his head. "Or so they think. 'Course, I haven't told them about the singles' minister, the guy in accounting, or the graphics designer, or the—"

Matt held up his hand to stop the discourse. "I've known you since our sophomore year and never met your folks."

"And I've known you the same amount of time and never even *asked* to meet your parents."

With arms crossed over his chest, he answered, "My parents are dead and you know it."

"And you are all the better for it, dear saint."

Matt pouted. "I thought…as close as we are…that it would be nice to meet them."

"Trust me, Mattie, there's nothing nice about meeting my parents."

"They must love you, or they wouldn't want to see you."

It sounded logical, but Thumper knew better. A tug of long-suppressed emotions requested recognition. It was a tenuous stew of nostalgia, guilt, anger and outright fear. As had become his habit, he refused to give in.

"They love *Jesus*," he countered. "Me? They feel I must be restored to my former state of sanctification. I'm sure they would call that the highest form of love." He looked back at Matt. "Tomorrow will be a day filled with Dad quoting the Bible, lots of weeping by Mom along with numerous invitations to repent of my sin and return to the fold."

This time, Matt hugged him. "Then don't go. We'll go out to a movie in a real theater. Afterwards, we could hit the bars and drink until we can't stand up."

"I like my idea better," he whined with a fake flutter of his eyes.

"Let me go take a shower," Matt sighed as he headed out of the room.

Thumper resisted a triumphant smile. "I'll help wash the hard-to-reach places," he offered, following into the bathroom, shedding his clothes on the way.

Thumper looked at Matt, sleeping on the other side of the bed. He let out a deep breath of envy at his ability to fall asleep so easily and sleep so soundly.

Now that lust had been expended—and cleaned up—it was too quiet to mask the clamor in his head and he had time to think. He was apprehensive about the impending visit with his parents, which was rarely enjoyable. The tension had developed over a period of time, but he could distinctly remember that it started out with a seemingly innocent decision.

"I want to go to Dallas-Southwest University," he'd told his parents early in his senior year of high school.

Dallas-Southwest University was located south of the city, in Oak Cliff, a once-thriving community that had seen—and endured—the ravages of ethnic, racial and economic changes. The school had a national reputation for business and management.

"Barnabas, that's so far away." His mom's voice indicated that tears would soon follow.

"Do they even have a degree in theology?" There was a typical sternness in his dad's voice.

He had prepared for the discussion. "Uh, I don't plan to study theology. DSU has an awesome communication program, and I plan to combine it with classes in nonprofit administration."

"We could sure use your help with the ministry," his mother said. "It's growing every year."

Barnabas had been in church since birth. His skills in leadership emerged early, and with his outgoing personality, he was well liked by those his own age and respected by adults. He worked extensively with the youth group in the unofficial role as assistant youth minister and spoke frequently to large gatherings of young people who attended his dad's evangelistic crusades across the country. Most people assumed he would follow in his dad's footsteps, possibly even one day taking on the pastoral mantle for the congregation in Birmingham his dad had built.

"I appreciate that, Mom. But I already have a ministry. I got a job...in Dallas."

His dad's right eyebrow went up. "Doing what? Where?"

He'd waited to spring this news on them until everything was settled. "I'm going to be the Minister of Youth at Inwood Worship Fellowship."

Now his dad smiled slightly. "Pastor Carl's church? When did all this come about?"

"In April, when our youth choir went out there to sing during spring break. He told me the church had budgeted for a staff member, to start in the summer and asked if I knew someone who'd be interested. I told him that I had applied to DSU, and he offered me the position." As Barnabas related the story, he talked noticeably fast.

"It's part time, but it'll help with school expenses. And I got an academic scholarship and a partial soccer scholarship that will also help. I didn't want to say anything until it was all official. The letter came last week, while y'all were at the crusade in Pasadena. The scholarships cover everything, except my meals. If I keep my grades up, I can apply for additional financial help next year."

Thinking it would help, Thumper also shared how a member of his dad's church—a successful DSU alumni and an elder in the congregation—had helped with the application process. The man wrote a glowing letter of recommendation, extolling Thumper's exceptional credentials: graduated top of his high school class, valedictorian, president of the student body, an award-winning member of the debate team, captain of the soccer team, and voted most likely to succeed.

Of course, what he didn't included in the story was that he *needed* to get out of Birmingham. As far away as possible from an affair that he'd recently ended. Guilt was crushing him and he felt if he could lose himself in school and the work of the ministry, God would eventually relieve the internal struggle. But he'd determined that if relief were not possible, distance would be the next best thing.

He watched for any negative reaction, then proceeded. "I really want to do this. I think a degree in communication would help me, no matter what ministry opportunities come along."

"The work of God doesn't just *'come along,'* son," his dad said with his typical solemnity. "God is in control of providence and He will guide you."

His mother looked as if she wanted to speak, but his dad continued. "My heart tells me that the move to Dallas is part of God's plan for your life and your own ministry. You have a great many gifts, son. Your ability to memorize Scriptures is beyond anything I've ever seen. Your passion and your leadership are a powerful asset—one that God will surely use for His kingdom. I trust you, Barnabas. And I trust the Holy Ghost in you to make these kinds of decisions."

He would always look back on that conversation as the first time he realized his father's much-hyped ability to know the Will of God by discerning the voice of the "Holy Ghost" was not infallible.

THREE

WHILE EARL SPREAD OUT THE BLANKET, Milton peeled off his tank top and put it on the ground. He was a tall, well-built man, developed from years of strenuous construction work. His tan made it obvious he liked to work without his shirt.

Earl was a stark contrast; at five feet, ten inches tall, he was shorter than Milton's six foot, one-inch frame. He was on the heavy side and self-conscious about it, as Milton once found out when he asked why Earl was still wearing a shirt in the ninety-plus degree temperature.

"Not everyone has the kind of body that looks good without clothing," Earl had answered. "You happen to be blessed with one. I'm not, so there's no reason to inflict the sight of my fat belly on innocent by-standers."

Milton sat down on the blanket and took out his Bible from the backpack. Earl grabbed two sodas from the plastic cooler and handed one to Milton.

It was becoming a weekly ritual, depending on Earl's weekend work schedule. They'd meet at the local IHOP for breakfast or lunch, then to the park for Bible study and discussion. Usually, they would listen to taped messages of their favorite preachers; most often, it was Brother Jimmy, since he was the one who'd made the biggest impact on their lives.

Earl had known Milton since they were kids living in Garland, a community about twenty miles east of Dallas. Though he was three years younger, they'd played together when they were kids. That is, until Milton got into high school and was too busy...or too cool...to hang out. After Milton graduated, he moved away from the neighborhood, and they'd lost touch.

About a year ago, he saw Milton again, in a most unexpected circumstance. Milton had spent an evening drinking, following his break-up with a girlfriend. While driving home, he over-estimated his ability to take a curve and crashed into a tree. He was taken by ambulance to the hospital in Garland. Once Milton had been moved out of the emergency room, he was placed in a room on the floor where Earl worked as a nurse.

The reunion did not start out cordial.

"I thought you wanted to be an architect," Milton chided when he saw Earl in the green scrubs.

Earl laughed timidly. "Yeah, and at one time I wanted to be an astronaut. People change."

He tried to appear busy with the machines around Milton's bed.

"But being a nurse is kinda sissy, ain't it?" Milton taunted with an alcohol slur.

He walked to the other side of the bed. "We can't all be manly and wrap our pick-up truck around a tree after an evening of drunken revelry."

"I diddunt mean anything by it, kid. I'm just a bit…" Milton didn't finish the obvious sentence.

Earl relaxed his scowl, then explained. "It's okay. After school, I tried to get on at the fire department, but I couldn't pass the physical. I thought if I went to nursing school, I might could eventually become an EMT. But I found I really like doing this, so I stayed."

"Actually, I'm glad you're here. I could use a friendly face. I figure I'm in deep-shit trouble."

He patted Milton on the arm. "Is there anything you need?"

"A priest would be nice," Milton muttered.

The next day, there was a marked difference in Milton's mood. The anger was gone, but he was visibly solemn. "My life's fucked up, Earl. I need to get it right."

Earl looked up from reading his medical chart. "I'll say! Do you know how dangerous it is for you to be drinking with the medication you're taking?"

Milton blushed slightly. "After talking with that preacher you sent—"

"He's the hospital chaplain," Earl corrected. "It was as close to a priest as I could find."

"I 'preciate it, man. He read the Bible to me and prayed with me. It felt good. I need to get myself right, man. That is, if I'm not in jail."

Earl held Milton's hand while he cried, talking softly to calm his anxiety and fear.

As it turned out, Milton didn't go to jail; the judge gave him a short suspended sentence. Earl was at the trial with him and had even spoken in his behalf, alluding to his bipolar disorder and suggested that Milton was unaware of the potentially deadly combination of medication and alcohol.

Leaving the courthouse, he asked Earl, "Do you still go to that church?"

"As often as my schedule allows. Why?"

"Think I could go with you on Sunday?"

Earl wavered. "I'm not sure you'd like it. It's nothing like the Catholic Church."

"I ain't really been a Catholic in a long time. But I know I need something."

"It's…Charismatic."

Earl then detailed for his unenlightened friend what that meant and what to expect. "The services are pretty contemporary, with lots of singing and clapping. Folks raise their hands during the music. Even speaking in tongues. It can get very, well…animated."

"I promised God," was Milton's only response.

"Sure. It won't be our regular preacher. We're having revival meetings this week, and we got this evangelist coming to preach."

Not only did he go with Earl on Sunday, but he returned for every service the rest of the week.

"I've never heard anyone like Brother Jimmy," Milton confessed to Earl about the guest preacher after one of the services.

Before the crusade was over, he'd made a public profession of his faith in Jesus and requested to be baptized as a member of the church.

The changes were almost immediate. His vocabulary went from profane to praise. Money once spent on his vices now went to various ministries and to an abundance of Bible study materials. His truck literally became a rolling testimony to his new-found devotion—the bumpers were replete with pithy proclamations of his budding faith.

"You have to listen to this one," Milton insisted, as he handed a cassette tape to Earl, who was laying out snacks on the blanket. "It's this preacher from Tulsa. He talks about hearing God. For so many years, I thought only priests could hear God."

Earl took the tape and promised to listen to it later. "Did you get any sleep at all last night?"

"I was in the Word until after three." He never looked up from his Bible.

"Milton, can I ask you a question? As your friend, but also as your nurse."

"You want to know if I'm taking my medication," he answered, this time glancing briefly at Earl, but quickly returning his attention back to the Bible. "Well, I am. I just can't believe how much there is to learn, and I'm so grateful that God is my strength for this journey. Brother, I am wired on the Holy Ghost."

Earl placed his hand lovingly on Milton's arm. "Please remember, Milt. Jesus also came to give rest to our souls. You should try to get some sleep. You won't be any good for the Kingdom if you collapse from exhaustion."

"'Those who wait upon the Lord,'" Milton quoted from the prophet Isaiah, "'will run and not be weary.' I love that you worry about me, brother, but I can do all things through Christ who gives me strength," he affirmed, now quoting the Apostle Paul.

FOUR

As THEY DROVE OUT OF DALLAS, Jim looked over and saw his wife wipe a tear from her eye. "We should be thankful," he said. "I sense in my spirit that the Lord sent this man to help Barnabas."

They were headed to a four-day revival at a large Pentecostal church in Tyler, about two hours outside of Dallas. The crusade would begin tomorrow, at the Sunday morning service and continue through Wednesday night. They'd just had breakfast with their son, which usually left Jim troubled and frustrated. But this time, he was feeling hopeful.

Jim Rivers—or more precisely, Dr. James David Rivers—was the Senior Pastor of Charisma Community Church in Birmingham, Alabama, the largest Pentecostal congregation in the denomination. He was a third-generation preacher and bragged about his pedigree: his grandfather had been part of the birth of the Pentecostal movement in California at the turn of the twentieth century.

Jim was the first to attend school to prepare for the ministry, though he'd only completed the three-year ministry training program at a small denominational school, then received his honorary doctorate from his alma mater after his ministry became successful and his donations increased.

Nationally recognized as a fiery evangelist and teacher of Pentecostal beliefs, he was known for his unwavering faith in the Bible as the absolute Word of God and his hardcore message on the necessity of a pure, chaste life for Christians. He was renowned for his insights into how cultural and political affairs related to—or were in violation of—the teachings of Scripture. He was regularly invited to be a guest on religious news programs, like *The 700 Club*, and had been featured several times on Fox News programs.

Also integral to his message were what was commonly known as "Word of Faith" principles. Like others in the movement, he taught that in order to receive the blessings of God—especially healing and financial prosperity—the believer must combine the Word of God with active, vocal faith.

"It matters what comes out of your mouth," he proclaimed. "With our positive words, we ignite faith to produce results, or with our pessimistic words we curse our lives. When we say the same thing that God says, we see His work manifested. When we moan and whine and complain, we reap the rewards of our own negative confession."

One of the reasons his church in Birmingham had grown over the years was due to its early involvement in television. The church's weekly worship services had been televised for decades, first on a local station and then expanding to cable. In recent years, the church also purchased air time on several religious networks for various evangelistic crusades, elaborate Christmas and Easter productions from the church and, most recently, weekly Bible studies taught by the pastor. His televised crusades were among the most popular in the country, and sales from his books and tapes were considered the backbone of the financial structure of the ministry. He operated the highly successful national television outreach ministry called *Rivers of Life* broadcast from the church's fifteen-acre facilities on Birmingham's far east side, and he and Gwen also hosted a weekly religious talk show. It was estimated that millions watched the various broadcasts.

Jim was a rotund man; people had too much respect to call him obese or fat. It was estimated his weight was pushing three hundred and fifty pounds, though no one but his private physician knew the exact number on the scale.

At fifty-eight years old, he still had a full head of thick, dark brown hair. His deep, resonant voice had several levels of loud and his round face would turn crimson when he was preaching. His hell-fire messages were accompanied by profuse sweating, no doubt due to his size and lack of exercise. He attributed it to the "anointing of the Holy Ghost," giving an intensity to his messages, but this was also something that brought voiced concern from his private physician.

Gwen wiped her eyes and gave Jim a gentle, loving smile. "I'm sure you're correct. I thank the Lord that he promised to help. Heaven knows, we've tried everything else."

Most of the time, Thumper was the epitome of hyperactive happiness. *Perky* would be an apt description, though he would reject that term because it wasn't butch enough. And being butch was important to Thumper.

"My parents inflicted me with the name Barnabas to instill a sense of purpose," he admitted once when asked about his always-up disposition. "The name means 'encouragement' and damned if God Almighty didn't see fit to build that very nature into my personality. I only get *down* when I'm dancing...or sucking dick!"

But that wasn't entirely true. Matt had seen him down on several occasions, and they always corresponded to a visit with his parents. His mood would turn uncharacteristically sullen and conversation would be nearly nonexistent.

This afternoon, as soon as Matt walked into the apartment from an aerobics class, he could sense the distinct difference. Thumper was sitting on the sofa, staring down at the *TV Guide* in his lap. It was apparent the magazine served only as a focal point for his empty stare.

Matt leaned over and kissed him on the head. "You want something to eat?"

His eyes never left the magazine. An ever-so-slight shrug was the only response.

Matt walked around the sofa and sat beside him, moving the magazine to force Thumper's attention. "Want to talk about it?" Based on past experience, he didn't actually expect an answer.

"How can Christians be so mean?" Thumper mumbled.

Matt waited for a further explanation.

Thumper exhaled heavily. "How can Christian parents be so selective in their love. Why can't they love me? Not the 'me' they want me to be. Just *me*."

Matt decided to lighten the mood. "Are we going to start singing *Just as I Am?*"

He looked over and wrinkled a slight smile. "They can accept an alcoholic. They can forgive an adulterer. I've seen them embrace drug addicts and visit murderers in prison, but when it comes to their own son..." He didn't even finish the sentence.

In reflex, he pulled Thumper closer and squeezed him tight. "I accept you, sweetie. Even though you can be an arrogant, self-absorbed, narcissist horn-dog, I accept you...just as you are."

Thumper huffed an actual chuckle. "You have a great future in grief counseling." His hand wandered toward Matt's lower region.

"Why don't I make us some dinner?" Matt stood up, deflecting the inevitable advances. "Do you want to tell me about it?"

Before Thumper could reply, his cell phone rang. "Oh, hi," he heard Thumper say. "Yes, they told me you'd be calling."

Matt couldn't hear much beyond that because he took the phone into the bedroom. But whoever it was, he heard Thumper agree to meet that evening.

Probably a hot date to release some of his anger and frustration, Matt concluded.

"Thanks for meeting with me." The greeting had a sincerity that Thumper couldn't deny. "Your father is such a wonderful man, and I was so honored that he asked me to talk with you."

His name was Winston DuMont. He stood to shake hands when

Thumper arrived, and he was at least six feet tall. His ink-black hair looked like it had fallen into place, with enough natural curl to make it appear slightly tousled.

He had all the classic features one would expect from the latest soap opera hunk: square jaw, tanned face, white teeth and what appeared to be a well-built body under his *Oral Roberts University* sweatshirt. Small, wire-rimmed glasses framed and highlighted his hazel eyes.

To Thumper, the imprinting on the front of that sweatshirt delivered a clear message, revealing as much about this man as any external visuals. Oral Roberts University was a Pentecostal school in Tulsa, founded by the well-known evangelist to train students in both academics and Biblical principles. *Conservative* would be an understated description of the school. The bold clothing billboard made him a bit self-conscious about being seen with Winston.

"I'm here because I promised my Mom. And that was only to stop her from blubbering in the restaurant. She was cramping everyone's happy meal."

They were sitting at a small, round metal table outside a coffee shop and bakery. The dining area, while actually inside the upscale NorthPark Mall, was made to resemble a sidewalk cafe somewhere in Paris. The items on the menu all had cute, French-sounding names, there was a fake wax-covered wine bottle on each table and the floors were even painted to look like cobblestone. The illusion was broken when the young, gum-chewing waitress arrived at their table.

"What ch'all gonna have ter-day?" she asked in her heavy accent, which would be keeping with the theme, if it were Paris, Texas.

They both ordered coffee, which only seemed to frustrate her. She left with a exaggerated huff.

"They care about you very much," Winston insisted. "You have to know that, don't you, Barnabas?"

He stiffened, and it must have been obvious.

"Is it okay for me to call you Barnabas?"

"My *friends* call me Thumper. I'm not sure what *you* can call me yet." His tone was terse and his gaze remained on Winston.

"Fair enough," the man said graciously. "I want you to know that I'm not just here because of your parents; I'm here because I've been where you are, and I think I can help."

"Dad's the one who thinks I need help," he emphasized. "Contrary to what my parents think, I'm content with my life."

This meeting was a mistake, he determined. *But I did promise Mom.*

"I have someone we'd like you to meet," she'd said while they were having breakfast earlier in the day. "He was a guest on our show a few weeks back."

He couldn't resist a quip. "Mom, are you tryin' to fix me up?"

"We need you to be serious about this, son." His dad's tone was gruff and impatient, which meant he should be quiet.

"This young man is extraordinary," she beamed. "He was…he's…uh, he has some wonderful insights from God's Word about your…situation. I think you would benefit from talking with him."

It suddenly became all too clear to him, and he reacted. "Is this one of those freaks who've gone through some kind of gay-to-straight-fix-it program?"

"It wouldn't hurt to hear him out," his dad said sternly.

He was going to object, but his mom started to cry. He released a sigh which he knew she heard, then mumbled, "If this guy doesn't mind talking to a brick wall, then fine, I'll meet with him."

Now, in spite of his resistance, he was totally fascinated by the man. It was rare that he was distracted by outward beauty, but this guy was so damned gorgeous he couldn't help but stare at him. Listening took extra effort.

"Then help me to get to know you. How did you get the name *Thumper*?"

He almost launched into one of his many well-rehearsed fabrications, but for some reason, decided to go with the truth. "My full name is Barnabas Taylor—Taylor is Mom's maiden name—and when I was young, the kids called me B.T. for short. Then, in middle school they started calling me Bible Thumper, since I was a bit, shall we say, outspoken in my zeal for the Lord. It later got shortened to *Thumper*….and that stuck."

"Yes, I've heard about your early involvement in the ministry from your mother. She goes on and on about what a powerful and positive influence you had on the young people of the church. They were…*are* so proud of you."

Though he didn't say anything, his mouth turned downward and he rolled his eyes. He took a sip of coffee, which was now lukewarm.

"You contend that I don't know you, but I believe I do, Barna…uh, I think I do. Truth is, I used to be much like you. I lived in New York, had a nice apartment, was on the fast track with my career—"

"Underwear model?"

"No, I'm an attorney," he answered calmly, though he did blush slightly at the concealed compliment. "Back then, while I was in school, I was into the bar and cruising scene. I did my share of sleeping around with lots of guys. The one-night stands were so casual and meaningless. Eventually, they all ran together. It reached a point where it was no longer about the sex, or the person. It was the chase and the conquest that mattered. I used those men to affirm that I was someone other people could love…even though love certainly had nothing to do with it."

"Stop," Thumper said with a snide smile. "You're making me want to book a trip to New York."

Winston gave him a sad look, then continued. "Deep inside, I knew I wanted more, but couldn't seem to find it. That's when I began going to a men's Bible study with one of the guys from school. They showed me that what I was missing was God's ultimate plan for my life. And I think the same thing is missing in your life. If you were truly honest, you'd tell me that casual sex is not what you really want. Am I correct?"

"Were you a top or a bottom?" Thumper wanted to see if he could rattle him.

Winston didn't skip a beat. "You can be as flip as you want about this, but I firmly believe you are throwing away the gifts that God gave you. God can change you."

"Bullshit!" was his only response.

"I can't believe that with all your knowledge of the Bible and your strong Christian upbringing, you doubt God's ability to bring about real transformation in a person's life. God did that...is doing that...for me."

Thumper leaned over the table. "So let me get this...*straight*. You *were* gay, but now you're a bona fide heterosexual-type man. You're telling me that when you beat off at night, you think of Angelina Jolie and not Brad Pitt?"

Winston crossed his arms onto the table. "I'm here because I care for your eternity—"

"That answers my question," Thumper concluded aloud.

"Do you think God is pleased with the way you're living your life right now? Look at all the opportunities and privileges you've been given. Your parents have devoted their entire life to the ministry. By the time you graduated from high school, you had more ministerial experience than most men in the pulpit today. There is still so much that you can do, if you'd let God heal you of this sin."

Thumper shook his head. "In my opinion, you're the one with the problem, Mr. DuMont." The contempt could now be heard in his voice. "You want *me* to be honest, but I think you're hiding the truth about yourself. Don't you know the Word, my brother? 'You shall know the truth and the truth shall set you free?' I think you still struggle with those evil lusts of the flesh, but you can't admit it. So, you recruit and try to reform others, hoping...wishing... that in the process, you'll convince yourself somewhere along the way. It's like some perverted form of Amway."

For a few seconds, Winston didn't say anything. He took a slow drink of water, then looked up at Thumper. "This is not about me. This is about you... and what God wants for you. With your skills, personality and overall charisma, there's no limit to what you could accomplish for the Kingdom—"

Losing patience, Thumper slammed his fist on the table. Several people in the cafe turned and looked. He leaned in and intentionally lowered his voice, though the tone clearly communicated his anger. "This is the *same* Kingdom of God that won't allow me to enter? That *is* what we're told in First Corinthians, isn't it? 'Do not be deceived. Neither fornicators, nor idolaters, nor adulterers, nor homosexuals, nor sodomites will inherit the kingdom of God.' I am a homosexual *and* a sodomite, Winston. I'm attracted to men and I love fucking men. That buys me an express ticket to hell."

Winston nodded with an obvious understanding. "But that passage gives hope that we can change—"

Thumper threw up his hand to interrupt. "Don't you think I've *tried* to change?" He let out a deep, long breath. "I've been to several therapists, all at the request of my parents. I've prayed and fasted and cried and begged God to take these desires away from me."

He drank the last of his coffee, then slammed the mug on the table. "You have no idea how much I've tried. I've confessed my sin, renounced my sin, written all my sins down on paper and burned them. I've even repented for the sins of my ancestors, because one person told me their sins had been passed down to me. Folks told me that I needed to believe more or to pray more or to read the Bible more. I've been told to hold onto to God. I've been told to let go and let God do it all. I've had the elders of the church anoint me with oil, claiming the promise of healing from the book of James. In the process, they cast out every demon they could name. But you know what? The desires were still there."

"I'm sorry for all you've gone through," Winston said sympathetically. "But I still believe that God can restore us to His original design."

"Several years ago, I paid money to attend a workshop on inner healing." His tone was now thoughtful and reflective. "Someone said the key to overcoming my homosexuality was dealing with past trauma. All the literature promised lasting results, and there was glowing testimonies of those who'd been change, so I was very hopeful. I paid extra to have one-on-one sessions with the counselor. And you know what happened? In our second session, the guy made a move on me." He laughed caustically. "I let him give me a blowjob, then demanded a full refund.

"Over the years, I've read countless books on the subject, and none of 'em can even agree on the cause, much less the solution. A smothering mother. An absent father or an overbearing mother. It happens as a result of sexual abuse. How can anyone be cured when no one knows the fucking cause? Short of cutting my dick off, I think I've done it all. But the feelings didn't go away. The goddamed desires are still there."

When Thumper finished the tirade, he was fighting back tears. He was surprised to see there were also tears in Winston's eyes and the lawyer gave a sympathetic nod.

"I understand. Believe me, I do."

Was that some kind of confession? Thumper wondered.

Before he could explore the meaning, Winston continued. "I certainly don't know what causes our same-sex attractions. It's complex, deeply rooted and obviously many people have strong opinions about the solution. You must not give up."

"No, you got it wrong! According to the Apostle Paul, God gave up. I'm sure you know that passage, don't you? 'For this reason *God gave them up* to their vile affections.' God…gave up…on me! That's the inspired Word of God…right? God gave me over to my unnatural desires of the flesh. So I am now determined to be the best homosexual there is."

Thumper leaned back in his chair and crossed his arms across his chest and grinned with pride. "And I am. Trust me, I give better head than a porn star and I can fuck like a robot. I'd be willing to show you…any time."

For a brief second, if that long, there was something in Winston's eyes.

Was it interest? Or did I finally startle the stunning ex-gay evangelist?

Whatever, there was an equally fast recovery.

The meeting didn't last much longer. Neither man yielded their arguments. Winston encouraged Thumper to give their discussion some serious thought and asked about the possibility of seeing one another again.

"I'm certain I'll see you in my wildest wet dreams," Thumper replied with a devious grin.

FIVE

MATT WAS IRONING SHIRTS WHEN THERE was a knock on the door. It was his Sunday afternoon ritual to get all his shirts pressed for the entire week. He sat the iron upright and slipped on a shirt. When he opened the door, he immediately recognized the young man from CFNI that Thumper had picked up one night a few weeks earlier.

"Jonah," he said. "Thumper's not here, if you were supposed to meet him."

There was obvious disappointment on his face. "No, I thought he might be...I just needed...well, wanted to talk with him."

They always come back, Matt remembered Thumper saying.

"Do you want me to tell him you came...uhm, that you stopped by?"

"Doesn't matter, I guess." Jonah shrugged, and turned to leave.

"Would you like to come in? I'm a pretty good listener." He stuck out his hand. "I'm Matt Martin, by the way...in case you didn't remember from the bar."

Jonah walked in as Matt closed the door. He was taller than Matt expected. The only time they'd met—at the bar several weeks earlier—Jonah had been sitting on a barstool. Matt was six feet, one inch tall and they were eye-level when Jonah passed him. At the bar, Thumper had described Jonah as "adorable and delicious." Looking at him now, Matt decided that was an understatement.

"You like him, don't you?"

"Uhm, excuse me?" Matt stammered.

Jonah looked young and preppy—his sandy brown hair neatly combed and his shirt tucked into his khaki pants, which Matt assumed was a requirement for the Bible College's strict dress code. Jonah's age was probably early twenties, Matt guessed.

"I saw the way you looked at him, that night in the bar. You like him...as more than a roommate. But he doesn't like you in *that* way, does he?"

Matt chuckled. "You ever think about switching from theology to matchmaking?"

"He told you I'm a ministerial student?"

"We're best girl-friends. He tells me everything."

Jonah's face reddened. He sat on the sofa and Matt took a seat in the chair facing him. Jonah was clearly upset.

"I know it hurts," Matt said. "You're now part of an exclusive club—those of us who've slept with Thumper. Probably not more than five or six thousand of us. And that's just here in the Dallas-Fort Worth area."

"That's all I was, wasn't I? Another on his list of conquests."

"Hey, don't let it get to you. I've been on the receiving end of his charm, too. Pardon the pun."

"I wasn't going to see him again. But..." Jonah's voice trailed off to nothing more than a deep breath.

Matt got up from the chair. "I think we're gonna need more than soda. Do you drink beer?"

"It's not allowed at school." He laughed. "But then, neither is going to a gay bar. I'd *love* one."

Matt walked to the refrigerator and grabbed two cans. "He has a way of getting inside you, and that has nothing to do with sex." He handed Jonah a beer.

"It was like he was reading my mind."

Matt smiled as he sat back down. "I've never understood it, but he seems to have some innate ability...a special awareness to those in—what's his term?—the ecclesiastical closet."

"That's for sure. He's a walking enigma. He can quote Scripture one minute and in the next breath, talk as nasty as a longshoreman."

"He says it helps him call forth the sinner inside every saint."

"I wonder why he's so cynical about the Christian faith."

Matt thought for a second. "I think it has to do with his upbringing. His father's a preacher and pretty strict."

"How long have you known him?"

"We went to school together. When we first met, he was as green as you were that night in the bar."

"I can't imagine that," Jonah said.

He smiled at the memories. "We were both too young to even get into a bar. It was about half way through my sophomore year..."

"Don't we have a class together? " he asked the cute guy sitting next to him. "American History, I think."

It was a Friday night and Matt had gone to Hunky's, a local hamburger joint, after a long day at the cable company where he worked in the customer service call center. The job allowed him flexibility for school: he could schedule his classes in the morning and then work five to six hours in the afternoon. It prevented him from taking a full load at school, but the money served to augment what he got from student loans.

The young man looked up from his dinner with an obvious panic on his face. "It's just…I've never…I didn't expect to see someone I knew…here."

The meaning was clear. They were in the gay section of Dallas. Situated on Cedar Springs Road, the four-to-five block strip was home to numerous gay-friendly eating establishments, with a wide variety to appeal to many tastes and budgets: hamburgers, American home-style, Chinese, Italian, Mexican and a couple of sandwich shops. There were also gift shops, clothing stores, a video store, a card shop, a tattoo parlor and a bookstore that had been the hub of the gay and lesbian community for more than twenty-five years.

Within the gay community, the section was known casually by the street designation—Cedar Springs or simply "the strip." Rainbow flags lined the street and it was the only place in the city where same-sex couples felt comfortable—and safe—enough to walk down the street holding hands.

Of course, there were many bars and clubs catering to the large gay and lesbian population of Dallas, but the Cedar Springs area had the most in a small proximity. Again, there was something for all interests: country and western, dance club, leather, piano and lesbian.

Hunky's was popular as a place to fuel up before going out to various bars in the vicinity or just to watch the endless parade of gorgeous men. On this evening, Matt was sitting at the counter since there were no tables in the small dining room.

"Don't worry," Matt assured the anxious man on the seat next to him. "I won't tell the teacher." He put out his hand. "I'm Matthew Martin, but I prefer Matt."

"My name is Barnabas Rivers." He took the extended hand. "But most folks call me Thumper."

"If I'd known that, I'd have used my cartoon name, too."

Thumper laughed and seemed to relax. "Okay, if you could have a cartoon name, what would it be?"

"If you're Thumper, I should be Bambi. Or maybe Roger Rabbit. Seems fitting, doesn't it? Two little boy rabbits…doing what rabbits do best."

Thumper gently placed a hand on Matt's leg. He felt a surge of energy and accompanying blood flow, rushing from where Thumper's hand was touching to the area that he hoped would become useful later.

"How'd you get that nickname?"

Thumper flashed a salesman smile, and with a totally believable tone, explained: "I get nervous around gorgeous men, and my legs start shaking, making a noise like the one Thumper made in the movie. It's happening now, you know." He winked at Matt. "If you don't believe me, put your hand on my leg and feel for yourself."

They didn't linger for dessert.

The entire weekend was spent together at Matt's small apartment near the strip. It wasn't just sex—though that happened often and with an intensity Matt had never experienced before. They went to a movie, walked around NorthPark Mall, ate almost all their meals together and talked for hours.

"What are you studying?" Thumper asked while they were waiting on the pizza to be delivered. It was Saturday afternoon, and they had finished enjoying one another for the second time that day. They were still naked in bed.

"Haven't totally decided. My Nanna…uhm, my grandmother wants me to be an accountant. She equates working with other people's money as being successful."

"What do your parent's want?"

"They both died when I was young. Car accident. I don't remember them. I've lived with her since I was three. What about you?"

"Unfortunately, my parents are alive and waging holy war against all things immoral and queer. My Dad is a old-time 'penny-costal' preacher and he would *not* be happy with my lifestyle choice these days."

"So they don't know?"

The sound that came from Thumper was something like a cough, mixed with a gasp. "No way! My father would call down the judgment of God on my sin!"

"Do *you* think it's a choice? And immoral?"

Thumper's tone got serious. "I was raised on a strict diet of hell-fire Bible teaching. The Scriptures are very clear."

"My church doesn't teach that, so I've never thought about it. I came out when I was in high school. Nanna even let me go out on dates with boys."

Thumper made a disapproving clicking noise with his tongue. "Dad would be quick to tell you that your church is wrong. The Bible declares it's an abomination for men to do what we just did. The Apostle Paul invokes the wrath of God on us and assures us that we will not see the kingdom of heaven."

A knock on the door interrupted the discussion, so Matt quickly slipped on a pair of gym shorts and went to get the pizza.

As much as he'd enjoyed their first weekend together, it was a couple of weeks before he saw Thumper again. They ran into one another at Crossroads bookstore, across from Hunky's where they'd first met.

"Hey, Mattie," Thumper greeted, bounding up to where Matt was perusing the magazine section. "How you doin'?" he asked like they'd seen each other just last night instead of six weeks ago.

Matt wanted to be cold and detached. After that incredible weekend together, he'd waited an acceptable amount of time and called, leaving

Thumper what he thought was a cute, sweet and casual voice mail message, but never received a return call. Nothing!

"I'm doing great," he exclaimed, in spite of his plan to be aloof.

Dammit, he scolded within. *Be cool.*

"Sorry I didn't return your phone call," he said, as if reading Matt's thoughts. "School has been crazy and I'm dealing with lots of personal crap. I'm starting a new job at a bookstore up in Preston Park Center. It's only part time, but the owner is flexible with my school schedule. I hope you'll let me buy you a cup of coffee to show my repentance."

How could anyone stay mad at this cute little guy?

Of course, the coffee only served as a stimulus for an evening of conversation, then back to Matt's apartment. At two in the morning, when Thumper was getting ready to leave, he promised to call. "Let's get together and do this again," he'd suggested.

It was evident that Thumper was enjoying his "coming out" process and was more interested in playing the field than having a boyfriend. Matt would see him occasionally around the strip, and they hooked up a couple of times.

It was Thumper who first suggested living together, a few months after they'd first met. "Hey, I need to find a roommate to help cut expenses," he announced one day when they were having lunch in the college cafeteria. "You interested…or know of someone who might be?"

He confided that he was reluctant to tell his parents about his current financial difficulties. "They did not like it that I left my last job. And my new job doesn't pay enough to satisfy all my…extracurricular needs."

Matt wanted to believe there was more to the invitation, but within a few months of moving into the two-bedroom apartment just off Cedar Springs Road, he could tell it was solely based on finances and friendship. He made the effort to move on in his own dating life, and enjoyed the occasional no-string-attached, always-intense sex with Thumper.

"Am I keeping you from something?" Jonah's question brought Matt back to the present.

"Yes, my ironing. And thank you," he answered with a smile.

"Have you eaten? I was about to fix something. It won't be much, just some pasta and salad, but you're welcome to stay." He couldn't believe how much he was enjoying spending time with Jonah.

Jonah followed him into the kitchen and they continued talking while Matt prepared the meal.

"What do you do?" Jonah asked.

"I'm a Customer Service Manager for Showcast Cable. I help oversee the call center, making sure you get prompt and polite service when you call to bitch about your bill."

"Do you like it?"

Matt rocked his hand from side to side. "I've worked there through most of college, so when I graduated back in December, they promoted me. My degree is actually in accounting, but after four-plus years with the company, it's hard to find anything else that pays as well with the same benefits."

Jonah didn't immediately reciprocate with his own details—Matt wasn't sure if that meant he was shy or ashamed—so he decided to take the lead. "How 'bout you? You go to school full time? Do they allow students to work off campus?"

"It's a Bible College, not a monastery. So yes, they do allow us to go out amongst the heathens…as long as we wear our protective armor." He smiled at Matt, and even gave a quick wink.

"I work part time as a web designer for SnynapTech. We're an IT company, and we contract with businesses to handle networking, installation, support and training, plus we do web hosting."

Jonah shared that he'd gone to community college in his hometown of Houston, where he'd gotten an Associate's degree in website design. He was pursuing ministerial training at Christ for the Nations because he wanted to strengthen his faith and possibly use his skills in some kind of ministry. The diploma from CFNI required five semesters, with the option to get an advanced diploma once it was completed. He would finish up the final semester over the summer, and was already planning to enroll in the advanced program in September.

"What's your church background?" Jonah questioned.

"I started going to a Methodist Church back home in Little Rock, and when I moved here, I found a nearby church. Between school and work, I haven't been that involved, but I'm there on most Sundays."

"Do *you* think it's possible to be gay and Christian?"

Matt stirred the spaghetti sauce. "You guys make my head hurt with all your deep theological discussions. I guess I'm too simple to worry about it. I've pretty much always known I was gay, and I've been going to church since I was a teenager. I'd never heard all the hoopla until I met Thumper. Or if I did, I didn't pay attention."

"That would be so nice," Jonah said with a reflective tone. " At least once a month, the subject gets attention at school—in the classroom, at chapel services. Even at meals. And the last two times I visited a church, it came up in the sermon. It's like that's all some folks can talk about. So in the past few weeks, I've decided to try to figure it out…for myself."

"You had a visitor earlier."

Thumper had entered the apartment after his shift at the bookstore and heard the announcement coming from the kitchen as he flopped down on the sofa. "Yeah? Who was it?

Matt came out of the kitchen, wearing a pair of shorts, no shirt and an oversized apron. "The cute little twink you met a few weeks ago—the one from CFNI. He wanted to talk to you."

"*Talking* was not what he wanted, trust me."

"Whatever. He was here for several hours, and now I'm behind in my chores."

"This sounds…intriguing. I notice you're half-dressed. Can I assume that you and preacher boy….?" If his meaning wasn't obvious enough, Thumper finished with a series of punctuated groans, moans and lewd finger-in-hole hand gestures.

Matt put his hands on his hips and huffed. "Stop writing me into your porno movie. He's mixed up and hurting. He thought you might be able to resolve some of his religious issues about being gay and Christian. I'm not good with that stuff, but I let him talk. And listened. He's really sweet."

"I'm sure you are just what he needed. Hope you got pictures."

Matt scowled at him.

"Okay, here's my advice to him: You don't get to do both. Pick one. Forget the other."

Matt rolled his eyes, then walked—loudly—back to the kitchen. When the phone rang, Thumper instinctively grabbed it, but then wished he'd checked the Caller ID first. It was Winston DuMont, the ex-gay zealot.

"I know it sounds trite, but I was praying for you. Since you were on my mind, I thought I'd call to see how you're doing."

"As long as I'm on your mind, that's all that matters," Thumper said with an unmistakable hint of flirting. "Maybe God will answer both of our prayers."

"Have you given any thought to what we talked about the other night?" Winston asked, without acknowledging the not-so-subtle innuendo.

"Let's just say I've thought of *you* often. And I assume you've given your negative to my parents?"

The man exhaled slowly into the phone. "Your parents only want the best for you, Barnabas."

"That's crap!" He spared none of the emotions he was feeling, and spoke loud enough to bring Matt out of the kitchen. "My parents don't want me to be an embarrassment to them and their reputation. How would it look if their devoted minions knew they had a queer son?"

"They love you. If you can't see that, you are truly deceived, my friend."

"That's where we differ. I'm seeing very clearly and I think it's you who distorts the truth. You don't know my parents…beyond their TV ministry. And you don't know me, beyond what you know about my sexuality. That makes you either the most arrogant person in the world, or the most naïve."

"I only want to help—"

"I don't doubt that, Winston. I think you're probably a nice guy and given another time and place I would welcome the chance to get to know you… especially in the biblical sense. God knows, you're gorgeous. But I think you see me as little more than another star in your crown for Jesus. Fact is, I'm not going to change, and I can't see you renewing your membership in the lavender boys club, so this conversation seems a bit pointless. Thank you for calling, but I have to go." He hung up the phone.

"That was…intense," Matt noted, still standing in the kitchen doorway.

Thumper took a deep breath and let it out slowly. "Sorry. My parents insisted I talk with this guy who claims he's been healed"—he emphasized the word with a high-pitched voice and hands raised toward the ceiling—"of his homosexuality. He's a bit pushy."

"And cute, I take it from your conversation."

Thumper fanned his face. "So pretty he makes my teeth sweat. At first, I thought I might be able to bring him back to the dark side, but none of my Jedi mind tricks work on him. I'll have to keep him as a fantasy when I whack off."

He looked up to see Matt with a strange expression on his face. "Everything okay?"

———————

Matt stood in the doorway, wondering how much to reveal.

"I know who your father is," he responded meekly.

There was a long silence. Matt was uncomfortable and wondered if he should have mentioned it.

"When did you figure it out?" Thumper didn't look up at him.

Matt walked into the living room. "Actually, not long after we moved in together. You got a card from your mom and it was embossed with your father's organization."

"But you never said anything?"

"It's always been clear that you didn't want to talk about it. I didn't want to pry."

Thumper finally grinned. "You're a good friend, Mattie. I'm sorry to be so secretive. Part of it is habit and part is guilt. Plus I reckon I'm tryin' to protect them. If word got out their son is gay, it might hurt Dad's ministry."

Matt sat down. "And you are a good son. I hope they know that."

"I wish I could be what they wanted me to be, I truly do," he admitted. "I would love to find a good woman, get married, have a family. I want all that, but know it can't happen. Why would I pretend to be someone else and ultimately fuck up some girl's life?"

"What about being happy with who you are? I think you are a wonderful, caring person. Can't you believe that you are exactly the way God made you?"

Before Matt even finished, Thumper was vigorously shaking his head. "It goes against everything I was taught. Deep inside me, I believe that the Bible is God's truth for our lives and our behavior. According to the Bible, homosexuality is an abomination. So, I can't accept my desires as anything other than sin against God."

"That makes me sad for you, Thumper. There's no way to be happy. You are destined to always feel like you've failed…your father *and* God."

"I've accepted that I'm gay." Thumper took in a deep breath and let it out slowly. "But I know I'll never be accepted by God, or my father."

"I've actually watched his program a couple of times. Thought it might help me to…" Matt shrugged his right shoulder.

"You figured if you understood him, you'd get to know me better."

"Something like that."

"So, what you think of dear ol' Doctor Rivers?" Thumper asked with a mischievous gleam in his eyes.

"Well, it's very…uhm, different than what I'm used to, that's for sure. He's…he is certainly a, uhm…powerful speaker."

Thumper howled in laughter. "Don't get much hollerin' and spittin' in your Methodist church? Did you feel the power of Holy Ghost convicting you of the heinous sin of ho-mo-sex-u-al-ity?" he mocked.

"What if your father is wrong? What if being gay is as much a part of you as the color of your eyes? I certainly don't know the Bible like you, but I'm gay, and I consider myself a Christian. I don't see it as an either-or proposition. It seems wrong to me that you can admit you're gay and cannot change, but you can't believe that's because God made you that way."

Thumper folded his arms. "I wish I felt that way. I've always admired how comfortable you are in your own identity." He leaned in and kissed Matt on the cheek, then picked up the remote control and turned the TV on.

"I put some pasta in the oven for you." Matt stood up, knowing the conversation was done. "Now I have to finish my ironing."

———————————————

When the phone rang, it woke him from a dead sleep. He startled up in bed and grabbed the receiver, mumbling his "hello."

"I'm afraid," Milton whimpered from the other side of the call. "There's so much to do. So many people, lost and dying without Jesus."

Earl hoped the sigh that escaped couldn't be heard by his distraught friend.

Here we go again, he determined. He looked at the clock. *Two-twenty.*

"There's too much evil in the world. How can we even make a dent in the power of the enemy, brother?"

They had been to church several hours earlier. As usual, Milton had participated in the after-service prayer time, so Earl had not gotten home until after eleven.

"You are doing something, Milt," he insisted, still trying to be comforting. "*We* are doing something. Every action makes a difference, especially in God's eyes."

"How can it ever be enough?"

He turned the light on and sat up in his bed, resigned to another late-night conversation. "What's got you all upset, Milton?"

"These new tapes from Brother Jimmy. They're so powerful."

Earl knew about the tapes; Milton had talked about them for several weeks. *America is Sick! What We Can Do to Bring Healing* was a series of Bible studies the TV evangelist had been hyping heavily for the past few months, with promos on each of his broadcasts. By ordering the entire eight-tape set, the ministry would also include a DVD of live praise and worship music recorded at Brother Jimmy's church. An additional bonus: each person who purchased the hundred-dollar collection, the preacher promised to put their name on his personal prayer list. Milton wanted to be on that list, and had been saving to purchase the tapes.

"When's the last time you slept?" Earl pressed.

"I can't sleep, brother. There's so much to do."

"And you can't do anything if you're exhausted, or if you make yourself sick."

"Jesus is my Physician and my Healer," he snapped. "He is keeping me well and giving me strength. Don't put those negative words of sickness on me; I refuse to receive that curse…in Jesus name."

This time Earl sighed without worrying about being heard. "Milton, I am not putting any curses on you with my words. And we both continue to pray for your healing. But if you remember, God revealed that until your healing comes, you need to take care of yourself and stay on your meds. Remember?"

It had happened last week, during a Sunday night service at a church they frequently visited. Milton went to the altar for prayer and as he was returning to where Earl was seated, a woman who was highly respected as a prophetess walked up and proclaimed that God had spoken to her.

"The Lord will heal you," she declared to Milton with Old Testament seriousness. "It will be in His timing and by His ways."

For a moment, Milton had seemed disappointed, but finally accepted her prophesy, and promised to keep taking his meds.

Was that only five days ago? Earl now wondered.

"We should hit the street," Milton proposed.

"Huh?"

"Brother Jimmy talks about all the problems in our world and how they're related to the lapse of national morality. We should go out and preach to those who need to hear the good news. We can hand out tracts and talk with those who will listen."

Earl agreed, mainly because the plan seemed to help Milton's mood, but also because he had to get up in a few hours.

Milton promised he would turn off the tapes…and the lights…and try to sleep.

SIX

"DO YOU HAVE ANY SELF-HELP BOOKS on how to craft a heart-felt apology?"

Thumper looked up from the cash register and was surprised to see Winston DuMont, the ex-gay eye candy. He was dressed in what Thumper assumed was typical lawyer attired. The white shirt didn't look as crisp as it probably did in the morning when he put it on, but that certainly didn't distract from the tailored fit over his athletic build. His tie had been loosened, showing just enough chest and hair to magnet Thumper's attention. But not more than the end of the tie; like an arrow, it pointed to an area that had assaulted Thumper's fantasies on numerous occasions since their first meeting.

Damn, he looks good, came the instant thought.

He forced himself to remember who this man was and what he represented.

"What the hell are *you* doing here?" He knew immediately he'd spoken too loud; several customers in line gave him a stunned look.

Sharon, the bookstore owner, walked up behind him. "Is everything okay?"

He turned to her, his angelic Sunday School smile securely in place. "Sorry, boss. He's uh...I know him. I'll take care of this."

"How did you know I worked here?" he demanded once they'd moved down the counter, away from the registers.

"You told me," was the too-casual answer. "Remember?"

"Showing up here is a little...*stalker-ish*, isn't it?"

"Not really. I had a meeting with a church board in Highland Park, and thought I'd come by."

"I assume you aren't really looking for a book?"

"I didn't like the way we left our last conversation. You haven't returned my phone calls, so I thought I'd drop by."

"You're persistent, I'll say that for you."

Winston did a slight, polite bow. "I like 'persistent' much better than 'stalker-ish.'"

He smiled, bringing such a kindness to his handsome face. "I really would like another chance to talk," he insisted. "How 'bout we get some dinner?"

Instinctively, Thumper looked at his watch. The store closed at nine, which was three hours and fifteen minutes away. "I'm scheduled to lock up tonight," he informed, as if he needed an excuse not to accept the invitation.

"I'll take care of that," Sharon interjected as she joined them at the end of the counter. "Why don't you balance your register and then you can go. We can't have you turn down dinner with such a *beautiful* man. It would be a tragedy. And so unlike you."

She tossed a flirty grin at Winston, then let out a silly giggle when he returned the gesture.

"You heard the boss," Winston said. "I don't want to be held responsible for any damage to your legendary reputation."

"Okay," Thumper huffed in her direction, then walked around the counter. "Why don't you browse around, sir?" he advised with artificial formality. "Might I direct you to our section of gay fiction? Should give you some conversation ideas for our dinner later?"

"I'll get some coffee and wait for you," Winston replied courteously, pointing to the in-house coffee shop at the front of the store.

After counting the money from his register, he walked to where Winston was sitting, reading a newspaper.

"I get to choose the restaurant," Thumper announced.

"Deal! But I won't pay extra for food served by male strippers."

The look on Thumper's face must have been a combination of surprise, confusion and a bit of intrigue.

"It's a joke, man," the lawyer clarified with a smile.

"So, here we are," Thumper said, once they were seated at Carlo's, a small Italian place near the bookstore.

"And I want to thank—"

Before Winston could finish, the waiter arrived at their table. "Can I get you something to drink," he purred at Winston, putting the water glasses on the table, but never taking his eyes off him. "Maybe a cocktail or glass of wine before dinner? We also have some specials, which I'll *gladly* tell you about."

The overture was as understated as a street corner hooker, though Winston seemed oblivious to the blatant flirting.

Thumper enjoyed watching. Strangely, he also realized that he was a little jealous. Which was annoying.

"I'd like a glass of Cabernet," he bellowed to draw the waiter's fixed gaze from Winston. He thought it would irritate his dinner companion that he was ordering alcohol.

It didn't. "Make that two," Winston said, giving a smile-infused nod to the fawning waiter.

"Don't let my Dad know you drink...even wine. In his opinion, all drinking is sin." He let out a laugh. "I reckon everything is sin to him."

Winston came back with "Jesus turned water to wine."

"Sure, and he'd rejoice at the miracle, but then request it be changed back before drinking it."

"Well, like the Apostle Paul taught, I believe there's nothing wrong with most things...in moderation."

"Moderation is so over-rated. Give me excess every time. More is better—especially when it comes to liquor...and men."

Winston waited a moment before speaking, in a kind voice. "You enjoy being provocative, don't you? You like to shock people. I think it's a defense mechanism, to avoid letting anyone see the *real* you."

A grunt. "So now you're a therapist?"

"Call it a concerned observer."

The waiter brought the two glasses of wine and sat them on the table. "Would you like something to...*eat*?" he cooed, again with full focus on Winston.

I might as well be invisible, Thumper lamented.

They ordered a large pizza. Thumper also ordered a double rum and Coke.

"I see what you mean about moderation?" Winston teased.

"Have you even noticed that our waiter is nearly doing a lap dance to get your attention? I'll be surprised if he's clothed when he brings our food."

Winston did a quick glance in the vicinity of the kitchen, then shrugged. "Maybe I'll invite him to the *Circle* as well. We could make it a threesome."

Thumper snickered. "And you call me provocative."

"Would you be willing to tell me about your background? I'd love to know more about your past, aside from the glowing stories I hear from your parents."

"You first," Thumper came back.

When he hesitated, Thumper taunted. "Oh c'mon. I'll show you mine, if you show me yours. Besides, you have the advantage of knowing about me from talking with my folks. I know nothing about you, except you used to live in New York and our waiter is ready for you to be dessert."

Before Winston could speak, the drink arrived and Thumper took a long sip, savoring the warmth of the alcohol as it went down.

"Tell me about your sexcapades," Thumper requested. "Start with your first time—"

"I decided a long time ago that talking about my sexual history is not healthy for me. Since it's in my past, and I'm not the same person I was back then, I find it serves me best to focus on the wonderful work of healing God has done since that time."

Thumper faked a yawn. "That explanation should not be taken while operating heavy machinery. It's okay to just say it's none of my business."

During dinner, he did learn that Winston was originally born and raised in Atlanta. His father was a successful attorney and his mother—a former

Miss America contestant—was a social worker. Using what Winston termed "courtroom interrogation tactics," Thumper was able to find out that Winston graduated with honors from Columbia Law School, one of the top schools in the country, and specialized in nonprofit law.

"My practice provides legal services to nonprofit organizations," he explained. "Most of my clients are religious, but I do some work for charities and foundations as well. To me, it's important at the end of the day to feel like it mattered that I went to the office."

The combination of striking good looks and a genuine desire to help people made him a difficult person to dislike. Obviously, with four years of college and three years of law school behind him, he was older than Thumper. After some coaxing and calling him "grandpa," he finally admitted that he was "much closer to thirty than to twenty." And to Thumper's delight, in the process of his personal discourse, Winston did divulge that though his parents had paid his law school tuition, he had supplemented his income with modeling jobs.

"I knew it," Thumper boasted. "Please tell me you did swim suits."

Winston shook his head, but Thumper wasn't sure if that meant he didn't or that he wasn't going to talk about it.

"But it was modeling that almost cost me everything. It's a lifestyle that can pull you down quickly. The glamour is exciting and the attention is flattering, but the temptations are many."

"One can only hope," Thumper said lasciviously.

"It felt so shallow and empty. Once I was going to the Bible study, I took fewer modeling jobs. As the reality of God's love began to sink in, I knew I wanted more than what's visible on the surface."

"Don't discount the fine job God did on the surface, though," Thumper remarked, causing Winston to blush slightly. "How did you get to Dallas?"

"When I finished law school, I had several offers. I considered a couple of places on the East Coast and almost accepted a job at a firm in San Diego. But each time I prayed about it, I couldn't get a sense of divine peace about the decision. Then when I interviewed with a national nonprofit organization here in Dallas, it felt right. I've been here about three years."

"What organization? I thought you had your own practice?"

Winston took a sip of his wine. "My primary client is the National Council on Religious Freedom, an organization of churches and religious groups all over the country who are committed to maintaining our religious liberties. I convinced them that instead of hiring me, they should put me on retainer. It was enough to get my practice up and running, and it allows me the autonomy to do work for other clients and keep up involvement with the restoration program."

There was an involuntary roll of Thumper's eyes. "That's the one where you go in as miserable queers and leave as happy heterosexuals?"

"It's not that simple, but we do try to help those hurting from sexual confusion, bad decisions, addictions...a whole host of issues."

The lovelorn waiter arrived with the pizza and hovered while Winston took a bite. "Is everything to your liking?"

"I'll have another drink."

The waiter left, without acknowledging if he'd heard Thumper's order.

"How do you find time to do your lawyering and lead this group?"

Winston held up a finger to signal a delay in his answer as he finished chewing a bite of pizza. "Oh, I'm not the leader, though I do serve on the board of directors. The group is part of *Full Circle Ministries*. They have an active outreach to the...to those with sexual brokenness."

Thumper couldn't resist. "I assume that 'full circle' doesn't refer to a circle jerk?"

Winston ignored the bait. "There are many aspects to the ministry. We have the weekly *Circle* meetings, which are open to anyone. When a person decides they're ready to change, they enroll in the *Full Circle* program."

"What happens when someone joins this merry-go-round?" He used his finger to make a circle motion.

"It takes a commitment. There's counseling, workshops, group sessions, accountability partners...and we all participate in the weekly *Circle* meetings as well. The ministry is a community for those of us with a common issue— our sexual brokenness. Once involved, we can share what's going on inside. There's a real healing power that comes from the encouragement, empathy and support of the guys in the group. It's a safe place, where we are free to talk about our struggles, our victories, our failures and our challenges."

That got Thumper's attention. "Failures? What does that mean?"

"We aren't perfect...and we're on a journey to wholeness."

Thumper was suddenly much more intrigued. "You...you've...uh, failed?"

"Not tonight."

The wisecrack brought Thumper instant amusement that mirrored on his face with an unintentional smile. He reminded himself that he was supposed to dislike this man. And that was more difficult than he'd imagined.

"Those of us in the program want to resist giving into the patterns of our brokenness, but sometimes we don't," Winston disclosed. "With the *Circle*, we can be honest. So when we need to discuss problems...or failures... the group is there for us. And we can do it with the assurance of complete confidentiality."

"How does it work?"

"I like to tell people it's more like forming a diamond out of coal and less like microwaving popcorn. It's a long term process, not a quick fix."

"But that doesn't tell me how y'all *'de-gay-ify'* a person."

"We're hooked into a national network of other reparative organizations. That gives us access to resources such as training, literature, professional therapists, seminars," Winston used his hand and fingers, as if counting the resources while he talked.

"Our executive director, who also came out of the gay lifestyle, is a licensed counselor and specializes in the treatment of sexual problems, such as orientation dysfunction, sexual addiction, abuse and gender identity, so we're able to provide one-on-one counseling as well. I help out with peer counseling, since I've been…well, I've been involved for a while."

"But…does…it…work?" Thumper's tone was intentionally firm, and he enunciated each word for emphasis.

Winston cocked his head to the side and looked confused. "Why else would I be here? The ministry has a proven success rate. More than three-quarters of those who enter our program will graduate to lives of healthy sexual expression."

Thumper's face must have conveyed his ongoing skepticism.

"I think if you came to one of the group meetings, you might be surprised."

Thumper's laugh was loud and mocking. "I'm sure that's true."

"You could come as my guest. No one would need to know your story, unless you decided to tell them."

His eyes got narrow and a sly grin formed. "Wouldn't the guys in the group be suspicious if you bring a date?"

"Only if we make out during the prayer time," Winston retorted. "But I do hope you'll consider it. I'd love to change your preconceptions about who we are and what we do."

To Thumper's surprise, the waiter had heard the order and his cocktail arrived. But not surprising, the waiter was able to set it in front of him without taking his eyes off Winston.

Winston looked at his watch. "Wow, we've been talking about me for way too long. It's your turn." Winston stared at him, waiting.

"I'll assume you want to know when I knew I was gay. Or are you more interested in my first gay experience? You may not talk about your sexual conquests, but I can give you explicit details of mine. It will take *hours*," he said with conspicuous pride.

The offer was ignored. "Your parents figure you experimented after you got to college. I suspect you were wrestling with it long before that."

Thumper grinned, and gave a quick wink. "You would be correct, lawyer-man. I knew the feelings were there since I was a kid. I was having wet dreams around fourteen, and they always involved being touched by other boys. I had my first actual sexual experience when I was in high school, the summer before my senior year. I was spending a couple of weeks as a counselor at a Christian retreat. One night, after the campers had gone to bed, a camp director invited me to his room. And that was my first sexual experience."

"It was an adult?"

Thumper shrugged his only reply to the shocked outburst. He took another drink from his cocktail, then waved his glass at the passing waiter to order another.

Winston was shaking his head. "That not only illegal, it's immoral. I hope you reported him."

"Hell, no. After that, we met on a regular basis. He taught me a lot. Liked to talk dirty during sex and loved it when I—"

Winston held up his hand. "I get the picture. There's no need to be explicit."

Thumper was relaxing from the alcohol, and for reasons he couldn't explain, decided to open up to Winston. "Okay, that's not completely truthful."

"So the waiter doesn't want to give me a lap dance?"

Why does he have to be so charming and funny? Thumper wondered. *It would be easier to dismiss him if he were a jerk, like most Christians I know.*

"No, about my affair with the counselor. He was the Minister of Music at a church in my hometown, and I wasn't as comfortable with it as I led you to believe."

Winston put down the slice of pizza and raised both eyebrows, giving permission to continue.

"At first, it was so thrilling and new. The feelings—those feeling that had been there so long—finally had a way of expression. But all the things I'd been taught made it hard…" He snickered at his pun. The alcohol was now making him silly.

"After a while, I felt bad about what we were doing. Yes, I did enjoy the sex. And he was so adoring of me and so complimentary of my body. But afterwards, I felt…"

"Guilty?" Winston filled in the pause.

Thumper wrinkled his nose as he considered the question, then took a big swig of his cocktail.

"I was ashamed and infatuated at the same time. It lasted a few months and finally I gave into the guilt and told him we had to stop. He was furious and threatened to expose. But I ain't stupid. He was married and on staff at a huge Baptist Church in Birmingham, so he had too much to lose."

"What did you do after that?"

"Once it was over, I threw myself into the work at church. I was there nearly twenty-four hours a day. As I said, moderation has never been my strong suit."

"So you were trying to…what? Appease God?"

"More than anything, I figured the busier I was, the less time I'd have to, you know, feel those feelings. And when the job here in Dallas came open, I thought maybe it was a sign that things were changing."

"How long were at the Inwood congregation?"

"Almost two years, started the summer before my freshman year and left at the end of my sophomore year. It was a difficult decision; I loved that group of kids and we had so much fun together."

"From what I've heard, you were very good at it. They still talk about you with such love and affection."

Thumper sat up in his chair. "I certainly hope you aren't doing some kind of spiritual background check on me. That would also be a bit stalker-ish."

Alcohol had loosened the controls on his volume and his words came out louder than he'd intended.

"Not at all," Winston assured. "But I work with one of the guys who used to be in your youth group. He has mentioned what an impact you had on his life."

"One of the kids works at your office? That's cool. Who is it?"

"It's not like that," he corrected. "But I want to stay with our conversation. For almost three years, you didn't have the feelings. You were serving God, you were happy, you were successful. You enjoyed working with the kids and you were doing something that you loved. What happened?"

"They came back," Thumper answered with a noticeable sadness. "The feelings came back. I tried to resist. Thought if I ignored them, they'd go away again. But we know that didn't happen. I got to the place where I would masturbate just to relieve the sexual pressures, so I could concentrate on other things. But since I was fantasizing about guys, it was little more than a treatment of the symptom…not a cure for the illness."

"When did you…you act on the feelings?"

Thumper thought about it for a minute. His brow wrinkled and his eyes rolled back as if responding to the calculations going on his mind. "It was about midway through my sophomore year, I think."

"Was it with someone in your youth group?"

Appalled, Thumper nearly shouted, "God, no!"

Winston's brow furrowed as he spoke in a matter-of-fact tone. "It happened to you like that, but you didn't think it was wrong for the adult minister who seduced you."

"I would *never* do that!" he repeated strongly. "I loved those kids and tried to help them. Even…" He stopped. "Wait a minute. I had a guy in my group who confided in me that he thought he might be gay. He was really struggling with it. Owen…Owen Daniels. Is that the person you know from the church? Is he part of your circle jerk?"

Winston was stoic, his legal training was obviously in control. "Our group values privacy and confidentiality. I cannot disclose anyone's name. I'm sure you can understand that."

Thumper was certain he was right. Moreover, he now knew he could never go to the group meeting, no matter the reason.

"Well, Owen's situation did stir up my own desires," Thumper confessed. "So, after I finished listening to him one night, I went to the gay section of town, met someone and we went back to his place…"

Thumper momentarily lingered on the happy memory of the first time he'd met Matt.

"And the guilt?" Winston interrupted the reminiscing. "Was the guilt there also?"

Thumper let out a long breath. "Yes, to a lesser degree. More than anything, it was now an internal struggle with my ministry. Should I even *be* in the ministry? What if someone found out? What could I say to Owen? I mean, how could I help them when I couldn't handle my own problems? Eventually, I decided to resign."

"Your parents wondered about that. That is, until you told them about your homosexual activities."

"Yeah, they took that really well," he murmured sarcastically.

"Barnabas—"

"Hey, I've poured out my deepest secrets to you. That earns you the right to call me Thumper."

That made Winston smile, and Thumper enjoyed that he'd been able to get that response.

"Ever been in love, Barna…uh, Thumper?"

"If this is a proposal, I'm not the marrying kind."

Winston didn't join his laughter, so Thumper got serious. "I don't believe in love. I'm gay, but I know that's more about sex than it is about love."

"What about before? Did you date girls before…before you chose this lifestyle?"

"I had a girlfriend back in Birmingham, while I was in high school. She was sweet and I truly cared for her. We talked about getting married once I got to college. But we know how that would have turned out."

"So you *do* believe in love," Winston pointed out. "You just don't think it's possible to be gay and be in love. Doesn't that tell you there's something wrong?"

"He is the very definition of an 'enigma,'" Thumper said to Matt, once he got home from his dinner with Winston. "Sometimes I think I'm getting signals from him, but there are other times when I feel like he's repulsed by me and the idea of all things gay. He throws my gaydar way off."

"Wow, that's never happened. But we both know your fondness for the religious type. Is this just your pecker over-ruling your logic?"

"There's no doubt that lust is involved. He's drop-dead gorgeous, but seems completely unaware of it. Which only makes him that much more attractive, dammit. He's a dyed-in-the-wool do-gooder, dedicated to making the world a better place to live. But I still don't think he's being totally...uh, straight with me. Pun intended. I mean, can he truly be *straight*? I can't get a clear read on him."

"You make him sound too yummy to be true," Matt said with a salacious grin.

"He is, in fact 'yummy.' But he's not only easy to look at, I actually enjoy spending time with him. I found myself being way too honest with him. Told him things that only you know."

"Well, I was surprised that you were seeing him again, after that conversation you had with him on the phone."

"Hey, no one was more surprised than me. He'd left like four messages on my cell phone, and I ignored them. I'd written him off as another of Dad's fanatic followers. But when he showed up at the bookstore today, being all sweet and such a gentleman...and standing there all handsome and humble. What could I do? And I'm glad I did. He's sensitive, charming and compassionate. He's the kind of guy you could take home to meet your mother."

Matt put both hands on his hip. "Don't make me quote *Fiddler on the Roof.* You cannot fall for this guy because it cannot work. You are from two different places. You're gay, and he's...well, he's...the *anti-gay!*"

Thumper waved him off with a casual gesture. "You know I don't do the falling-in-love thing. I mean, talk about a doomed relationship. I can't see him going sixty-nine with me and I sure as hell ain't planning to go straight for him. But if he called right now and invited me to meet him again, I'd go in a New York minute."

Matt gave him a serious look. "And that's what bothers me."

SEVEN

"GOOD EVENING, WINSTON. THIS IS GWEN Rivers. I know you're busy, but I was calling to see how the meeting with Barnabas went. You may have tried to call us last week, but we were out of town at a revival meeting in Wyoming, of all places. The cell reception was terrible, so we might have missed your call. But we are looking forward to hearing about your visit with Barnabas. Have a blessed day, dear."

The phone message greeted him when he got home from the office. He felt guilty. It was the third call he had not returned. *Ignored* would be more accurate. He wasn't even sure what to tell them. Or if he wanted to report at all. And for now, he refused to examine why.

That first meeting with Thumper had happened because the Rivers had asked him to meet with their son. It was after he'd appeared on their TV show. One of the show's producers had heard him speak at a Christian conference in Atlanta. The famous preacher and his wife hosted a weekday program called *Down at the Rivers*, which was basically a talk-show format, similar to what had been done by Jim and Tammy Faye Bakker with the *PTL Club*.

"We're here today to talk about an extremely important topic," Dr. Rivers had told the audience, as he stared into the camera.

"From my intensive study of God's Word, and my observation of current events, there are several grave issues affecting our country."

He paused for effect, and to allow the camera to move in closer.

"But I can't think of a bigger threat today than the evil goals behind the homosexual agenda. The liberals in Hollywood and left-wing politicians tell us that we're being intolerant when we refuse to accept this perverted lifestyle. Well, I tell you this: as Christians, when we stand up and speak out against this dangerous tide of darkness, we're not being homophobic, we're being wholly obedient Ambassadors of the Lord Jesus Christ."

The in-house audience jumped to their feet in deafening screams and applause.

"The leaders of this insidious movement tell us it's the way they were born." Dr. Rivers' voice took on an affected, effeminate whine. "We can't change You need to accept us. We're weak and can't help ourselves—"

Angry shouts and booing from the audience interrupted the preacher.

47

Dr. Rivers looked over at his wife. "Praise God, I see we have an army of agreement with us today."

Gwen smiled sweetly. "And Jesus said where two or more agree on anything, it shall be done. We're claiming victory over the works of the devil." She dabbed her eyes with a handkerchief.

The preacher pointed to the audience and his stern expression burned with holy ire. "Don't believe the lies of the enemy," he instructed. "The blood of Jesus changes lives every day. And that includes the homosexual. We have two men with us today who can testify to that truth."

More applause.

"My first guest is Dr. Thomas McAvoy, the director of *Restored Image*, a ministry to those in bondage to sexual perversion." He looked over at the guest. "In his new book, *From Street Hustler to Street Preacher,* he chronicles his life as a male prostitute. In 1990, he accepted Jesus and his life has been miraculously turned around. He now goes back to the street and rescues those still caught in the grip of sin. Thank you for being with us."

"Praise Jesus!" the man shouted. The loud, sudden exclamation startled Winston, who jumped in his seat. But the crowd seemed to instantly love him.

McAvoy pontificated about the success of his ministry's program and monopolized the show, speaking about issues beyond the assigned subject matter. And regardless of the topic or the question, he had *the* definitive, not-to-be argued-with answer. His dogmatic rants included the immorality of rock music, the evil influence of video games, the undeniable role of women in the home and the uselessness of public schools. Winston saw Gwen Rivers flush with embarrassment when the street preacher did a tirade about masturbation.

His tone was harsh and his manner confrontational. According to him, America was under divine judgment and the church was to blame for being soft on sin, particularly and especially the egregious sin of homosexuality.

"In the book of Leviticus, God's law demanded death for those caught in this sin. Today, we tolerate their damning behavior and vote to give them special rights to practice their perversion. Like we know better than God!"

Winston was stunned and decided to get some clarification, though he'd not even been introduced to the audience. "I'm sure you're not advocating the death penalty for homosexuality," he said, hopefully in a tactful way that allowed McAvoy to explain his position. "After all, the love of God and the power of the Gospel can change lives, where the law of Moses could not."

Without blinking, McAvoy looked at the audience. Or more precisely, the camera. "The Word of God is very clear. Yes, God wants to transform those who come to Him in repentance. Praise Jesus, he changed me from a homosexual hustler to a born-again, Spirit-filled, tongue-talking Child of God." He lifted his hands toward the ceiling as the crowd gave loud approval to his proclamation.

"But let's not lose sight of the other truth," he continued. "Homosexuality is an abomination to the heart of a holy God. Did you hear that word? A-bo-mi-na-tion." He uttered it slowly for some kind of impact.

"The Apostle Paul tells us this behavior is unnatural and those who practice it will not…I repeat…will *not* enter the Kingdom of Heaven. So, let's not make it less than God says it is." He then looked accusingly at Winston.

Winston didn't blink. "I think we do a disservice to the Gospel if we give the impression we want them dead—"

McAvoy slapped his hand on Dr. Rivers' desk, bringing a surprised sound from Mrs. Rivers.

"Love doesn't mean we coddle them. That's the root of their problem. Most of these guys have been smothered by an over-protective mother, so they don't need us to give them more of that 'poor-baby' kind of pseudo-love."

Dr. Rivers shifted and was about to speak, but McAvoy didn't give him an opportunity. "It takes discipline and willpower to crucify the deeds of the flesh and do battle with the principalities of darkness. God rewards diligence and perseverance. But make no mistake: those who ignore the truth and turn their back on God…those who choose that lifestyle…that *a-bo-mi-na-tion* … deserve death."

He leaned back and folded his arms across his chest. "Not my words, dear friends, that's God's Word."

Winston was about to challenge, but following the audience's overly appreciative, thunderous and extended response, it was time for a commercial. During the break, a woman wearing a headset came to the sofa and quietly instructed him to switch places with McAvoy. She apologetically whispered that the show was running long, so the final segment would be cut short.

"Let's continue this spirited discussion with our next guest," Dr. Rivers announced when the camera's red light came on.

"Like Dr. McAvoy, he's seen firsthand the power of God. He was once a practicing homosexual, but now he's a practicing attorney." The audience laughed at his wordplay. "Please welcome Winston DuMont and hear his wonderful testimony."

Winston took a deep breath and deliberately smiled.

"My life has not been nearly as dramatic as my brother over here," he gestured toward the other side of the sofa, but didn't look in that direction. "I knew there was something missing and I sought to satisfy that emptiness— with alcohol, with nightlife, with the attention of others. But to paraphrase the philosopher Pascal, it's a God-shaped vacuum, so only God can fill it."

There was a gentle smattering of applause and a few weak "Amens."

"I don't have all the answers, but I do know this one thing: God loves me, and it was that love that drew me. I think if we spend our time condemning people, we run the risk of driving them away rather than drawing them in. The Apostle John tells us that the essence and nature of God can be summed up in one word. It's not *abomination*!" He resisted the temptation to look at McAvoy. "It's love."

He felt McAvoy move beside him and knew the man was going to interrupt, so he didn't stop talking. "In fact, in Saint John's letter to the church, he says those who claim to know God but don't love...well, they aren't telling the truth. God is love, and love is the proof that we truly know God."

McAvoy immediately leaned in front of Winston. "Are you suggesting that we not teach responsibility for sin?"

Winston hesitated for a brief moment, but not long enough to let McAvoy answer his own question. "We must never compromise the Gospel message." He looked at Dr. Rivers. "But the word 'gospel' means 'good news,' and I think that means our message should be more than sin, condemnation, judgment and death."

"But sin is extremely serious. Especially this sin, and we should never take that lightly," McAvoy pressed.

Winston wanted to explore why "this sin" was more heinous than others, but knew it would eat up the rest of his time. So he intentionally turned toward the desk, facing the hosts. "You'll get no argument from me, Doctor Rivers. But even more serious is God's love...and the good news that our sins have been forgiven."

For the first time, Winston looked directly at the audience. "I don't think anyone would call Jesus soft on sin, but if we read about His life, He spent much of his free time with those who'd been rejected by the established religious community of His day. He didn't condemn them and He certainly didn't tell them they deserved to die. He loved them unconditionally. And they followed Him. People already know what their sin is; let's show them what love is. I believe our message will have a much greater impact when it's presented as good news, not as a threat. It worked for Jesus."

He heard a "pffff" beside him, but Gwen gave a hearty "Hallelujah!" and there was finally enthusiastic clapping from the audience. Dr. Rivers thanked both guests and the camera moved in for his close up. During the time when the hosts talked about upcoming crusades and the books and tapes on special this week, the young producer escorted Winston and McAvoy behind the stage.

Once they got back to the green room, Winston figured he would have to listen to a lengthy theological dressing-down by McAvoy. However, after grabbing an apple from a bowl on the table, McAvoy left the building, all the time talking loudly into his cell phone.

He was not the least bit upset at the absence of a good-bye from the arrogant minister, but was annoyed that he'd not been able to talk about the *Full Circle* group. He also wished he could have challenged some of the street preacher's radical interpretation of Scripture.

Two weeks after the show, Gwen Rivers called him at work. "Winston, dear, I hope I'm not bothering you, but we're coming through Dallas next week, on our way to a crusade in Tyler and we would love to take you to dinner on Friday night, if you have the time. Jim and I want to learn more about your testimony and your ministry."

They'd met at an upscale Italian restaurant near the Galleria. The food was excellent and the place was quiet, allowing for conversation. It was while they were eating that Dr. Rivers asked him to talk to Thumper. And the request wasn't subtle.

"I'm sure you don't know, but several years ago, our son rebelled against the teaching of Scripture and has chosen to live a homosexual lifestyle."

"We love him so much," Gwen said with trembling voice. "But we don't know what to do. We've paid for him to see several specialists, but it didn't help. Now, he just won't listen to reason."

Thumper's father actually harrumphed, and the sound almost made Winston laugh.

"His mind has been darkened by the work of the devil. He knew the truth, but turned his back on it. We fear for his very soul."

"We were hoping you might talk with him," she pleaded. "Maybe if he meets someone who's living in victory..." She was sobbing before she finished.

Winston took a sip of water. "Of course, I'd be happy to help in any way I can."

"We'll be seeing him tomorrow, and we'll let him know he can expect to hear from you, if that's okay."

She was now giddy, and pulled out a pen and wrote on the back of a business card. "Here's his home number and the number for his cellular phone. Don't call him until tomorrow afternoon, after we've had a chance to tell him about you."

On the front was the contact information for the *Rivers of Life* ministry offices. She had written her son's information on the back, and also included their private home number in Birmingham. Winston put it in his pocket and again expressed gratitude at their confidence in him.

After the check arrived, before they said their goodbyes, Dr. Rivers suggested a return visit to their television show, which Winston didn't expect because he wasn't sure what kind of impression he'd made, compared to the outspoken and arrogant Thomas McAvoy.

"And if your schedule would allow, we'd also welcome you as a guest at our crusades. Your testimony would have such an impact on those entangled in this sinful behavior."

"I would be honored, sir."

Looking back now, Winston was glad he'd agreed to talk with Thumper. There was an obvious need; the kid was clearly mixed up. And it was another chance to share what God had done for him personally. Like he'd done so many times in the past.

He was surprised by an internal query: *So why does this feel different?*

He was also a bit annoyed when no answer came.

Thumper was on his way to work, but his mind was replaying the events of the past few hours. He was confused, and a little pissed off. With himself.

Why did I do it? What did I hope to accomplish?

It had not been planned. The events that led to the snap decision were so happenstance. He'd gotten ready for work and then realized he was not scheduled until one o'clock, not ten. He looked through the mail and there was a note from his mom, and she mentioned Winston. The idea was born.

Thumper grabbed the phone book and looked up the address. On the way, he picked up a couple of coffees and some bagels. He wasn't even sure if Winston would be in the office or if the hunky lawyer would be able to see him when he showed up.

"May I tell him who you are and what this is regarding?" the receptionist had questioned with skillful efficiency. According to the plaque on the counter, she was *Sasha Childress*, though her plain appearance didn't match the exotic name.

Thumper held up the cardboard tray holding the two coffee cups in one hand and showed the bagel bag in the other.

"I have a delivery. Could you tell him…uh, tell him it's his favorite cartoon character." He finished with an exaggerated, all-the-front-teeth, comical grin.

She was not amused, but did pick up the phone and delivered the message. Almost immediately, Winston came around the corner.

"Thumper? Of all the cartoon characters in the animation universe, you are not the one I expected. What are you doing here?"

As he walked away, he turned and smiled again—for real, this time—at the receptionist. He took out one of the bagels, wrapped it in a napkin and laid it on the counter.

"Thanks for your help, Miss Sasha. Have a glorious day." He got the response he wanted from her that time.

Turning to Winston, he said, "Hey, you dropped by my place of work, so I thought I'd return the favor."

Even though that visit had been several weeks earlier, Thumper hoped it would sound valid. He held up the tray. "And I brought food!"

Looking back on it as he drove to work, he determined it was a good visit. Winston was as charming and gracious as ever. But more than anything, the visit served to further confuse his gaydar.

They enjoyed the coffee and bagels, while talking about everything from the recent horrible remake of *War of the Worlds* to favorite TV shows. Winston liked *The Amazing Race*; he liked *South Park*. They both liked *Lost*, and spent some time discussing the intricate storyline.

"Is everything okay?" Winston asked after a while. "I'm thrilled you came by, but if you needed something specific, I don't want us to miss the chance to talk."

I can't stop thinking about you, was what Thumper wanted to say. He also didn't tell him: *I constantly fantasize about what your body looks like without Oral Robert University sweatshirts or business professional attire.*

"Have you been thinking about our previous conversations?"

"I can't lie, I have thought about it. A lot. It's all a bit…unsettling."

Winston got up and went to the wall of bookcases, where he selected a couple of books and then knelt down beside Thumper's chair.

"These are some good resource materials. All biblically based."

He handed one of the paperbacks to Thumper. "I heard this man speak a few years ago and he's terrific. This is his personal story of how God transformed his life. He's now married and heads up a ministry in Phoenix."

Winston placed the book in Thumper's lap, and brushed against his arm, causing him to turn slightly. They were face to face. If this had been a scene in a Tom Hanks-Meg Ryan romantic movie, the two would have slowly moved closer and kissed, to a swell of violin music. Thumper thought he detected a slight movement from Winston, and instinctively tilted his head.

Winston jerked back suddenly. He stood and walked back behind his desk.

"And that one's a book about counseling those with sexual brokenness. It's a bit heady, but with your background, I think you'll appreciate it."

Before he left, Winston also gave him a list of other books on the subject. "After all, you do work at a bookstore," he reminded.

Thumper did promise to look over the books. Winston suggested they get back together and talk soon. And though he had little interest in the content of the books, Thumper was motivated to fulfill the promise if it meant seeing him again.

To say that Thumper was not what he expected would be too simplistic. Winston could not get the surprise visit off his mind.

The guy was a mixed bag of glaring incongruity. At first, he'd seemed comfortable—even militant—in his gay lifestyle, but apparently he struggled with the divine implications. He was caring, but could also be scathing and cynical. There was an obvious intelligence and he was an interesting conversationalist. Of course, at times, he was bawdy and brazen, but Winston still felt that was Thumper's way to get attention. Regardless, he did it all with an endearing personality that was infectious.

He's incredibly hot.

The words jumped into Winston's mind without warning. Immediately, years of training kicked in and he was able to exile the rogue thought to that self-imposed, long-ago-constructed dark region where such now-forbidden feelings were imprisoned.

Rehearsed self-talk quickly took over.

It was only a thought. A thought or a feeling is not a failure.

He would confess it to his accountability partner, and together, they would pray for continued strength to resist temptation. That would be the end of it.

The internal dialogue worked, as usual. He didn't give in, and that was the goal of all the program's teaching, discipline and counseling. Once again, he'd made the right choice and not allowed a random, carnal thought to grow into a more destructive force. It was a battle won.

Doesn't feel like a victory, came a new, equally disturbing thought.

EIGHT

MATT CAME IN FROM WORK AND noticed Thumper was seated in the wingback chair, wearing shorts and a ratty t-shirt—not his usual Friday night bar attire.

"You going out tonight?"

"Nah," Thumper mumbled back. "Think I'm gonna stay in and uh…do some reading."

The option to read would not be unusual for Thumper; he was an avid reader. But on a Friday night, it presented an obvious departure from the customary routine. And something about Thumper's tone told Matt there was more to the decision.

"Is everything okay?" he asked, taking a seat on the ottoman in front of the chair. He saw a book on the table next to Thumper: *The Unbroken Circle.*

Thumper saw him looking at the book. "It's about those who've been through that group that Winston goes to. Ten guys who've successfully completed that fix-it program tell their story of how they were healed of their homosexuality. Winston's story is chapter six. I picked it up at the bookstore today."

Matt knew that in the past few weeks, Thumper and Winston had met several times; as always, Thumper had related all the details. After Winston's initial visit to the bookstore, Thumper had dropped in at the law office. One afternoon, Winston showed up again at the bookstore and they had a snack at the in-house coffee shop. They had brunch one Sunday, after Winston got out of church. Last Saturday they went for a jog, and then breakfast.

"Why?" Matt made sure he masked his concern.

"Don't worry, I'm not about to enroll in straight-school. Guess I thought it might help to get a handle on Winston—to get some idea of who they are and what they do."

"Again, why? You know there's no chance of a sexual relationship with him. The best you can hope for is to be friends. You don't have to change who you are to be his friend, do you?"

"It's not that I want to change, it's just that…" Thumper didn't finish the thought.

"Why not get books by those who've been able to successfully integrate their sexuality with their faith? Jonah said he's reading—"

"I should take theological counsel from a closet case hiding in Bible College?" Thumper smirked.

"I'm suggesting maybe there's more than one way of looking at the issue. I get that you have a school-girl crush on this guy, but he's wrong on this. And wrong for you!"

Thumper pushed the book slightly with his index finger. "I hear what you're saying. So tell me this…" He waited for several seconds, as if giving Matt's conclusions some consideration. "How is it that you know what *Jonah* is reading these days?" He looked up with mischievous smile on his face.

Matt had hoped that slip had gone unnoticed.

"I ran into him the other day, at Blockbuster's over on Lemmon. We talked for a while; the subject came up." It was the truth, though Matt had failed to mention they'd left the video store and had dinner at a nearby restaurant.

"Anything else…come up?"

"One of these days, a house is going to fall on you," he shot back.

"I'm just gonna skim over this book, but I'll also check at the bookstore to see if we have anything on the other side of the argument. Perhaps you could ask *Jonah* to recommend a reading list for me?"

Matt flipped him off and walked into his bedroom to change. He was meeting some friends from church for dinner, and was now running late. Thumper didn't need to know that Jonah was joining them. Not yet.

Thumper was finishing his workout. The combination of the summer heat and the work he'd done on the machines had him drenched in sweat. When the weights from the bench press machine crashed down for the final rep of the set, he sat up with a grunt.

Time to shower, he decided.

In the locker room, he peeled off the sweat-soaked shirt and tossed it on the floor next to his bag. He had just pushed down his shorts and strap when he looked up. At that exact moment, Winston DuMont stepped out of the shower and their eyes locked.

"Thumper," he exclaimed. The lone towel that he was using to dry his head was hurriedly wrapped around his waist. But not quick enough to deny Thumper a peek.

"What are you doing here?" he asked Winston.

"I had a morning meeting not far from here." The crimson in his face was fading as he casually walked to the locker area.

Thumper was still naked, so Winston took the lead and handed him a towel. Thumper thanked him, then draped it around his neck.

"I guess that makes me the welcome wagon. I'd gladly show you around, spot you in the weight room...save you a seat in the steam room."

Winston appeared to be struggling to maintain eye contact. "Is this where you normally work out?"

Thumper decided to be kind and wrap the towel around his waist. Because of his schedule at the bookstore, his workout routine varied each week, though he made sure to get to the gym at least three times a week.

"It's my first time to ever visit a gym," he lied.

Winston actually looked up and down Thumper's body. "We both know *that's* not true." He placed his hand on Thumper's bare chest. "You don't get this kind of definition by accident."

He took a deep breath, pushing his chest into Winston's hand.

Is he making a move? Thumper wondered hopefully.

As if reading his mind, Winston quickly withdrew his hand and cleared his throat. "Well, I need to get dressed and head out to my meeting. It was good seeing...uh, so glad to talk with you again. Let's get together soon. It's been a while."

Before he could reply, Winston turned and left the area.

The ex-gay has some ex-quisite equipment, Thumper observed.

As he'd imagined, it was an amazing body.

Now I have lots of reality to flesh out my fantasies, he concluded, tempted to follow him to the other part of the locker room.

"If we keep this up, folks are gonna think we're going steady."

"We're two friends, having coffee," Winston snapped back. "Doesn't have to mean anything."

He was glum, and the words carried a sternness Thumper didn't understand. He wondered if it had to do with the *revealing* meeting at the gym last week.

"Lighten up, Matlock. I was only kidding."

He did manage a slight smile, but not with his usual confidence. "I'm sorry. It's been a crazy week. I was out of town part of the week and it put me behind."

"You spoke at Dad's crusade in Shreveport," he said without looking at him.

"How did you...? Oh, you talked to your mom."

Thumper laughed. "She's your biggest fan. Like the son she never had."

"That's not true and you know it. They both love you very much. You are all they talk about."

The 'yeah, sure' grimace was his rebuttal.

Winston got still and looked at Thumper for several seconds. "I have something I'd like to talk with you about."

He was still confused with Winston's solemn mood. If they'd been dating, given Winston's disposition and the we-need-to-talk statement, he'd figure they were breaking up.

Winston pushed his coffee aside and crossed his arm on the table.

"We both know that I agreed to meet with you as a favor to your parents. Then…well, you were not what I expected. I found that I enjoyed spending time with you."

The past tense of the sentence was noted.

"And that's a bad thing?" Thumper probed, uncertain why there was such a grim tone in Winston's voice, matched with an out-of-character somber expression. "I like spending time with you, too. I know we disagree about stuff, but so what? I disagree with Mattie, and we're best friends."

Winston slowly shook his head. "I can't be your friend…" His words could barely be heard. "And we have to stop meeting."

It took several seconds, but Thumper's reaction was intense. "What? You figured out that I'm not going to fall in line with your little circle of Stepford straights, so you decided it's time to move on to the next mark?"

Thumper stood to leave. Winston looked up at him with an observable sadness, but said nothing.

Thumper took a deep breath to help diffuse his anger and waited. He glared at Winston, demanding a further explanation.

Still, none came.

"This is so typical." His voice was already quivering and he felt his face flush. In spite of his effort to prevent it, his eyes filled with tears.

"I thought…" He fought giving into the flood of emotion he was feeling. "I thought you were different, but you're just like the rest of my father's cronies—fucking hypocrites. I'm outta here!"

He slammed a five dollar bill on the table.

———

It's not like that.

That's what Winston wanted to say. But how could he tell him the *real* reason?

"I don't have to tell you about triggers," the counselor had told Winston, then commenced summarizing the concept, as if neither of them had heard it.

Winston had requested the session after running into Thumper at the gym. After *touching* Thumper at the gym. But even before that, the internal struggles were there.

At first, he ignored them, like a mild headache.

After all, he reasoned, *the idea was absurd.*

He exercised his long-standing pattern of self-examination and affirmation. But the thoughts persisted, and grew into discernable feelings. So it was time for more drastic action.

Of course Winston understood triggers. In the early stages of his work to overcome his sexual brokenness, they had been drummed into him. He could recite by rote the explanation:

Triggers are those influences that cause me to engage in…or want to engage in…inappropriate sexual behavior. I may not be able to eliminate the trigger, but I can control how I respond and what I do to fulfill the actual need that prompted the impulse.

Some triggers were apparent, like talking about sex or watching pornography. Others could be less obvious, such as feelings of loneliness or even the smell of a certain fragrance. The *external* ones could usually be avoided by careful planning; *internal* triggers needed to be controlled by determination and discipline.

Since triggers would normally vary from person to person, each individual in the *Full Circle* healing program was taken through an inventory process of self-examination. That way, they could address dangerous emotions or moods and avoid situations or people that could lead them—or trigger them—to act on temptation. The majority of group discussions in the weekly *Circle* meetings typically revolved around this subject, especially for those who had failed in the prior week.

For the first two years of the program, Winston had worked meticulously to identify his personal triggers, and was diligent about keeping himself out of situations that might engage them. Alcoholics Anonymous had done groundbreaking work in this area by identifying the most common feelings that could trigger the desire to drink. They used the simple acronym: H.A.L.T.—Hungry, Angry, Lonely, Tired. He'd effectively adapted the model and was regimented enough to maintain a schedule that didn't facilitate these areas: he ate regularly, got plenty of rest, worked out diligently and surrounded himself with plenty of people from church and guys from the ministry.

As far as overt temptations, he simply did not put himself in those situations. He was highly selective about his movie and TV entertainment, as well as the books he read. He didn't go to bars and rarely drank. Because of his success, he taught a workshop about triggers to those entering the *Full Circle* restoration program.

"What is it about this guy that brings up the feelings?" the counselor had wanted to know.

That was the problem and what had caught him by surprise.

Obviously Thumper was attractive, with his dark red hair, expressive blue eyes and well-toned body, but he didn't fit the pattern for Winston's typical trigger. In his past, he'd been attracted to older, mature men: successful, affluent and refined. He'd preferred the quiet, more submissive type. And typically they were tall, at least close to his six-foot stature.

That was certainly not Thumper, who was brash, aggressive and coarse, to the point of crude at times. He was at least five years younger and four inches shorter. He was not affluent, successful and definitely not submissive. And yet, Thumper had stirred up some area that he had obviously not explored.

A new trigger? Winston had wondered.

That possibility was not only inconvenient, it was troublesome and frustrating.

But whatever the cause, Winston knew that Thumper was occupying too much of his energies—monopolizing his thoughts, invading his dreams and even the occasional, unexpected fantasy. It was not healthy. Or safe.

The counselor emphasized what Winston already knew: it was best not to see Thumper outside of some kind of protected environment, like church or the *Circle* meeting. Winston left that counseling session resolved that their agreed-upon plan was the best course of action to maintain and protect his sexual recovery.

So he had arranged the dinner meeting with Thumper tonight to implement that plan. He'd hoped to explain why the friendship was unhealthy, and once again invite Thumper to visit the *Circle* meeting, perhaps even enroll in the *Full Circle* program.

Now Thumper was gone—from the restaurant and from his life. And even though the counselor had discussed that as a possible outcome, the amount of sadness Winston felt was unexpected. Moreover, that internal sense of divine peace the counselor had promised would result from following the plan was missing.

A crashing noise in the living room unexpectedly interrupted his sleep. Matt was immediately afraid someone was breaking into the apartment. His heart was racing with panic as he reached for the phone, hoping he could quietly call 9-1-1 before the intruder came in and murdered him. Then he heard another noise, followed by the familiar sound of Thumper's voice, cussing like a sailor with Tourette's.

Matt walked to his bedroom door and saw Thumper standing next to the cast-iron umbrella stand which he'd apparently knocked over when coming into the apartment.

"What the hell are you doing?"

"Sorry," he slurred back.

He was fall-down drunk. Again. It was the third time in as many weeks.

Since his blow up with Winston, Matt concluded.

"Where have you been? It's after three."

The fragrance that wafted from him was a bizarre combination of alcohol, sweat, incense, spent sex and chlorine.

"I was…working out." He flexed both arms, as if that would be proof. "At Metro Spa."

The Metro Spa advertised as a private club for men, complete with a gym, indoor pool, billiards, a full bar and steam room. But beyond those conventional, marketable perks, Metro Spa was primarily a bathhouse—a place where casual, anonymous and abundant sex was practiced by those who enjoyed an abundance of casual, anonymous sex.

Going to a bathhouse was definitely out of character for Thumper, who made fun of those who frequented such places. "Anyone can get laid there," he once told Matt, who confessed he'd never been to a bathhouse. "Where's the skill in that?"

"You went to…" Matt chose not to finish the pointless inquiry.

"Need to keep *the muscle* toned." Thumper chuckled at his joke. "Wanna feel my muscle?"

He pulled his pants down to complete the invitation, then reached for Matt. "I'll exercise your muscle, if you like."

Matt closed and locked the front door, then put his arm around Thumper and helped him to his bedroom, where he fell across the bed.

"I hope you didn't drive in this condition," he scolded, as he worked to untie Thumper's shoes. But it was too late; Thumper was asleep on the bed. His pants were partially down and his shoes were still on.

"Screw it," Matt muttered, leaving him in that condition.

NINE

"I'm worried about Thumper," Matt said.

Jonah looked up from reading the menu. "What do you mean?"

It had been a couple of months since Jonah showed up at the apartment looking for Thumper. That night, they'd talked for several hours. Before he left, they agreed to meet again and continue talking. And over the past few weeks, they'd met or talked on the phone almost daily. Tonight, they were having dinner and planned to go to a movie afterwards.

Matt grabbed a packet of sugar. "He's messed up, and I don't know what to do. He's out whoring around almost every night—"

"And that would be different *how?*"

Levity aside, Matt knew there was more to it.

"Thumper is always drinking and always getting laid. Hell, that's his strong suit. But lately, he's doing it with a bit more...oh, I don't know the right word...a bit more *abandon* than usual. Last night, he went to a bathhouse."

"Any idea what's bothering him?"

"He's been talking to a guy involved in one of those ex-gay groups. His parents set it up initially, but then he began spending lots of time with the guy. I think Thumper was infatuated and some of the stuff he was hearing had him mixed up. A few weeks ago they apparently had some kind of disagreement, and since then, he's been surly, unhappy and difficult as hell to get along with."

"That's surprising. Wouldn't think he'd give that ex-gay crap a second thought. The way he quotes the Bible gave me the impression he had it all figured out."

"I don't get it, that's for sure," Matt said. "I was raised to believe that God created me this way and loves me unconditionally. It was all so simple... for my simple faith. Not like you guys, with all your hardcore theology and profound Bible questions."

Jonah reached across the table and took Matt's hand.

"I hope that you think about me in *other* ways...besides my theology and my questions. I know that I've come to have some...well, less-than-holy thoughts about you that verge on a different kind of *hardcore*."

A quick warmth rushed over Matt. *Nice to know I'm not the only one with these feelings.*

He wrapped his own hand around Jonah's. "Well, at least now we have our next topic of conversation. I want to hear all about those 'less-than-holy' thoughts. And spare no details!"

Matt knew he needed to talk with Thumper about the recent developments with Jonah. As he rolled out of bed and headed to the kitchen, he decided to have the conversation over breakfast. Thumper was not always alert in the morning, especially after a Saturday night. But since he knew Thumper had to open the bookstore, breakfast would be a good occasion.

About twenty minutes later, Thumper padded into the kitchen and kissed in his general direction before reaching for the coffee pot.

"What time did you get in?" Matt asked.

Thumper took a deep drink of the black coffee.

"Sometime before the sun came up. Had to drive back all the way from North Dallas, near the Addison airport. But he was so worth the effort, if you know what I mean."

"Mannequins in Macy's window know what you mean," Matt quipped. "In other words, a typical Friday night?"

Thumper stretched. "There was nothing typical about this guy. Bob… Joe…whatever his name was. Dark hair, swimmer-bod, young and hung. Makes me hungry thinking about it."

"Good, I made us some breakfast. There's pancakes and bacon. I'm making some eggs, too. Thought we could have a nice breakfast and, you know…talk."

"Does it have anything to do with you and that kid? What's-his-name from CFNI?"

Matt dropped the whisk into the bowl of eggs and spun around.

"How did you…who told you…?" he stammered, trying to regain his composure. "What do you mean?"

"I saw y'all at the restaurant last night. Is it serious?"

He took a deep breath. "We've been spending lots of time together the past few months, but I'm not sure where it's going."

"If you like him, go for it."

Matt looked long at Thumper. "But will it be weird for you, if he and I are together?"

"Can't imagine it would. I think it's cute. Besides, it'll give me and him something to talk about, since we've both seen you nekkid!"

"For the record, he hasn't seen me naked. I don't want to move too fast, especially since he's still processing so much."

"Why not?" Thumper put a piece of bacon in his mouth. "He's adorable, and has a dick that's pleasingly proportional to his height."

Matt laughed mockingly. "You can't remember their names, but you remember dick size? That's priceless."

Thumper took a slight mock bow. "What can I say? I'm the Rain Man of cocks. But you didn't answer my question. Why haven't you slept with him?"

"I wanted to talk with you first."

"That's sweet, and so like you. But totally unnecessary. If you remember, he left before we did anything...*significant.* So I'll rely on you for those details, once you and preacher boy have done the nasty."

"For the record, his name is Jonah. We haven't done anything. It's still early. He lives with roommates in a house down near the school. They are also students at CFNI, so we wouldn't be able to go there when...if...anything were to, uhm, you know."

"You can bring him here. Just let me know and I'll be scarce or quiet. Or handle the video camera. I live to serve...and to service."

Matt slapped him with a dish towel.

Thumper looked back at him. "I hope he knows how lucky he is to have someone like you."

"For that, you get extra pancakes."

Thumper got up and wrapped his arms around him from behind and pulled him close.

"I'm glad for you, Mattie. I really am."

Matt turned around and looked him in the eyes. "I appreciate that, Thumper. You are my best friend and I love you."

"And I love you, Mattie. I know you always wanted...more, but I just couldn't give that to you. I hope I didn't hurt you. I do cherish our relationship. And I'm not talking about the sex."

Thumper kissed him on the cheek. "I reckon since you got yourself a man, pancakes are about all I'll get from you now. 'Cause I know you'll be everything I could never be—a faithful boyfriend."

"I had a talk with Thumper this morning."

Matt looked over at Jonah, who was reading the latest issue of the *Dallas Voice*, the local gay newspaper. They were having lunch at a small sandwich shop on Cedar Springs Road.

"About us," he added with more emphasis.

It must have taken a moment for the statement to register, then Jonah looked up with eyes widened, demanding more details.

Matt smiled. He could spend hours staring into those huge brown eyes.

"He was very supportive. And already suspected it, the little shit."

"I know you've always had feelings for him…" Jonah let his voice trail off, but intently looked at Matt for a response.

"I'll always care for him," he said, nodding his head in agreement. "Because…well, because he's Thumper. But I've known for a long time that there was no future with him."

Jonah got serious. "Do you think there's a future with…me?"

"I'd like to think so—"

"Me, too," Jonah interjected, cutting off the sentence. He was smiling.

"But," Matt interrupted, causing Jonah's happy expression to vanish. "I'm not gonna lie to you. There are…challenges."

Jonah stiffened in his chair. "Such as?"

He reached over and took Jonah's hand. "I care for you very much. But let's face it, there's a big difference in our—"

"You're not that much older than me."

"It's not about age. It's more about experience and perspective. I've been out since high school. I've done my time whoring around and had sex with plenty of guys. I'm ready to settle down. You're just now coming to terms with your sexuality. And what, you've slept with *one* guy?"

Jonah's mouth tightened, his eyes narrowed and his brow wrinkled. "First, I reserve the right to come back to 'all the guys you've had sex with,' but for now, let's see if I can address your concerns. Thumper was not my first; that happened in high school. Most folks thought we were best friends, but we were a secret couple for almost three years, until he went away to college in California. After high school, I had several one-night stands, but once I decided to go to Bible College, I tried to put that part of my life behind me."

"Damn!" Matt exclaimed, with bewildered surprise. "Thumper told me it was your first time in a gay bar."

"That part is correct. I'd never been to a gay bar before that night. I'd had a really bad week at school. My systematic theology professor veered off the lesson plan and spent every day talking about homosexuality in the Bible. He said it came to him in a dream that we needed to be prepared with the truth so we could fight the war of morality."

He let out a nervous laugh. "For me, it drove the feelings back to the surface. I gave in, and that night, met Thumper. When I went to the bar that night, I…" Jonah shrugged, then flushed red.

"You had an itch and needed someone to scratch it?" Matt suggested, completing the sentence.

Jonah paused, then nodded. "I met Thumper, and I think I responded to his knowledge of the Bible. Anyway, I regret that it happened, except I met you."

"And that leads to my other concern: the fact that you're still wrestling with the whole Christian-gay-morality issue. How do I know that you won't be overcome with holy guilt and try to go…you know, straight? Straight back to Jesus and the church."

"For one thing, I have no intention of excluding Jesus or the church from my life. Unlike Thumper, I think I can be gay *and* Christian. Ever since that night I came over and we talked, I've been doing some serious study on the subject of the Bible and homosexuality. I found some great material from a wonderful group of gay and lesbian Christians called *Evangelicals Concerned*. In fact, after this semester, I've decided to leave CFNI. I can no longer support their mission in good conscience."

Matt was stunned. "Jonah, what will you do?"

"I'll have my ministry diploma, but I'm ditching the idea of the advance degree. I have to be honest with myself. If there's a ministry for me that won't compromise who I am, then God will show it to me."

Matt got up and moved to the other side of the table. He leaned down and gave Jonah a long kiss. "You are amazing," he marveled when their first kiss ended.

"I think you're pretty wonderful, too. Now, can we get back to 'all those guys' you've slept with?"

Thumper walked up to the table and greeted Matt and Jonah. "Howdy, you cute lil' lovebirds."

Jonah looked down at the menu, his face red.

In the weeks since Matt had divulged what was going on, Thumper could tell the feelings were real, so he was openly supportive. He was truly glad for his friend. But there was also a little jealousy; he knew that besides Matt, he didn't have any real friends.

"You wanna a drink?" Matt offered.

"Thanks, I really need it."

"What are your plans for the evening?" Matt asked Thumper.

Thumper took a deep draw off his cocktail.

"I met a cutie last night at JR's and we're gonna meet up for some boot-scootin' at the Round-Up and then some boot-bumpin' later at his place." Then he added with a devious grin: "That means y'all have the place to yourselves tonight."

He winked at Matt, then put his elbows on the table, cupped his face in his hands.

"So, have y'all had sex yet?" He didn't address the query to anyone in particular, but was looking at Jonah. He loved to see him blush.

His question got the intended response.

Matt answered firmly, "Not everyone feels the need to—"

"Ask him again in the morning," Jonah said, with his own smile.

Once Matt and Jonah got back to the apartment, there seemed to be no hurry for what they both knew was inevitable. Matt got them a beer, and for several minutes, they sat on the sofa and kissed. Jonah managed to get Matt's shirt off and was slowly moving his hand over his flat stomach, stopping frequently to toy with his nipples.

Matt was unbuttoning Jonah's shirt, when he pulled away slightly.

"Can we talk first?"

"Is this going too fast?" Matt asked, even moving over a little and leaning back in the sofa.

"Not at all," Jonah assured sincerely. "I'm undressing you, so I am under no delusion of what's about to happen. It's just that..." He seemed to be struggling with what to say next.

"If you're worried about HIV, I'm negative and I always practice safe—"

Jonah cut him off. "It's not that. And I also don't want to discuss who's top and who's bottom. I need to tell you something."

Matt took a deep breath, wondering silently if he wanted to hear what Jonah had to say.

"I told you about my boyfriend in high school and about the encounters in college. One thing I learned from those experiences is that casual sex is not for me. I believe that it's more than 'insert tab A into slot B.' Am I making sense?"

Matt squinted and rocked his head back and forth. "You think we should slow down before we go any farther?"

Jonah moved over and put his arm around Matt. "No, but I want what we do together to, you know, mean something. I don't want to be another one-night stand in this apartment."

Matt pulled him close and kissed him. "I wish I had the words to tell you how much I care for you. I've never had a relationship like this one. We met, became friends and our feelings grew. How rare is that? I definitely don't see this as casual."

Jonah was smiling. "I'm so glad I'm not freaking you out. I don't want to be corny or sound like some religious fanatic, but I am giving myself to you tonight because I believe it's the right thing to do and it's the right time." After staring at him for a few seconds, Jonah added: "And the right person."

Matt responded, kissing Jonah tenderly—first on the lips and then down his neck.

Jonah leaned close to his ear and whispered, "But just for the record: top or bottom?"

TEN

"I GOT EVERYTHING WE'LL NEED."

Earl stood in the doorway of Milton's apartment and looked in shock at the piles of supplies. He'd assumed they would go downtown, hand out some tracts, then call it a night. But apparently Milton had a different idea, and had enough supplies for a city-wide Billy Graham crusade.

"You found more folks to go with us?" he asked hopefully.

"Nope, but the Holy Spirit will empower us and multiply our efforts. I've been prayin' about it since early this morning."

He walked over to a huge sign, like those used in picket lines. On one side was emblazoned the words *Repent, it's a short trip back to God* and the other read, *We're here because God loves you!*

"You've been busy, I see," Earl commented as casually as he could muster.

Milton moved around the apartment incredibly fast, detailing all the supplies. "I got us several boxes of Bibles and Gospel tracts. We'll give out the tracts to everyone who passes by and when they stop talk with us, we'll give 'em a free Bible."

Earl opened the flaps on one of the boxes and his eyes landed on the pamphlet, printed on bright yellow paper. Large pink letters said it all: *Straight Talk: God Can Heal Your Homosexuality!*

Earl shivered and turned to Milton. "Where exactly are we going?" He feared the answer.

"To where all the queers hang out."

"I...uh...I thought we were going downtown."

"I was listening to Brother Jimmy, and he says homosexuals are the biggest danger we face in our country." Milton was talking fast. "We must confront them about God's wrath against their immorality. Their sin will bring about the destruction of our nation if we don't do something."

"I don't think I can go...*there*," Earl protested.

Milton walked over and put his arm around Earl's shoulder.

"I know it's a creepy place, brother. And it's disgusting to think about all the unspeakable immorality that goes on there. But as Jesus said, it's not the healthy who need a Physician. As a nurse, you know that. We have to take God's healing power to their sickness."

"But, I'm not sure it's a good idea for us to go—"

"I promised God, brother. I made a solemn promise to God that I would make it up to Him. Don't you understand? I promised." Milton was nearly shouting when he finished. He was sweating, which was running down his face.

"Relax, Milt. Please calm down so we can talk about this."

But Milton grabbed a box of Bibles and headed for the door.

"I have to do this. I promised God and He sent me on this mission. And you promised you would go with me, brother. I told you about this, and you promised. We both promised." Without turning around, Milton exited the house with his arms loaded.

Give me courage, Earl prayed silently.

Taking a deep breath, he grabbed the "picket" sign and followed his friend out the door.

"Why are you here?" the man snarled as he walked by. "We don't want your hateful Jesus."

Earl gave the obligatory grin—now little more than pursed lips strained into formation—and withdrew the Gospel leaflet the man had refused to take.

"Thank you," he said politely.

"Jesus is *not* hateful," Milton hollered back, pumping the picket sign up and down. "Your mind is deceived by sin. Jesus loves you and died for you."

They had been on the corner of Cedar Springs and Throckmorton—considered the center of the homosexual district—for more than an hour, positioned near a bookstore called Crossroads. In the time they'd been there, no one had stopped to talk with them so they had not given out a single Bible. Some who passed mocked and ridiculed them; most merely ignored them as if they were invisible.

"We are blessed," Milton reminded, when it became apparent the verbal assaults were affecting Earl's mood. "Jesus taught, 'Blessed are you when they revile and persecute you, and say all kinds of evil against you falsely for My sake. Rejoice and be exceedingly glad, for great is your reward in heaven.'"

But while Earl became discouraged, Milton got more agitated and confrontational with those who passed. He hoisted the "repent" sign, waved his huge black Bible and shouted Scripture at a volume that could have been heard over the airplanes from nearby Love Field airport.

"This is the Word of God in First Corinthians: 'Do not be deceived—homosexuals will not inherit the kingdom of God. Flee sexual immorality. Your body is the temple of the Holy Ghost? You were purchased at a price; so glorify God in your body.'"

Earl walked over to his friend. "Milt, I don't think screaming achieves our goal to show the love of Christ."

Milton calmed for a moment, but then his attention was distracted by a man walking down the street.

"Praise God, the Jesus patrol is out in force tonight," he sneered as he passed. He didn't stop, but began to sing *Onward, Christian Soldiers* as he waited on the corner for the light to change.

Milton walked over and stood by the young man. "You are correct. We are soldiers in a war. But we don't struggle with flesh and blood, but with the forces of Satan, who have a hold on your life."

The guy turned and looked up into Milton's face. "Jesus said that if you preach the Gospel and folks refuse to listen, you should shake the dust off your feet and move on. You are wasting your time here."

"Jesus loves you and died for your sin. Your unholy choices can be covered in his precious blood."

"Don't you know that God has given up on us homosexuals?" the man said. "We're reprobates and an abomination to His heart. That's what the Bible teaches in Leviticus twenty-two, isn't it? Why are you wasting your time on us?"

Earl walked over and tried to gently move Milton away from the man.

"Is this your boyfriend?" the belligerent man asked Milton.

Turning to Earl, the man crooned: "I can't blame you for lusting in your heart for this one. He's got a great body and I bet, a huge dick. Talk about fellowship of the saints."

"You are a God-forsaken pervert!" Milton screeched. "Your mind has been darkened by the lust of your own flesh and deceived by the enemy. You are going to hell." He was panting and red-faced.

"That's true," the man agreed calmly. "But at least I'm enjoying the ride. Unlike your boyfriend here"—his head gestured toward Earl—"who's afraid to let his true feelings show."

Earl was so shocked he didn't have a response.

"It's okay," the man said. "You can pray all you want, but the dark desires won't go away. Trust me, I know." The man winked at Earl, then turned and walked across the street.

Milton screamed Bible passages until he was out of range.

———————————————

"Did you see the Jesus-ites across the street?"

Thumper flopped down in the booth seat across from Matt and Jonah.

They were having dinner at the Bronx, a local restaurant on Cedar Springs Road.

"The hunky one is your typical angry fundie," he said with a sharp grunt. "But the younger one's a closet case who's crusading for Jesus and hoping to eradicate his own self-doubts."

"Some queers have gaydar," Matt snickered. "Thumper has sanctified sonar."

Thumper looked at Matt and Jonah. "Y'all going dancin' tonight?"

"Nope, I've got finals coming up," Jonah answered. "Have to hit the books."

"Should we even try to guess your plans?" Matt asked.

Thumper rubbed his stomach. "I've been invited to dessert by a Pastry Chef I met at JR's. Sweet and tasty, I'm sure."

Jonah looked over at Matt. "Is he talking about the chef or the dessert?"

"I'm sure both will be consumed before the evening is done," Matt said.

As Thumper was walking to his car, he saw the two street preachers packing up their stuff in the parking lot behind Crossroads. He couldn't resist walking in their direction.

"You're quitting so early in the evening," Thumper accused.

The hunky preacher turned and, upon recognizing him, glared with what could only be called holy hatred. The young, stockier guy looked terrified.

"This is the time serious queers will be coming out. We're like vampires, you know," Thumper said. "Creatures of darkness."

"We're just being obedient to our hearts." The younger man's voice was quiet, his tone sincere. "We know the love of God and we're here sharing it. We don't want to offend and we don't want to debate."

"But you're also hoping that this godly devotion will somehow overpower your lustful, carnal desires. And you're here with him—" he looked over at Milton, who was putting boxes in the truck—"because you're secretly hoping that one day he'll return your feelings. Perhaps share your passion. And your bed?"

The shock was evident, as Thumper had intended.

"Look, you got your way, we're leaving." The young man turned and headed in the direction of the truck.

Thumper followed, taunting. "But Jesus said if you put your hand to the plow and then turn back, you ain't worthy of the kingdom of God. Hey, that kinda puts us in the same boat, doesn't it? I'm not worthy 'cause I'm queer and you're not worthy 'cause you're quitters."

The big man threw down the sign he'd been carrying, turned and pointed at Thumper with fury in his eyes. "In Jesus name, I command the demons of lust and perversion and immorality to come out of you. I speak healing, freedom and redemption in the powerful name of the Lord Jesus Christ. Loose him, Satan, and let him go!"

Having been raised in the Pentecostal Church, Thumper was familiar with this kind of antic. He faked a shudder that would pass for a grand mal seizure, then suddenly stood very still, defiantly crossed his arms over his chest.

"How 'bout that. I'm still queer. Guess your Jesus-spell didn't work. I reckon homosexuals are immune to your puny Pentecostal incantations." He laughed his best impression of the Wicked Witch of the West.

The man rushed over, grabbed Thumper by the shoulders and shook him forcefully.

"Come out, Satan. Set him free, Jesus."

Thumper suddenly realized the situation had escalated beyond what he intended. Terrified, he looked pleadingly to the other man for some kind of rescue.

"Stop it, Milt!" the young man shouted. "Let him go!"

He rushed over and tried to push the big man away, but was struck in the chin by the hunky preacher's elbow, sending him to the ground, stunned by the impact.

Thumper swung both arms—full strength—into the sides of his attacker's chest. The man fell to his knees, trying to catch his breath.

"You're a crazy person," Thumper snarled. He was panting, trying to catch his breath. "If this is your idea of evangelism, you should have lived during the crusades."

Thumper turned to leave, but stopped when he heard the young man on the ground shriek "No!" He looked back, and in that instant felt the impact of the wooden pole from the "repent" sign hit him in the head.

Everything went black.

Earl saw Milton kicking the man who appeared to be unconscious. By the time he got himself up off the pavement, Milton was on top of the guy, still casting out demons while punching the man in the face over and over.

"Stop it, Milt. You're going to kill him!"

He used the only thing he could find—his Bible—to slam Milton in the back of the neck. His friend crumpled onto the sidewalk, sobbing uncontrollably.

Earl moved quickly to the side of the injured man and leaned in to listen for breathing. He looked over at Milton. "You need to get out of here," Earl ordered. "Grab the rest of the stuff and go home. I'll call you later."

"But I—"

"Listen to me! This man is hurt and I have to stay with him. Do you understand me, Milton? Just go home. Now!" he screeched.

Milton whimpered, but did as he was instructed. As he got in the truck, Earl noticed someone coming out the side door of the gay bookstore.

"Please call 9-1-1," he instructed with calm authority. "This man's been injured and we need an ambulance."

He gently took the injured man's hand and found a pulse.

"I am so sorry. It wasn't supposed to be like this."

He quietly began to pray. He was still praying when a paramedic pulled him off and began treatment.

PART 2:

Put to death the deeds of the flesh

Eleven

Jonah was lying asleep in his arms when the phone rang. Matt gently reached over and answered it.

"You sorry bastard," the caller snarled.

Matt almost hung up. "Who the hell is this?"

"Thumper?" The voice on the other end now had less venom.

"No, he's not here."

"Tell that little fucker that I don't like being stood up. I went to a lot of trouble to make this dessert."

Matt sat up in bed, pulling his arm from under Jonah, waking him in the process.

"I'm sorry. We had dinner with Thumper and when he left us, he was going to your place. What time is it?" He turned the light on to see it was nearly midnight. "That was hours ago," he thought aloud.

Matt heard a click, ending the call. He immediately dialed Thumper's cell number.

"What's wrong?" Jonah grunted in a just-woke-up voice.

Matt wasn't exactly sure if he should be concerned.

"Thumper never showed up for his date. That was the guy he was supposed to meet, and he's pissed about being stood up."

He turned and saw Jonah on the side of the bed, putting his pants on. "Let's head down to the strip and look around," he instructed.

"It's probably nothing," Matt mumbled without much conviction. "He's not picking up his cell."

As they drove the short distance down Cedar Springs Road, Matt found himself getting more frantic.

"Any idea where he parked?" Jonah asked as they approached the strip.

"When he left the Bronx, he was headed across the street, probably to the parking lot behind Round-Up." Matt pointed in the general direction of the popular Country-Western bar.

Jonah steered past Hunky's and turned left on Throckmorton. Just past Crossroads bookstore, he turned right into the parking lot. As they were looking for a parking space—no easy task on a Saturday night—Matt spotted the car.

"Maybe he met someone and changed his plans," he suggested.

"Doesn't seem likely," Jonah said, shaking his head. "He was pretty stoked about having that chef for dessert."

After finally finding a parking place several blocks away, they walked the distance back to the strip. Crossing Cedar Springs Road, they went to JR's, one of Thumper's favorite bars, but the bartender had not seen him.

For nearly thirty minutes, they went into every bar on the strip, looking around and asking if anyone had seen him. As they were leaving Throckmorton Mining Company, a denim and leather bar, Matt overheard a conversation that stopped him. Jonah moved in closer to listen as well. One of the bartenders was talking to a couple of customers at the bar near the door.

"Terry told me that three guys jumped him behind the Round-Up."

"I heard it was over by Crossroads," one of the customers corrected.

"Probably just a lover's quarrel," the bartender said with indifference.

Matt and Jonah immediately left the bar, walking quickly to the other side of the street to Crossroads bookstore. It was the cashier—he didn't know Thumper—who knew the story.

"I didn't actually see what happened, but when I saw the ambulance lights, I went outside. It was behind where the leather shop used to be." He gestured back and over his head.

"By the time I got there, they'd taken him away, but I heard the cops talking. It was three guys arguing, then two of them got into a fight. They aren't even calling it an attack."

He looked at Jonah with obvious concern. "Do you think...?

But Jonah was already on his cell phone, calling the local police department, where he learned that one "victim" had been taken to Baylor Hospital. They rushed back to the car and were at the hospital in less than thirty minutes.

When they entered the emergency room, they walked up to large counter. Off to the side, Matt saw a police officer talking to a young man with a blood-stained shirt. The man was seated, while the officer was standing, towering over him. Matt willed himself not to look at the gory stains.

Don't panic, he told himself. *This is Saturday night in an emergency room. Could be anything.*

Matt and Jonah stood for several minutes before the young woman glanced up at them with an annoyed expression, like they were interrupting some task more important than the job posted on the overhead sign: Information Desk. She didn't speak, but finally raised her eyebrows and intensified her glare, which he took as a demand for him to speak.

"Uhm, I'm looking for my roommate. He might have been attacked. I'm not sure it was him. The police...we called them before we left...the police said someone was brought here—"

"What's the name?" she asked without looking away from the computer screen.

"Thumper...uhm, I mean, Barnabas. Barnabas Rivers."

"Can I help you?' the officer asked when he heard Matt speak the name.

"I'm so sorry," the man seated in the chair whimpered. "It was an accident."

The cop shushed him and turned back to them.

"He's in there," pointing past the nurses desk, to an area behind closed double-doors, confirming Matt's fears.

It was obvious he wasn't going to get much from the cop, so Matt addressed bloody-shirt guy. "What did you do to him?" he demanded in a loud voice.

The policeman imposed himself between Matt and the seated man.

"He's a nurse who was with your friend when the paramedics got there. I'm questioning him at the moment, so I suggest you sit down and wait until we get an update on your friend."

His tone was professional, and firm. But mostly firm.

Matt turned to go back into the waiting area.

"Do you know how to get in touch with a relative?" the cop asked, as if an afterthought.

"His folks live out of state, in Alabama. Their number should be in his cell phone."

"His phone was damaged in the fight. Any idea how to find them?"

"I have it in my phone." He scrolled through the directory. "His father is a TV preacher...Reverend James Rivers—"

When Matt gave the name of the preacher, he heard bloody-shirt guy gasp. At the same instant, Jonah vocalized a surprised "What?"

Matt found the number from his cell phone directory and recited it to the officer.

"Thanks," the cop said. "I'll let you know if I need anything else." He turned and resumed his conversation with bloody-shirt guy.

"Thumper is the son of Jimmy Rivers, the TV preacher?" Jonah asked as they walked away. "That can't be easy, since I know how his father feels about homosexuals."

After an hour of waiting with no updates, Matt nudged the sleeping Jonah. "This is crazy. C'mon, I have an idea."

They walked outside and he called the hospital on his cell phone.

"May I speak with Joe Rodriquez? He's a nurse, but I'm not sure what floor he works on."

Joe was one of Thumper's former tricks who'd essentially spent an entire weekend at the apartment. Matt would occasionally see him at the bars. One evening, Joe unloaded his hurt feelings about the weekend tryst and the fact that Thumper never called back. As usual, when he had to deal with the broken hearts Thumper left behind, Matt had been sympathetic and supportive.

When Joe got on the phone, Matt said, "I'm downstairs in the emergency room. They brought Thumper in earlier—"

"An STD?"

Matt decided to let that go.

"He was attacked, Joe. I don't know the details and can't get anything from the nurse—"

"Oh God, Matt. I'm such an asshole. I am so sorry. What can I do to help?"

"Is there any way you can check on how he's doing?"

"Let me see what I can find out," Joe offered. "I'll come down and find you."

Within twenty minutes, he saw Joe come through the double-door and gestured with his head to go outside. Matt and Jonah followed him through the double-doors to a small garden area.

Joe looked around cautiously, then took a deep breath. "I could get in real trouble for telling you this, Matt. It's against the rules."

Matt forced his tone and volume to cooperate. "How is he?"

Joe shook his head, in that slow, sad way people use when they have bad news. "It ain't good, dude. He was real beat up. Trauma to his head, a couple of broken ribs, stuff like that. He's on a respirator 'cause he's not breathing on his own. Right now, he's unresponsive."

He paused and took a deep breath. "I have to tell you, they're very worried about him back there."

The emotion Matt had been holding back—the fear, the worry and the concern—came forth in a surge of tears. Jonah held him, softly speaking words of comfort.

"Let me know if there's anything I can do." Joe patted Matt on the arm as he left.

"Let's go." Jonah led him back inside and down one of the halls. They entered the chapel, where they sat on a pew. Jonah prayed softly, though Matt couldn't understand the words he was saying. He silently voiced his own prayers.

A phone call in the middle of the night is not unusual for a minister, but since he now had several associates on staff, it hadn't happened in a long time. He was awake instantly as he reached for the phone.

"Is this James Rivers?" the voice asked.

"Yes, I'm James Rivers."

"Are you the father of Barnabas Rivers, who lives in Dallas?"

Jim sat up in bed. "May I ask who's calling?"

"This is Sergeant Randall Mitchell, with the Dallas Police Department. I apologize for the late hour—"

"Is my son in some kind of trouble, officer?" The tone in his voice could not hide his growing concern.

"He's in the hospital, sir. He was attacked and—"

"What?" The outburst woke up Gwen. "Is he alright?"

"What's happened to Barnabas?" she gasped.

"It would be a good idea if you come to the hospital," he suggested firmly. Then he added with seriousness: "I think you should come...*now!*"

When the chapel door opened, Matt looked up to see bloody-shirt guy come in. Jonah looked up, too. At the same time, the guy also saw them. He hesitated momentarily, as if he was going to leave, then walked over and knelt beside the pew.

"I am so sorry," he stammered through his tears. "This wasn't supposed to happen. It was...he didn't mean to hurt your friend." He talked so softly it was difficult to hear.

Jonah moved past Matt. "My name is Jonah and this is my boyfriend, Matt. Why don't you tell us what happened?"

Jonah treated Earl with a gentleness that impressed...and annoyed Matt.

After a brief introduction, Earl related the story of how he and Milton came to Cedar Springs. "We were only supposed to be handing out tracts. I didn't want to go to *that* part of town, but Milton insisted. He was convinced that God wanted us there."

Matt gave a grunt that was intended to be heard. "Why attack Thumper? What did he do to deserve that?"

Earl took in a deep breath. "It happened so fast. Milton just seemed to come...unglued. Your friend kept antagonizing us. Twisting Scripture. Challenging him. Said all kinds of dirty stuff. Accused me of...how could he know? I am so sorry."

"Fanatics." Matt spit the words at Earl. "You're telling me that he's here because he refused to take your religious crap like a little sissy. I guess you think he got what he deserved."

"Milton is...he's bi-polar," Earl told them, as if providing an explanation would help. "I think he's off his medication." He let out a deep breath that quivered with emotion.

"Why don't you sit up here?" Jonah patted the pew in front of them.

The young man complied, then got thoughtful. "Your friend...what's his name again?"

"Thumper," they said together.

"He was telling me things about myself that...telling me things he couldn't possibly know."

"It a quirky knack he has," Jonah explained.

"How could he know *that*?" Earl asked with a soft sadness in his voice. "I never told anyone. I've prayed about it for years, but it won't go away?"

Jonah answered. "I think it's a gift from God. He's like an Old Testament prophet, seeing into the heart and calling out the deception. He helped me to face my own lies and live my life with integrity."

"It can't be from God," Earl said, shaking his head in disagreement. It just *can't* be. The feelings...those kind of feelings. God says they're wrong."

"How do you even know what God thinks? " Matt snarled, exasperated.

Jonah deflected the conversation. "Why do you think your friend was so fixated on Cedar Springs and homosexuals?"

Earl seemed to be struggling with a response. "He's been listening to some tapes, you know, about the spiritual decline in America. He became obsessed with the gay agenda. The bizarre thing is...." He was glancing back at the door, as if expecting someone to come in.

"It okay," Jonah consoled. "You can talk to us."

"The tapes. The ones Milton's been listening to. Well, he got them...they were preached by...they are by Brother Jimmy Rivers."

"Thumper's father?" Matt exclaimed.

Jonah put his hand on Earl's shoulder, but looked at Matt. "Listen, I think it's best if we keep this to ourselves."

"I'm not sure what you mean," Matt said.

"I mean, when Thumper's parents get here...well, this would only add to their pain, don't you think?"

"*Their* pain?" he snapped, in full volume. "It was his teaching that caused this to happen."

Jonah remained calm. "And hurting them is not going to solve anything, is it? We need to show some compassion."

"Someone certainly does," Matt snapped.

Earl stood up. "I have to go to the police station and sign my statement. Milton should be there by now. I just came in here to pray for him...and your friend...before facing it all."

"How did they catch him so quickly?" Jonah asked.

Earl dropped his head. "I gave them his home address. I want to be there to make sure he's okay. I also want the police to know about his meds."

Jonah patted him gently. "We will be praying as well. Go, be with your friend. He needs you. Here's my cell phone number," Jonah offered. Earl did the same. "If anything happens here, I'll give you a call. And if you need us for anything, just call."

"You might want to change shirts." Matt indicated the red-splattered stain.

Earl looked down at his shirt. "I live forty minutes away. Not much I can do."

"I think I can help."

Matt pulled out his phone and called Joe again. Within a few minutes, the nurse brought down a scrub top for him to wear.

"Thank you. I appreciate all you've done." Earl's voice had a sincerity that was hard to ignore.

"Can't have you walk into the police station all covered in blood," Matt replied sheepishly. "Might cause the cops to faint."

"That was nice of you," Jonah complimented, once Earl had left. He put his arm around Matt and they sat back down on the pew.

"Yeah, well you're too nice," he said. "He was there, when Thumper was being beaten by that maniac. He should be locked up with his crazy boyfriend."

"Earl's not a bad person. And he's not a criminal. He was in the wrong place. Definitely with the wrong person. It's obvious he's scared…and struggling. He needs us."

"I say it again: you are too nice." A tired, faint smile appeared. "But that's one of the reasons I love you."

He laid his head on Jonah's shoulder.

He felt a soft kiss on his face as Jonah spoke softly into his ear. "I love you, too."

It was the first time either of them had verbalized their feelings.

Thanks, Thumper, Matt acknowledged. *You brought us together and I'll forever be grateful.*

TWELVE

"MY NAME IS DOCTOR MILES STERN. I was on duty when they brought your son in."

Jim Rivers stood when the young doctor walked into the ER waiting room and greeted them. His wife, Gwen, was holding on to his arm supportively.

It was nearly five in the morning. They'd arrived a half an hour earlier, and were told to wait until the doctor could meet with them. After getting the phone call, it had only taken them a few hours to get to Dallas from Birmingham, with the generous assistance of a private jet from one of the church's wealthy members.

"How is my boy?" Gwen whimpered.

"I won't lie to you," the doctor reported. "He's in bad shape. Most of the injuries should heal fine: a broken wrist, a fractured pelvis, couple of cracked ribs, cuts and bruises. What concerns us is the head injury. There's been some swelling around the brain, and it looks like some trauma to the skull. We relieved the immediate pressure on his brain, but we don't know the extent of the damage."

"What does that mean, doctor?" He determined to remain calm.

The physician took a slow, deep breath. "There could be brain damage—"

Gwen gasped, and her hold on him loosened. "Oh, dear Jesus, protect my baby!" Jim put his arm around his wife's waist and pulled her close.

"Right now, he's unconscious. We should know more in the next few hours."

As the doctor turned to leave, Gwen asked, "When do you think he'll wake up?"

The young doctor stopped, looked back at her and then down at the floor. "We're not sure he will."

"Can we see him?" Her words gurgled with emotion.

"As soon as they get him into a bed, I'll have the nurses let you know so you can be with him. Again, I'm so very sorry, but please know that we're doing everything possible."

"I appreciate that, Doctor Stern," he said before the doctor could walk away. "And I think you should also know that *we* will be doing everything as well. I will be putting out a national call to my ministry supporters, who will bathe this place and all your staff in the power and presence of God's healing power. God will show His mighty power with an undeniable miracle."

Gwen whispered quietly. "Yes, dear Lord. In the name of Jesus, we speak it into reality."

"That's him."

"Huh?" Matt mumbled, bleary from lack of sleep.

They'd finally left the hospital around four o'clock, went home, showered and had some cereal. Now they were back, still waiting for any information about Thumper.

"That's Doctor Rivers, Thumper's father," Jonah informed in a soft voice. "I recognize him from when he preached at CFNI last year."

Matt looked over the large man standing to the side of the emergency check-in desk. A petite woman was standing beside him. He also recognized him from having watched a couple of his TV programs.

"Stay here," he told Jonah.

When Matt walked up, Thumper's father was talking on a cell phone, so he stood a few feet away. He could hear enough of the conversation to know they were deciding how to handle today's Sunday morning broadcast, which apparently was supposed to be done live, but a repeat of a past sermon would be substituted. The minister instructed them to wait until they knew more about Barnabas' condition before making any public announcement.

As soon as the man hung up, Matt moved closer.

"You're Reverend Rivers." It was less of a question than a statement. "My name is Matt. I'm Thump—, uhm, I'm Barnabas' roommate."

The look he got from the minister caused Matt to shudder. The unrelenting glare—combined with tightened lips and clenched jaw—radiated contempt and anger. The man's face turned crimson as he stared without saying a word.

"Thank you for being here."

The greeting came from behind the hefty minister.

"I'm Gwendolyn Rivers, Barnabas' mother," she said as she stepped closer to Matt. "We are so grateful to know that his friends are here." It was obvious she'd been crying.

"We were here right after they brought him in. I gave the police your phone number. Thumper gave it to me, in case I ever needed it. I hope that's okay."

Her tight expression softened a bit and the corner of her mouth turned slightly upward.

"He still goes by Thumper? I never liked that name, but he always did."

"Have you heard anything?"

"They're doing what they can." There was a tremor in her voice. "The doctor told us—"

Thumper's father loudly cleared his throat, an obvious signal to his wife.

"We don't know much yet," she finished.

He decided it was best to address her. "I've known him since our sophomore year at DSU. He's my best friend. That's Jonah over there—" he motioned in the general direction where they'd been seated on the far side of the waiting area. "We're here if you need us. And there's a chapel down the hall. We were there earlier, praying for him."

Her face suddenly displayed genuine gratitude.

"Hallelujah! I've just come from the chapel myself. We'll join our faith, rebuke the devil and claim my son's healing. We speak it so in Jesus' name!"

"Uhm…sure. We're here if you need us," he repeated as he slowly backed away.

About an hour later, Matt saw an attractive man walk up to the couple. Unlike his own encounter, he noticed that with this guy, Reverend Rivers was overtly animated. He didn't want to stare at the family in their time of grief, but he did see Thumper's father point in their direction. The handsome man looked at them, then back at the preacher.

"I think I'd like some coffee," he said to Jonah, who'd dozed off again.

"I'm so glad you called me. Have you seen the doctor yet?"

When Winston arrived, Gwen stood and gave him a huge hug, accompanied with sobbing. He held her and let her weep, struggling to hold back his own feelings.

"They're not saying much," Dr. Rivers informed. "He's unconscious, and has some injuries to his skull. We have folks all over the country praying for him, so we are not fearful."

"We will not allow the opinion of doctors to sway our faith," she pronounced, with an obvious attempt at bravery. "We're standing on the Word of our Great Physician."

Dr. Rivers shared that two men had been involved in the attack and one had been arrested. The pastor also complained that there were friends of Barnabas in the waiting area. He pointed out the two, who were seated near the nurses' station.

"I need them gone," he demanded with unhidden emotion.

Before Winston could say anything, Gwen spoke up. "They are his friends, Jimmy. It's not our place to tell them they can't be here."

"I sense in my spirit they are bound by the same dark desires as my son. They could hinder the work of healing that God wants to do here."

Winston didn't understand the preacher's logic.

Even if they are gay, how could that be stronger than God's power?

He looked over at the area, but the guys had apparently left.

"I brought you some snacks."

Mrs. Rivers looked at Matt with obvious gratitude. "Thank you, dear. That's so kind."

Matt shrugged it off. There were several people in the ICU waiting room, so he put the bag of sandwiches and homemade cookies down next to her chair. Reverend Rivers was sitting a few seats away, talking to the good-looking man he'd seen earlier in the week.

It had been a couple of days, and Matt wasn't sure if Thumper's parents had even left the hospital during that time.

"Is there anything I can do?" Without waiting for a response, he added: "If you need to shower or wash some clothes, you're welcome to use our place. It's not that far from here."

"That won't be necessary." Reverend Rivers' tone was gruff.

"He's just trying to be helpful, Jimmy."

Mrs. Rivers looked up at Matt. "We truly appreciate it. We've rented a hotel room near here. But we try to stay here, since they only let us in to see him every few hours. When Barnabas gets better and has his own room, we will need to get him some pajamas to wear."

He didn't mention that Thumper never slept in pajamas. Or anything, for that matter. Instead, he gave a barely negligible nod in her direction.

"Just let me know, and I'll be glad to help. And we got his car from the parking lot where he…uhm, where he left it."

She gave him a motherly pat on the arm. "You are such a dear. Thank you very much."

"Have you heard anything else from the doctors?"

"There hasn't been any change. He's in a…he's still not awake yet. But we're believing for a miracle."

"I put him on the prayer list at church. He has lots of folks praying—"

Reverend Rivers ejected himself from the chair and confronted Matt. "We have hundreds of *godly* believers standing with us. Those who *truly* believe in the power of God."

He took in a deep breath and let it out audibly. This face was red.

"We stand with those who live in the authority of God's Word."

Matt was fairly certain he was being challenged. Possibly reprimanded. But he chose not to engage the preacher in his time of crisis. "Well, we will continue to pray. And my offer stands, if you need anything, give me a call."

As he left, he looked back at Reverend Rivers and rolled his eyes in disdain.

"I think I'll get some coffee. Can I get you anything?"

Winston waited, but both declined. He walked quickly out of the waiting area and almost had to run to catch up with the man who'd just left the waiting room.

"He's not trying to be mean," Winston declared, causing the man to stop before pushing the elevator button. There was a perplexed look on his face as he turned and looked at Winston.

"Doctor Rivers. He's under a lot of stress right now. I'm sure he wasn't trying to be so...*crotchety.*"

Winston extended his hand. "My name is Winston DuMont—"

"Of course you are! Exactly as Thumper described." He didn't complete the sentence and didn't receive the handshake.

Winston withdrew his hand. "From the conversation back there," he gestured back toward the waiting room. "I assume you're Matt. Thumper told me about you. I'm glad to finally meet you, but wish the situation were different."

"I do think you're wrong, though," Matt said cryptically.

"Wrong about what?"

"I believe Reverend Rivers is every bit that crotchety. Since the day they arrived, he's been nothing but snide to me. I mean, I get it. I remind him that his son's a queer, and he hates me for that. But it's not like I'm the one who hurt him. The person who did this was one of...*you*"—he spewed the word with intense contempt, and for emphasis, wagged his finger at Winston—"a religious fanatic thinking he was doing the will of God."

"How do you know that?" Winston questioned with sincere interest. That was not part of the story Doctor Rivers had related.

"I met one of the guys involved when the police were here. Right after they brought Thumper in." Matt's voice was now quivering with emotion. "Reverend Rivers can hate me if he wants, but I care about Thumper and I only want to help."

"I understand. Thumper is a wonderful person and certainly didn't deserve this."

Matt's eyes narrowed. "But if he were an asshole—which he could be at times—he *would* have deserved this?"

Winston felt a deep sadness come over him that brought an extended sigh. "That was insensitive of me. I apologize. It's not what I meant, but I should have phrased it differently."

Matt's expression didn't change, nor did the irritated tone of his voice. "You know, there will be some folks who'll think he got just what he deserved. I suspect his parents have even had those fleeting thoughts."

Winston stiffened. "Please believe me. I am not one of those people. I truly cared…care about him. As a friend," he clarified.

"Bullshit," Matt retorted with discernible annoyance. "Friends don't kick you to the curb, like you did to him. You really hurt him, you know?"

Matt glared at him, daring him to defend.

He wanted to feign ignorance, but was sure a wave of emotions would override even his rigorous attorney training.

"I know," he whispered.

Matt did not let up. "He liked you. Trusted you. Thumper doesn't let a lot of people into his life, but he thought you were his friend."

"What did he tell you? About our last meeting?"

"He said you told him y'all had to stop hanging out together. He figured it was because he wouldn't go to that ex-gay group with you."

"There was more to…it's…complicated. I never got to tell him that, but it's the truth." Winston words had little volume, but much feeling.

"He liked you," Matt repeated. There was an escalating anger to his words. "Not as a boyfriend or nothing. He knew about your…your straight oath…but he respected you and said that you challenged him and made him think. Then you dumped him and it messed him up."

And he had a similar effect on me, Winston concluded silently.

To Matt he only extended another heart-felt apology.

Matt turned to leave. "If you'll excuse me, I need to get to the apartment for some recon. His parents will be coming over to get some of his stuff, and I'm his sweeper."

Winston's confusion must have shown on his face.

"It's a pact we made," Matt explained. "Just in case something happened to one of us. As his sweeper, I'm designated to clean up anything that might be, you know…embarrassing. Those things that boys who play with other boys use, but don't want momma to find."

"Listen, why don't I give you my cell phone number? If you don't hear anything about Thumper, call me. I'll see what I can do to keep you updated on what I hear from the parents. Is that okay?"

Matt programmed the number into his cell phone. He looked up and remarked, "Well, I gotta get home. Thanks for the phone number."

He once again turned to leave, but looked back at Winston. "I know I'm a jerk, but he's my best friend and I hated seeing him hurt like that."

"Trust me. I deserve everything you've said."

THIRTEEN

HE TRIED TO OPEN HIS EYES, but they seemed glued shut.

Where am I? was his first thought.

No answer came.

He forced his eyes to open, but the intense light in the room felt like shards of glass, and amplified the immense headache that now came to his attention.

He tried to speak, but there was something in mouth. The garbled words brought pain to his throat as well. He was getting frustrated. And annoyed. The aggravation only increased when he attempted to grab his throat, only to discover his arms were strapped down. The irritation switched to fear and he began shaking and twisting to get loose.

"Relax, Mr. Rivers. If you promise to settle down, I'll take off the restraints."

Her voice was quiet and soothing. He opened his eyes slightly, and saw a woman in a medical uniform. Her badge gave her name as Wilda Morris. Once again, he attempted to speak.

"Don't talk yet, I need to remove your tube."

She reached up to a stainless steel panel mounted above his bed and pushed a red button. Within seconds, a static-laced voice boomed from the box: "This is the nurses' station."

She glanced in his direction and gave a reassuring wink. She then turned back to the panel and spoke in a firm voice, "Page Doctor Stern, please. Tell him the patient is awake."

She gave him a big smile. "Let's take that tube out, how 'bout it? It will be a little uncomfortable, so be very still."

It was more than "a little uncomfortable" as she slowly withdrew the hose which was down his throat. He gagged a couple of times and thought he was going to throw up, but once it was out, he took a deep breath and the nausea passed. His throat felt scratchy and dry, so he pointed to the yellow plastic water pitcher beside the bed.

"How about some ice?" the nurse suggested. "Not too much, though. Now, I'm going to unbuckle the straps, but be sure not to move around too much. You have an IV in your arm, and we don't want to pull it out, do we?"

He shook his head, as if she expected an answer. The ice felt wonderful in his mouth and going down his parched throat.

"Thank you," he mouthed.

"You have some visitors waiting to see you, but the doctor wanted to give you a thorough exam first. So why don't you rest and I'll come back and check on you in a few minutes."

"Where am I?" he said as loud as he could to prevent the pain and still be heard over the machines in the room.

She was reading his chart at the end of his bed.

"You're at Baylor Hospital. And we are very, *very* glad to see you."

"Hospital?" He was suddenly frightened.

How did I get here? he screamed to himself, knowing to do so out loud would be painful.

"The doctor will answer all your questions, honey."

She patted his leg and turned off the lights as she left.

He closed his eyes and enjoyed the cooling flow of the ice melting down his throat. He tried not to acknowledge his growing panic.

"We're moving him to a private room, per your request. You'll be able to see him as soon as they get him settled." The doctor was standing with the Rivers in a consultation room near the ICU.

"There appears to be some...some memory loss," he said, then added quickly: "We figure that's due to the cranial swelling. It should pass as he gets better. That's our hope, anyway."

Dr. Stern chose his words carefully, having learned from previous interactions that Reverend Rivers would forcefully challenge any prognosis that disagreed with his desired outcome. The TV preacher had trumpeted to the medical staff that God had spoken to him and the patient was headed for a full and miraculous recovery. Any opinions, data or diagnoses to the contrary were met with adamant sermons about faith in God's promises, or a string of Bible verses about the dangerous power of negative words.

"Memory loss?" Reverend Rivers questioned.

Dr. Stern nodded, but included a slight smile to make it seem less dire. "It's quite common with this kind of head injury. Usually resolves itself, assuming there's no permanent damage. He got a bit anxious earlier, so we gave him a mild sedative. He should be awake and more alert in a few hours."

"I need to see him," Mrs. Rivers declared, to no one in particular. She reached for her purse and needlework.

"What happens now?" the father asked.

"I've called in some experts and we'll run tests to determine the extent and the permanence...if any...of his memory loss. We'll also need to see if he needs rehabilitation—"

"Rehabilitation?" Reverend Rivers interrupted. "What does that mean?" His wife stopped gathering her personal items and listened intently.

Be careful, the doctor told himself.

"It's just a precaution. The broken pelvis will probably require some physical therapy. And *sometimes...*" He emphasized the word to avoid a confrontation with the preacher. "...sometimes with head trauma, there can also be damage to motor functions. Talking, walking, things like that. We just want to be prepare—"

"That is not going to happen!" the preacher boomed, as if his tone and volume would influence the outcome of his son's recovery. "I have heard from God—the Great Physician—and He will restore my son. It will be quick, it will be complete...and it will be miraculous." He used his finger to punctuate his points. "I have the promise of Almighty Jehovah on that."

The doctor let out the breath he'd been holding during the tirade. "I understand, sir."

"I'm ready to see Barnabas now," Mrs. Rivers announced resolutely. "Thank you so much, Doctor."

She didn't wait for a response, so the minister followed his wife out the door toward their son's room.

Dr. Stern was exasperated as he left the room. Another doctor who'd been brought in for a psychiatric evaluation of the patient was standing nearby, apparently waiting for him.

"I hope you can come up with a good report for their son," Dr. Stein said to him. "That man won't accept anything less than a miracle."

"Then let's give him that miracle," came the confident reply.

———————————

"Barnabas, it's Momma. Can you wake up for me?"

"Momma?" He slowly opened his eyes.

Talking was still uncomfortable. And though most of the pain was gone, the tube down his throat had obviously left him hoarse. He was surprised the first time he heard his own voice at how deep it sounded.

The room was bright enough to get a tan, so he found himself squinting. But as his vision focused, he saw the two people standing at the right side of his bed.

Yes, those are my parents, but something is...different.

He tried harder to focus in the harsh light. He immediately recognized the distinct difference in their heights; she was standing closer and his dad was looming over her. His father's face had the usual stern look, with that ever-present shade of red that made him look like he'd been running.

"We are very glad to see you." His dad's voice was unmistakable.

His looked up at his mother and saw she was crying.

"Am I in trouble?" He took her hand. "Have I done something wrong?" She fell on him and wept.

"I'm sorry, Momma," he repeated over and over. "Please don't be mad at me."

"Do you mind if I speak to him?" It was the man he'd met earlier—the doctor.

She moved and the man stepped in closer. "Barnabas, do you remember me? I'm Doctor Stern."

He said yes, but kept his eyes on his parents. He was still trying to figure out how the light was causing such strange effects on their faces.

"Do you know where you are?" the doctor asked.

He looked around, and gave a smirk. "It ain't McDonald's."

Everyone laughed, but the doctor asked again.

"I'm in Balford Hospital."

"It's Baylor," she corrected, but the doctor held up his hand, indicating he didn't want anyone to help.

"That's right, Barnabas. And do you know how you got here? Do you remember why you are in the hospital?"

His chin quivered and tears formed in his eyes. "Did I wreck the Pontiac, Daddy? Is Marti okay?"

His mom gasped and both parents quickly looked over at the doctor, who again used his upheld hand to keep them from talking. "Can you tell me the last thing you remember? Something or some place that you can clearly recall?"

"Sure," he replied confidently. "No prob."

He closed his eyes for several seconds, as if less florescent light would summon the requested memories.

"Hmm, I think...I went to..." His embarrassment triggered a weak, nervous laugh, but he tried to focus his mind. "It's all jumbled up. I can hear songs...and see pictures, like on a slideshow."

"That's good," the doctor complemented. "Do any of the places in the slideshow seem familiar to you?"

"Well, I think I remember going to my soccer game." Long pause. "Or maybe it was practice..." He raised his arms and slammed them to his side. "God dammit, this is fuckin' stupid."

"Barnabas! We do not use that kind of language."

"I'm sorry, Daddy."

The doctor moved closer to the bed. "It's okay, Barnabas. Just concentrate."

I can do this, he affirmed to himself.

"Marti and I went to a movie, but I can't remember the name of it. I had a student council meeting and we have a Bible study with the youth group coming up." He knew he was rambling. But the jig-sawed fragments of memories would not fit together into a solid image.

The doctor smiled. "You're doing great. Don't worry about it right now. Your injury has affected your memory, but we're going to try and clear it all up. Can you be patient for me?"

He shrugged, though it hurt his shoulder. "I guess since I'm in the hospital, I have no choice but to be...*patient*."

Before he had the chance to learn more about the accident, he heard the doctor invite his parents to go out into the hall. He figured they wanted to talk about him, without him hearing. He didn't like being left out.

Why can't I remember the accident?

He took a deep breath. An alarm sounded within as it dawned on him.

Why can't I remember anything?

Once in the hall, Dr. Stern motioned for the parents to follow. It was obvious they needed to talk, but he wanted to get them to a private place, so he took them to a small family counseling room, used by doctors and chaplains for private consultations.

"I know you must have lots of questions," he said compassionately, once they were all seated. Mrs. Rivers was already starting to tear up again.

"You told us about the chance of memory loss." The father's tone was serious. "But he's talking about things that happened years ago."

"Like the Pontiac?" The doctor glanced down at the chart in his hands.

"I had one, right after he turned sixteen," Mrs. Rivers related. "It's the car he learned to drive in."

He wrote the details in the chart. "And who is Marti?"

A pleasant smile came to her face. "They were sweethearts. Known each other since kindergarten. They were going steady all through high school. We always expected them—"

"Is this kind of confusion normal?" the father interrupted.

"Sometimes, yes. When we tell him what happened—"

"Does he need to know?" Reverend Rivers had a look of concern on his face.

The doctor put the chart on the small table. "It could help reduce his anxiety and frustration. You saw how agitated he got. I think when he knows, he'll be more active in his recovery."

"Do you think the memories will return?" There was anxiety in her voice.

He wanted to instill some hope. "He has some intact memories, which is a good sign. We're waiting on a full report from one of our psych doctors. We haven't seen any initial signs of motor dysfunction, but we won't begin those tests until he's stronger."

The doctor stood and picked up the chart. "I think we should go in together and let him know his situation. Then I'll begin to work up a treatment program—"

"Before we go…" Reverend Rivers remained seated. "I want to discuss precisely what we're going to tell my son about what happened to him. There are some aspects of that night…some facts that he doesn't…that we don't want him to know."

Dr. Stern remembered the police in the emergency room the night of the attack and had heard the gossip around the floor about Barnabas' sexual orientation, so the meaning became clear.

"As you wish, sir," he said, sitting back down and opening the chart.

"August seventeenth, two thousand and six."

He clicked off the micro-cassette recorder. He'd heard his own voice and it sounded shaky. It was imperative that he not communicate weakness or uncertainty.

We're too close now, he reminded himself.

He had been working non-stop for nearly a week, stopping only for short, periodic naps. It was after midnight, and he was tired from lack of sleep but also a bit jittery from excess coffee. He took a deep breath and told himself to relax.

Dr. Randall Davidson, known as "Doctor D" to his patients, was forty-four years old and because he'd spent so much of his adult life excelling in school—with two Master's degrees, a Ph.D., a medical degree and his psychiatric residency—had never married. With a dogged dedication to his practice, he still had little time for a social life, beyond attending church.

Aside from his vast educational accomplishments and higher-than-average IQ, the one word that would sum him up was *average*. He was five feet, ten inches tall and one hundred and fifty-two pounds, with brown hair that was thinning on top and seemed to be in a constant state of rebellion against staying in place. When he talked, it was always slow and precise, choosing every word for clarity. If he looked at you when he talked—usually his grey-blue eyes darted around the room—it was over thin glasses with no frames.

95

Holding the recorder near his mouth, he willed his voice to speak slowly as he pushed the 'on' button. "August seventeenth, two thousand and six." His tone now carried an authority that he hoped others would recognize and appreciate.

"The patient is a twenty-three year old male, admitted eleven days ago with multiple facial lacerations and contusions, several broken bones and a severe head injury, resulting in cranial swelling. He was unconscious for ninety-seven hours. Upon regaining consciousness, the patient demonstrated confusion and disorientation, with symptoms of memory loss, particularly surrounding the events causing his injuries."

His thumb pressed the 'pause' button.

"*Dis*-orientation," he repeated aloud, though he was alone in the room.

Let's hope that stays the case, came the thought that brought a slight grin to his usually serious face.

He could not believe his good fortune. After waiting years to test his full treatment protocol, he'd never expected an opportunity like this one. It was nearly perfect. And the way all the pieces had fallen into place could not be coincidence. He was convinced God had orchestrated the circumstances.

First, he had been asked to consult on the case. Nothing unusual there. But then he learned that not only was the patient suffering from significant memory loss, he was a practicing homosexual. It seems one of the male nurses, who was inquiring about the patient's condition, disclosed that they'd been sexually involved at one time.

If all that wasn't enough, the patient's father was one of the most respected evangelists and Bible teachers in the country. The doctor had many of the preacher's tapes and had attended numerous crusades. He felt certain this great man of God would be supportive, given the desired outcome was clearly God's will.

Taking a breath, he released the 'pause' button.

"I was brought in by the on-call physician for a comprehensive psych-eval. Upon further assessment, there was clear evidence that the memory loss was much more extensive, and included significant events of the patient's past as well. Two days after he woke up, the patient submitted to medically enhanced hypnotherapy. I witnessed positive results with an implanted memory. It's been four days, and he recalls the memory as if it actually happened to him."

He turned the recorder off.

He's a prime candidate, the doctor concluded silently.

FOURTEEN

"Excuse me, sir."

Jim Rivers looked up from his Bible and saw a nurse standing in the doorway. He quickly looked over at his son to see if he was awake again.

"This was left for you at the nurses' station. I was instructed to give it to you when you arrived, but we got busy. Sorry for the delay."

She walked to him and held out the plain, white envelope. He could see his name and the hospital room number written on the front. The sealed envelope was marked 'PRIVATE' in red letters. He thanked the nurse as he took it.

Gwen had gone to the hotel room for some rest. It was almost impossible to get her to leave the room, but he convinced her it would be fine. He put his Bible on the window ledge and opened the envelope to find a handwritten note:

> *Dear Brother Jimmy,*
> *You don't know me, but I'm one of the doctors here at the hospital helping to treat your son. I know the other doctors are giving you little hope. But we both know that God is our Healer and He's the One who confounds the wisdom of men to show Himself strong.*
> *I want to do more. Please meet me tonight at ten, in the consultation room down the hall from your son's room. I hope you'll hear what I have to say. In your heart, you'll know that God has given us this answer. For now, I ask that you keep this communication and the meeting just between us.*
>
> *I have some exciting things to share with you. Your ministry's had a great impact on my life and now, I want to help you and your son.*

It was signed, "Randall," but included the full title as well—Randall R. Davidson, M.D., Ph.D.

Jim had spent his entire adult life in the Pentecostal Church, and though he loved the church's emphasis on the supernatural work of the Holy Spirit, he had learned that it often brought out the immature of the faith, as well as those who relished the spotlight. Since this man was a doctor, and apparently well-education, he wasn't sure what to make of the note or the promise.

He looked at his watch, noting it was already nine-forty. He said a quick prayer.

"Why do you think you can help my son?"

Randall Davidson stared at the well-known preacher, a man he'd admired for so many years. "I've devoted the bulk of my adult life to two primary pursuits: my relationship with Christ and my career. But I don't see them as segmented; they are connected. My work as a doctor and therapist is an extension of my faith. More like a calling than a job."

"What is this treatment that you are proposing?" Brother Jimmy asked. The dispassionate tone in the father's voice didn't expose whether there was interest or mere curiosity.

"My approach is rooted firmly in the standard practices of medicine, psychology and counseling. However, the guiding principle comes from the Bible, particularly passages like Romans, twelve, two: 'Be not conformed to this world, but be ye transformed by the renewing of your mind.' I'm convinced I have an approach that will restore your son."

The preacher gave a single nod, but still did not betray his interest or intentions. "How would you define 'restore?'"

Randall hesitated, not wanting to offend this great man of God. "I know what happened to your son, and I know *why*." He waited to gauge a reaction, but when there was none, he proceeded. "I know that your son is...gay."

Expecting to be grilled how he came upon this fact, he waited. Again, the preacher displayed little reaction beyond the barely visible raising of his right eyebrow.

"Sir, I don't want to be presumptuous and I certainly don't want to add to your grief in this difficult time. I'm not here to judge your son. I believe God allowed me to learn this about your son because I can help."

For the first time, he detected a minute sign of interest. The evangelist's eyes widened and his head cocked ever-so-barely to the right. He chose to interpret it as permission to keep talking. "Brother Jimmy, I've heard your sermons and read your materials, so I know you believe in the power of God to change a person. I admire the fact that even though your own son chose this...uh, path, you never wavered from your convictions."

"I love my son, Doctor. But truth cannot...does not...change to cater to our personal circumstances."

The pain in the father's voice touched him.

"What I'm wanting to do with my program is repair the damage—both the identity damage that caused your son to turn to a life of immorality, as well as the emotional and behavioral damage that has resulted from living in that lifestyle."

"You've worked with homosexuals before?"

"I have several who are patients in my private practice. But I have not had the chance to fully test my comprehensive approach. Truth is, there aren't that many opportunities like this one. Your son is a prime candidate for my protocol."

He didn't tell the pastor of his personal crusade to fight this insidious sin—a vow he'd made the day he stood at the casket of his older brother. After college, Harold had strayed from the faith and slipped into the sin of perversion. The family rejected him, but Randall always held hope for his brother's repentance and restoration. But Howard died of AIDS before God could bring that identity healing.

"Are you talking about restoring his memory?"

One of the problems with hospitals is the doors open quietly. The question came from behind them; they both looked up to see Mrs. Rivers standing in the doorway. She was holding the letter he had written to Brother Jimmy.

"I thought you were resting." Brother Jimmy stood to greet her.

"Couldn't sleep, so I came back and found the note you'd left on your Bible. I don't like being kept in the dark, Jimmy."

She looked at the doctor. "My husband tries to protect me. Keeps things from me when he thinks I'm not strong enough. I'm Barnabas' mother and I *will* have a part in his recovery." Her tone was now forceful, with no chance of being misunderstood and probably no chance of being dissuaded.

"I assume you are…" She glanced back at the note in her hand. "Doctor Davidson?"

He stood and motioned to a chair beside Brother Jimmy. "It's Randall, please. Or if you prefer, my patients sometimes call me Doctor D."

"Please continue, Randall," Brother Jimmy instructed.

"To answer your question, Mrs. Rivers, I cannot promise that we can get the memories back. Amnesia is not like on TV, where the person suddenly remembers everything…just like that." He snapped his fingers for the effect. "Your son's condition was caused by trauma to his head. We'll have to wait to know the full extent. It appears he has what we call retrograde amnesia, which means that events and details prior to the accident have been damaged— that's why it's called *retro*grade. I've seen cases where there is absolutely no recollection of the past, but that's not the case with your son. He remembers some past events, and he recognized both of you."

"Thank you, Jesus," she said quietly. "So he could get his memory back?"

He didn't want to lie, but knew that prognosis was unlikely. He also didn't mention that outcome would severely hinder the success of his proposed plan, so he framed his words carefully.

"We will certainly pray for the very best outcome," he told Mrs. Rivers.

"Our tests have shown that Barnabas has the ability to form new memories, and that's the good news for you and for him. I believe we can restore your son to a place before he made the destructive decisions that led him into his lifestyle. And the very reality of his memory loss will help in that process."

There was confusion on their faces. He took a deep breath and prayed for the wisdom to communicate so they would understand. So they would *agree.*

"Maybe the fact that he can't remember the past few years works to our advantage. I've had a couple of sessions with your son, and from all I can learn, the details of his lifestyle since leaving home are gone. That's a good thing for us and for my treatment protocol. Perhaps it's in his best interest that he doesn't remember the bad life choices."

There were indicators on Brother Jimmy's face that this was making sense. "He remembers high school and he remembers his girlfriend, Marti. You're saying we don't try to recover his most recent memories?"

"Exactly!" he replied eagerly. "I recommend that we reinforce and augment the good memories: his ministry, his girlfriend, his normal desires...and we suppress those involving his life of sin and darkness. I firmly believe that if we re-structure what he remembers, we can literally erase his homosexual identity, along with the desires and impulses. We work in tandem with the Holy Spirit to renew his mind."

"This could work," Brother Jimmy said to his wife. "This could heal our son."

It was now difficult to contain his excitement. "Not only your son, sir. Think of the great victory this would be for the Kingdom of God," he said, sliding forward in his chair. "We could adapt this treatment protocol and use it for others trapped in that sinful mindset, curing them of the deviant behavior."

Brother Jimmy was finally nodding. "It truly is like being 'born again,'" he mused aloud, to no one in particular.

"I think of it in terms of *transformative*," Randall responded enthusiastically. "Like in the passage in the book of Romans, where God calls us to 'be transformed by the renewing of your mind.' I know I'm not telling you anything you don't know, Brother Jimmy, but that word in the original language is the same word we use for the *metamorphosis* of a caterpillar into a butterfly. Your son is once again a caterpillar and we can form a protective cocoon around him and help him emerge as the butterfly God intended him to be."

With both of them now interested, he outlined his recommended procedure. "My approach is multi-faceted and multi-layered. We will utilize some of the best methods of psychotherapy, psychology and medicine, within a decidedly Christian framework."

He waited a moment before informing them of one significant dimension of the program. "We will also be relying heavily on the latest methods of hypnotherapy to—"

The protest came, as he'd expected. "Hypnosis?" Brother Jimmy questioned. "I'm not comfortable with that."

He knew that many conservative Christians had serious reservations about hypnosis, due primarily to misinformation and misrepresentation. Because they thought hypnosis somehow surrendered control of a person's will, they preached that someone could be unduly influenced by Satan, or even possessed by a demonic spirit while hypnotized. And there was the well-known entertainment variety, where a hypnotist would make people cluck like a chicken on stage. Both outlandish perceptions made him cringe.

"Why do you need to *hypnotize* him?" Mrs. Rivers uttered the word like it was an ancient, pagan method of voodoo.

"I understand your concern, Mrs. Rivers," he said in a gentle, sympathetic way. "But it's a valid means to achieve our goals. We will use hypnotherapy to reinforce those important past memories. And if there are sinful or harmful memories that we don't want him to recall, we will use the hypnosis to help him *not* remember. It's perfectly safe."

"What if he can't be hypnotized?" When her husband huffed, she looked over at him. "I've heard there are some people who can't."

He gave his comforting, practiced doctor-smile and placed his hand on her arm. "I have done this many, many times, Mrs. Rivers. It's true that some people try to resist, but that's usually when they want to hide something. We shouldn't have that problem with your son. But I also plan to use a mild benzodiazepine sedative during my sessions with him. It's an anti-anxiety medication that will help him relax, and it's been shown to facilitate hypnotherapy by making patients more receptive to disclosure and suggestion. I'm very confident about this treatment plan."

Mrs. Rivers still looked concerned, but before she could voice those reservations, Brother Jimmy stood up.

"Thank you, Doctor. I believe God is telling me that He sent you to us. Our son was on a road of destruction. This sounds like a way to not only heal him, but to protect him from falling into the trap of the devil again."

Randall also cautioned them about letting guests visiting their son. "I know he was once...uh, involved with a nurse in this hospital, who's been trying to find out about his condition. That's how I learned about your son's... chosen lifestyle."

"His friends have also been trying to visit him." Brother Jimmy spoke with his well-known serious firmness. "We have not allowed it, because in my heart, I knew they were a corrupting influence."

"I think you're doing the right thing," the doctor assured Brother Jimmy. "As we begin the treatment, we will definitely want to restrict exposure to his former life." He let them know they could request a ban of all non-approved visitors, then promised to make sure it was enforced.

"His life is in your hands," Brother Jimmy said as they were leaving. "Do what you think is best to restore our son."

And so the treatments would begin, with a carte blanche he had not expected. It freed him to use some of the more non-traditional aspects of his treatment, should the need arise in the future.

FIFTEEN

"I WANT YOU TO RELAX AND listen to my voice. Can you hear the waves?"

The patient's entire body seemed to relax into the overstuffed chair. His arms were motionless on his lap, his shoulders drooped and his head reclined on the high, padded headrest.

Barnabas liked the ocean, and that was one of the reasons the sound machine was incorporated into the sessions. The white-noise also masked distractions and helped the patient relax, especially combined with the mild sedative.

"I want to talk about Marti," Dr. Davidson instructed. "Do you know who that is?"

He perked straight up. "Of course. Her real name is Martha, but she prefers Marti. We've known each other for...like...forever."

"You and Marti are sweethearts, aren't you? It's okay to tell me the truth."

The fact that the patient blushed was encouraging. Randall quickly wrote on his pad.

"You two have talked about marriage, isn't that correct?"

Barnabas looked cautiously around the room. "Yeah, but we ain't telling my folks. They'll think we're too young."

"Yes, you two planned to be married. Do you remember making the plans, Barnabas. You talked about getting married after you got to college. You discussed how great it would be once you two were finally together. I mean, we both know, it's not always easy to resist the temptation to go beyond a little kissing after the soccer game."

So far, he'd had five sessions with the patient. Four were conducted with hypnosis, designed to enhance strategic recollections. Vague or fragmented memories were strengthened and augmented using dialogue, coaching, meticulous descriptions and visualization. Where there were gaps in recall, the doctor would suggest additional memories and fill in with fictional details, all based on the ultimate, intended behavioral goals and the promise he'd made to the parents to restore their son's normal, healthy sexual identity.

After those four sessions, he had another one with the patient to measure the results. Barnabas had clearly recalled the implanted memories, and expressed the accompanying feelings that had been suggested during the hypnosis.

The treatments are working beyond my expectations, he concluded with pride.

"Were you ever intimate with Marti?"

"She said we had to wait until we got married. I respected that."

"But you tried, right? I mean, you're a guy after all." He forced a laugh, giving the statements a less threatening tone.

The patient's face turned slightly red. "Well, uh…sure. We had a couple of times where we were making out, hot and heavy. I was so turned on…"

Oblivious to his surroundings, the patient began to rub himself. The doctor noted a distinct change in breathing pattern; a bulge was evident in the front of his linen pajamas. He made a note in his pad, since this was one of the memories he had reinforced at an earlier session.

"You were turned on when you were making out with your girlfriend Marti. It's only normal, we all know that."

He moaned. "Oh, yeah. I wanted to fuck the daylights—"

"Barnabas," he interrupted calmly. His tone was firm, but with a maintained volume. He wanted to correct, not punish. "What would your father think of that kind of language?"

"I'm sorry," he said remorsefully. "It just slipped out."

"Those feelings are normal, Barnabas. You have sexual desires for your girlfriend and that's acceptable. We just have to find an appropriate way to express them."

That seemed to calm him down.

"You both agreed to wait until marriage before having sexual relations. Marti told you that she's a virgin, isn't that right?"

"She loves me enough to save herself for me."

"That *is* special. And you also wanted to give her the same gift, right?"

"It's not easy," Barnabas admitted, shifting nervously in his chair. "But it was something she…uh, we wanted to do."

"Because it's the right thing to do," the doctor pressed: "You and Marti are waiting until marriage because it's the right thing to do. As a Christian man, sexual purity is our responsibility and our obligation."

There was a confused look on his face. "It's the right thing…I don't think…I seem to remember…"

The sedative was obviously wearing off; the patient would become more alert soon.

"You do remember the accident, don't you, Barnabas? We talked about it?"

His head cocked to one side and he looked at the doctor, first with uncertainty then with obvious annoyance. "Yes, I remember. I have a head injury that took away my memory." His tone was terse and petulant. "How many times do you have to remind me?"

Dr. Davidson employed his professional, reassuring tone. "I have to remind you, Barnabas. There are times you remember things that may not have happened to you personally. It might have been a movie you saw or a book you read. Because the accident damaged your memory, it's possible to believe those things actually happened to you. I am here to protect you."

"He's being a bastard."

Jonah agreed. "But I think in his mind, he's being a father. Perhaps a bit over-protective, but he's concerned about his son. And his rigid beliefs dictate how he handles it."

Matt was furious that Thumper's parents had banned them from visiting and also put a restriction on the hospital giving any updates on his condition. It had been three weeks since the attack, and they'd gotten no updates.

"I only want to know how he's doing," he whined.

"Why don't you call your friend who works at the hospital and see if he can find out anything? He was so helpful that night in the emergency room."

Matt immediately hopped off of the sofa. "That's a great idea!" He grabbed his cell phone and dialed the number. "Hey, Joe. It's Matt. Sorry if I'm calling too late."

"Not too late for me. 'Bout to get off work and head to the strip for a drink. How's Thumper?"

"That's why I'm calling. His folks have frozen us out. I don't want to get you in trouble, but is it possible for you to—"

"Consider it done. Give me fifteen minutes and I'll call you back."

Matt flipped the phone closed and sat back down. "You're a genius. He's going to check and call us back in about fifteen minutes."

"Hmm, I can think of a few things we can do while we wait," he said as he playfully rubbed his hand across Matt's chest.

"Me, too. I'm starved. Let's eat."

They were in the kitchen, enjoying a turkey sandwich when the call came through. "I don't have great news," Joe began. "Once he regained consciousness, they found he has significant memory loss. You know, amnesia."

"You mean he doesn't know who he is?" It sounded to Matt like the plot from some cheesy *Lifetime* TV movie.

"Not exactly. A few weeks ago, I spoke with one of his doctor, but he's a dick and wouldn't tell me anything. Ordered me off the floor and reported it to my supervisor. Tonight, I talked with a nurse on his floor who's a friend of mine and she told me that Thumper has no idea where he is or how he got here. She says he has no memory of the past eight to ten years. I'm not sure of all the details; she told me they have a clamp-down on his chart and his computer records are restricted."

The past ten years? Matt replayed in his mind.

"I need to see him," he declared with a trembling voice. "Maybe it will help. Help him remember."

"They won't let you in, Matt. According to the nurse, they're under *strict* orders from the parents and the doctor about any visitor who hasn't been approved. Besides, they're moving him on Friday."

"What? Moving him where?"

"She doesn't know."

"Thanks, Joe. I'll take it from here. I appreciate all your help."

"Hey, it was nothing. When I look back on it, Thumper was…fun. I wish him all the best. Anything else I can do, let me know."

The next day, immediately after breakfast, Matt went to the hospital. It was a Sunday, so he wasn't sure if the parents would even be there. He waited for more than an hour until they arrived.

"Can I talk with you?"

Thumper's father kept walking, but Mrs. Rivers stopped.

"What can we do for you, dear?"

"Why can't we visit him?" Matt asked bluntly. "We're his friends and we care about him—"

Suddenly, Reverend Rivers did stop, and turned abruptly. "Our son is not your concern!" His response matched Matt's bluntness, but with more volume.

"Satan tried to destroy him, but God has delivered him back to us. We will not allow the corrupting influence of your chosen lifestyle to pull him back into that darkness." He pointed a chubby, accusing finger at him.

The words stung. "I am not a theologian, Reverend Rivers. But I *am* a Christian. I'm his friend, and I love him—"

"How dare you invoke the purity of love to describe what you feel. What you do…together…well, there's nothing Christian about it. I will not allow that unholy affection to once again contaminate my boy."

"I didn't make him gay!" His words were louder than he'd intended. Several nurses stopped to listen and one patient stepped out of her room to investigate the commotion. "And I'm not responsible for what happened to him." He stopped, remembering his promise to Jonah not to tell them that the man who did this to Thumper had been listening to Reverend Rivers' sermons just before the attack.

"You have been a blessing during this ordeal," Mrs. Rivers consoled. "But we only want what's best for our son. You can understand that."

"No, I don't understand." He forced control on his emotions. "Can't we just see him?"

"We want...no, I *demand* that you respect our wishes," Reverend Rivers ordered. "Leave our son alone."

With that, he turned and walked away.

"Where are you taking him?"

Without looking around, the man bellowed, "Again, that is none of your concern."

Mrs. Rivers patted him on the arm in a motherly manner. "Bless you, son. This is for the best. Please believe that. It's for the best."

She turned and walked briskly to join her husband.

"I'm sure Thumper would disagree," he yelled. "He would want to see me."

A large security guard walked up and directed him toward the exit.

Sixteen

"They're moving him today." There was a discernible sadness to his voice.

Jonah put down his backpack and sat down on the sofa beside Matt. He made it a habit to come by Matt's apartment on his way to work. Matt would usually make breakfast, but this morning Jonah had brought them coffee and Danish from a local pastry shop.

"I'm sure when he's better, he'll call you. We're talking about Thumper here. No one tells him what to do for long, right?"

He was not satisfied, but didn't answer.

Jonah leaned over and kissed him. "I gotta get to work, babe. And you better kick into gear, too. Don't you have to pick up a cake for work today?"

"Yep," he replied. "The monthly employee birthday celebration."

"Think about what you might want to do this weekend. I'm going by my place after work, but I'll call ya' later. I told my roomies that I was visiting family until Sunday night, so I'll get clothes while I'm there."

After Jonah was gone, Matt busied himself getting ready for work. An idea stopped him as he was about to get in the shower. He wrapped a towel around his waist, got his cell and scrolled though the numbers in the phonebook until he found it: Winston. No last name, but it was all he needed.

Winston picked up almost immediately.

"I'm sorry to bother you," Matt began. "I'm Thumper's roommate, Matt Martin. We met at the hospital."

"Yes, I remember you, Matt. Has something happened to Thumper?"

Matt noted the alarm in the man's voice.

"I wish I could tell you. His parents aren't letting us see him. And they're moving him today. I was hoping...well, do you know anything?"

There was silence at the other end of the phone and Matt thought they might have been disconnected.

"This is all news to me, Matt. I was at the hospital several times that first week...before he woke up. Did you try talking with them?"

"Yes, I had a rather loud discussion with his father at the hospital, right before I was escorted out by a giant security guard who probably moonlights as a Humvee."

He heard Winston snicker. "I'm sorry. I don't mean to make light of it. But the first thought that occurred to me was how Thumper would have loved to see that—what did you call it?—that *discussion*."

At that instant, Matt could see the humor, and they both laughed.

"Listen, I know I was a complete bitch at the hospital when we met," Matt admitted. "I said some pretty harsh things to you. Please forgive me."

"You had every right," Winston said graciously.

"I never meant to hurt him." His tone was now hushed and pensive, as if he were thinking aloud. "What I did to him was selfish. I wasn't much of a friend, and it's something I sincerely regret. I'm glad he has real friends like you."

Not knowing what to make of the amount of emotion from Winston, he decided to lighten the mood. "He can be a shit at times, but he has a way of burrowing into your heart like...well, like a little rabbit."

"I can attest to that," he agreed with a quick chuckle. "And I promise, if I hear anything from the parents about his condition, I'll let you know."

Like the rash decision to make the phone call, Matt suddenly had an idea. "Why don't you come over for dinner? I'm a great cook. That's what Thumper always said, anyway. A way to make up for my bad behavior at the hospital. I'd love for you to meet my boyfriend, Jonah. He's a graduate of CFNI and you two would probably have lots to talk about. He needs someone who can speak his language and challenge him, especially now that his biggest adversary is in the hospital with major memory loss."

He realized when he finished that he was out of breath from talking so fast.

"That's very kind, but you don't need to do penance to me, brother. Your actions were both warranted and needed. But that sounds great. Why don't we wait until after I have some news about Thumper and then set it up?"

"Deal. And if you do see Thumper, give the little pecker a hug from us. You probably don't need to tell his folks who it's from, and he probably won't know who we are..."

The reality of it dawned again, and he choked up. "I can't believe he doesn't remember me."

"Thank you so much for coming, Martha. I hope the flight wasn't too difficult."

Jim and Gwen Rivers were waiting when she arrived at the hotel, and escorted her to the room they'd secured—down the hall from the room where they'd been staying since Barnabas' accident.

The girl still seemed a bit overwhelmed at the whirlwind of events over the past days. Jim's secretary had made all the arrangements, including having a car pick her up at the airport and bring her directly to the hotel. She worked as a bookkeeper at her father's construction company, so getting the time off was not a major problem.

"It was my pleasure, Mrs. Rivers. You know I would do anything for Thumper. I am so sorry for...I mean..." She ended with a shrug.

Martha Denise Deaton preferred to be called Marti, but Jim was always careful with that kind of familiarity. She was a lovely young woman, with green eyes and brown hair that was kept in a modest style. The same could said of the way she dressed—not like some girls in his congregation who wore dresses too tight or too short...or both. She had always presented herself as a Christian woman of dignity, conviction and high moral values. He was glad to have her as part of the plan to restore his son.

Gwen reached over and patted her on the hand. "That's very sweet, dear. He goes by Barnabas now. But it is *we* who are grateful to you. And please, call me Gwen."

The young woman smiled shyly and laid her oversize purse on the bed. "Thank you, Gwen." She giggled. "That'll take some getting used to. But you..." She pointed at him. "You will always be Brother Jimmy."

"We think you could be helpful in helping Barnabas regain his memories," Jim said as they all sat in the room's small conversation area.

"So much has been lost," Gwen told Martha. "But he does remember you, so we thought it would be good for him to see you."

"I still care for him, you know. I suppose you never get over your first love. What's he been up to since he left Birmingham?"

Before Gwen could speak, Jim launched into a prepared, truncated history of their son's life in Dallas. "He finished college, with honors, of course. His degree is in communications, which we all know was one of his many strengths. He was still in the process of deciding how to use his training."

"Did he have a...was he dating anyone?"

Gwen smiled as she answered. "As you said, you never get over your first love. Of all the people in his life, besides his father and me, you are the only other one he remembers. I know he still has strong feelings for you."

Jim was surprised at his wife's participation in the conversation. She'd been a little wary of bringing Martha to Dallas and more than vocal in her objection to the short-term deception that would be required to proceed with this phase of the treatment. But Dr. Davidson had convinced them it was necessary to determine if the feelings suggested to Barnabas while under hypnosis would manifest in person.

Martha blushed, which only highlighted the happiness on her face. "I always wondered why we lost contact after he left his job at the Inwood Church."

"I'm sure that was difficult, especially with the...*plans* you two had made before he left." He let that revelation sink in.

Martha gasped slightly. "You knew that we talked about getting married? He didn't think you'd approve, 'cause we were too young."

Gwen was consoling. "He should have known that we also loved you, my dear. Our dream has always been for him to marry a Christian woman who would support his ministry. Yes, you two were young...back then."

"He's being moved today to a private facility where he can get more personalized care," Jim said. "We wanted you to be with us this weekend, to help during the transition to the new hospital."

"What should I say?"

Jim looked at his wife and the two exchanged a knowing look.

"Just be yourself," he advised. "Let him talk about what he can recall. And talk about your memories too."

"Help Barnabas remember his life before this awful tragedy," Gwen pleaded.

Matt was stunned when he came home and found Jonah with *him*. Surprise instantly turned to anger.

"What are you doing here?" he asked Earl, one of the guys who had been involved in Thumper's beating.

"I invited him," Jonah answered.

"Maybe I should go," Earl mumbled, standing up.

Jonah also stood. "I wish you'd stay. I promise, Matt will be civil." Jonah glared at Matt. "Right, dear?"

Matt shrugged, then walked over and kissed Jonah, long on the lips.

Jonah used the proximity to deliver a quiet, but terse message in his ear. "He's hurting, and I think we should try to help. I couldn't meet him at my place, so I figured we could do it here. Okay?"

Matt agreed, though he included a huff, and they both sat down on the sofa.

"Earl was telling me about the outcome of the hearing."

The nervous guest looked at the two of them on the sofa, then quickly diverted his eyes as he spoke. "Milton is in a...facility, undergoing treatment. I found out when he was arrested that he'd been off his meds for several weeks, even though he promised me he was taking them. He'll be there until they determine he's stable, and then a judge will decide his punishment."

"What about you?" Matt asked, with clear hostility.

"Earl didn't hurt Thumper," Jonah emphasized. "He was there when his friend freaked out."

"That's not entirely true," Earl said. "After all, I'm the one who told Milton to leave after the attack. I was only trying to protect him, but it was stupid now that I look back on it. And at the hospital, I didn't give all the facts to the police."

Jonah leaned over and patted Earl's hand. The action caused him to recoil his hand as if he'd been scalded.

"You were upset," Jonah said, moving back into the sofa. "And afraid. When you calmed down, you did the right thing. And we appreciate that."

"The judge took everything into consideration. And I was given a small sentence of community service. It won't show up on my record, once I complete it."

"So how are you doing?" Jonah asked with his usual compassion.

Earl rocked his head from side to side. "Good days and bad days. I'm still working at the hospital, but I've cut my hours significantly. I'm seeing a Christian counselor to help me deal with…well, to help me with my…uh… you know…*those* feelings."

Matt and Jonah looked at each other.

"Is there anything we can do?" Jonah inquired. "We've both had to deal with those same feelings, and we're here if you need us."

Earl stared at the floor.

"I can't," he muttered.

"You can't…what?" Jonah probed.

"I can't have the feelings. I need them to go away."

Jonah glanced quickly at Matt, who gave a single nod for him to continue. "I know it's not easy to hear this, Earl, but those feelings are part of who you are. They aren't going to go away. You can trust me on that, brother."

There was no immediate response from Earl. Jonah could see that he was crying. When he did speak, he still didn't look at them. "My counselor recommended that I go into a resident program in Denver. I need these feelings to go away."

Jonah fought to keep from reacting too quickly. "I wish you'd reconsider, Earl. I know things are tough, but please believe me. That's not the solution. God is big enough to show you how reconciliation extends to this area as well."

"We could help," Matt offered. "And I promise not to be such a prick."

Earl finally looked up with a tear-stained face. "I've already enrolled. I leave on Monday. It's the right thing for me. I can't be like you. I just can't."

Matt tried to object, but Jonah interrupted. "I understand, Earl. You have to do what you think is best. But please hear me. Are you listening?"

He waited until Earl actually looked at him.

"If you find that it's not what you wanted…not what you hoped it would be…please know that you can come to us. We will be here for you. Do you hear me, Earl?"

Choking back tears, Earl stammered, "It *has* to work."

SEVENTEEN

WINSTON GRABBED HIS KEYS AND ONCE again checked the address. He still wasn't sure about this. But in the same way his friendship with Thumper had started, he'd agreed to the visit because Gwen had asked him. *Insisted* would be a better description.

The Rushdoony Clinic—the private medical facility where Thumper had been taken—sat on several acres near an older hospital in Dallas, north of Interstate 635, known to most residents simply as LBJ Freeway. It wasn't far from Winston's office, but traffic was always heavy in that part of town. When he finally arrived, he wished it had taken longer.

The well-renowned hospital was a converted mansion built back in the sixties when the area was far enough away from downtown to be considered elegant. Admission was for those with wealth beyond the benefits offered by standard health insurance. Rushdoony especially catered to an elite class of patients whose status, fortune or fame came with a privileged sense of entitlement that demanded the need for privacy to recuperate after a delicate, albeit not-for-public-knowledge medical condition or enhancement.

An exquisite oriental rug softened his steps on the marble floors as he entered the grand foyer. There was no "Information Desk" and no kindly white-haired volunteer to greet him. He glanced around the atypical waiting room. Absent were the standard utilitarian steel chairs, linked tightly together for greater discomfort. The motif was more reading room than waiting room, with wingback chairs, ottomans, oversized sofas, bookcases and even a beverage cart.

"Good afternoon, how might I help you?"

He turned to see a woman dressed in an outfit that looked like it could have been purchased at a vintage shop for dowdy women. Her nametag identified her as *Gertrude Barrett, Guest Services.*

"I'm here to see Thum—, uh, Barnabas Rivers. My name is Winston DuMont. I was told he'd be expecting me."

Gertrude used her entire arm to direct him to the lavish, dark-paneled waiting area. "I'll let them know you're here. Please be seated." She took a couple of steps, then turned back around. "Can I get you anything? Perhaps a fruit plate and some tea?"

He declined, then sat down in a fluffy chair, near the fireplace.

When Gwen called and invited him to visit, she was clear that they did not want anyone or anything to bring up memories from their son's "sinful past"—that was the term she used repeatedly.

"And please don't call him Thumper. The doctor thinks it's best to use his given name to help bring up those memories from before his rebellion against God."

She'd also reported that they were not allowing anyone from his "sinful past" to visit, which he already knew from talking with Matt.

"His friends were trying to see him, but we didn't want that influence in his life again," she said. "That's one of the reasons we moved him. His doctor recommended this place and was able to get him admitted."

He leaned back in the chair and took a deep breath to relax.

There it is, he thought as the unmistakable smell registered.

The presence of plush furniture and a décor that clearly suggested an over-paid decorator could not disguise the antiseptic odor that exposed the true purpose of the facility. It may look like an old Georgian mansion on the outside, and the inside may have the feel of "stately Wayne Manor," but it was essentially and primarily a hospital.

"How much does he remember?" he'd asked when Gwen called.

"He knows there was an accident, and we told him that it caused damage to his memory, but we aren't telling him how it happened to him."

Or why, he reasoned.

"He does know who we are, but his memories are scattered and most date back over eight years ago." She let out a breath that quivered. "The doctor is still working to figure out how much of our boy is…lost."

She had openly cried. He couldn't *not* agree to the visit.

From Gwen's description, he'd surmised that Thumper would not remember him or the time they'd spent together. That realization caused him enormous sadness, and it took days for him to actually schedule the visit. But now he was genuinely excited to see Barnabas again. He was still trying to convince himself that the feelings came from a sense of Christian concern and compassion.

Gertrude walked back in. "Please follow me," she instructed with a professional formality.

She escorted him to the back of the building. Along the way, he was able to see a fully equipped gym that exceeded the high-priced one where he belonged. They also passed a kitchen that would cause a five-star chef to salivate, an immaculate garden encircling a massive pool and numerous patient rooms that were obviously part of the many additions and renovations. When they arrived at the room, Gertrude again indicated with her arm, then bowed slightly and left him.

"There you are," Gwen exclaimed when she saw him in the doorway. She rushed over and gave him a breath-restricting hug. "We are so glad you came."

Winston was about to respond when they walked into the room, but then he saw Thumper. The sight brought him to a halt. His intended words of greeting stuck in his throat, except for the sound of a sharp gasp he hoped no one heard. He was not prepared with how the once-vibrant man looked.

"This is Winston DuMont," Gwen introduced, looking at her son, but pointing to Winston. "Do you remember him, Barnabas?" Her tone was earnest, with the obvious concern of a mother.

Sitting on a recliner by the one window in the room, he was wearing pajama pants and a tank top, with the logo from his father's church emblazoned on the front: Charisma Community Church. His hair was buzz-cut short. There was no cast, but his arm was in a sling. A cut over his eye was well on the way to becoming a scar.

Or a reason to visit the plastic surgeon, he figured the old Thumper might say.

The most obvious change—indeed what shocked Winston—was the weight loss. "Skinny" would be the word that now described the guy who was once built thick, solid and strong.

"Momma said that you are one of my friends here in Dallas. I've only met one other person from my past, and she's from back home in Birmingham. Thank you for coming." There was a slight limp that became evident in the short trip from the chair to where Winston was standing.

"So sorry that I don't remember you. That happens a lot these days." He smiled and extended his left hand, since the right one was incapacitated.

The eyes mirrored Thumper's lack of recall—the kind of look you'd get from a guy on the street you'd just asked for the correct time. No recognition. No familiarity.

This was not the person he'd met six months earlier—the person who'd brought up long-suppressed desires and driven him back to counseling. Any resemblance to that cynical man who had challenged all facets of Winston's self-imposed identity was gone. There was no glimmer of the person who flirted shamelessly, made crude comments and boasted unapologetically of his sexual prowess and many conquests. Nor was there that lustful flicker, teasing of possible shared passion. His eyes no longer blazed that belligerent defiance to all things religious. And there was an absence of that knowing ability to look beyond all facades.

Winston felt many emotions at the same time: compassion, concern and sadness, of course. There was also regret over the way their last meeting had ended.

He pushed down the feelings and manufactured a return smile as he took Thumper's hand. "It's good to see you again…Barnabas."

"Please, have a seat," Gwen invited, motioning to the area near the window.

As he'd expected, the ample-sized room was unlike a typical hospital room, aside from the standard-issue hospital bed and some medical machines. The small sitting area had a rattan ceiling fan overhead, a loveseat, a wingback chair and the recliner where Barnabas was sitting. There were flowers and gift baskets on most every flat surface. The walls were painted a soothing pale, pastel blue and decorated with several pieces of contemporary art as well as a large-screen TV. Music—instrumental versions of Christian hymns—could be heard playing softly in the background.

"How do we know each other? What did we do together?" There was eagerness in both Barnabas' words and face.

Winston expected the questions and had struggled to prepare appropriate answers. Gwen had hinted that lying was acceptable. He didn't want to lie, but he still wasn't sure his rehearsed responses would fall outside the definition. Glancing over at her, she was wide-eyed in expectation of his reply.

"We go to dinner. We both like to talk, so we have discussions about everything from current events to the historic tenets of the Christian faith. We have a mutual interest in books, in television, movies and the Bible. We're friends, Barnabas."

"'A friend loveth at all times, and a brother is born for adversity,'" Gwen interjected, quoting Scripture. She was nodding her approval of what he'd shared.

"Proverbs, seventeen-seventeen," Barnabas inserted, giving a Biblical reference to the verse she'd quoted.

He must have noticed Winston's stunned look. "Bizarre, isn't it? I can't remember going to college, but I can remember Bible verses I learned as a kid. Makes no sense to me either."

"The doctor is actually encouraged by it," Gwen gushed. "He thinks the fact that there are patches of intact memory could mean others will emerge as the healing continues. And we serve God, the Healer, so we will not fear." She closed her eyes and raised her hands toward heaven, as if by instinct.

"That's exciting. Do they know how long it will take?" Winston's question was initially directed at Gwen, but she'd entered her own private prayer service, so he looked over at Barnabas.

"He's not sure. In the meantime, I'm doing physical therapy, plus my daily relaxation sessions—"

"Relaxation sessions?"

"Mostly counseling." Barnabas looked over to where his mother was sitting, still in her personal worship experience. "Helping me deal with the frustration of not remembering. I get a bit angry at times, so the doctor is teaching me some techniques to relax."

Barnabas' voice was strong, though his speech pattern was a bit like having a conversation with the order-taker at the hamburger counter—cordial, but perfunctory. There was something else—a distinct difference in the way he talked—but Winston couldn't quite pinpoint what it was.

"And we have people from all around the world praying not only for his healing, but for that divine 'peace that passeth all understanding.'" Gwen was back from the mountaintop and joined the conversation.

"Good thing it doesn't rely on mental ability, right?" Barnabas huffed. "I'd be shit outta luck."

"Barnabas Taylor Rivers!" Gwen reprimanded, her volume nearly matching her obvious shock. "We do not use that kind of language. Remember?"

Barnabas looked confused, but dropped his head in remorse. "I'm sorry, Momma."

Winston suddenly realized what was different in the way Thumper talked. It wasn't like a man in his twenties; the rhythm and cadence, even the way he spoke, was more like a teenager.

"The doctor said his injuries also let down some of his…what was that term he used?"

"Internal monitors," Barnabas answered. "I speak words without maybe knowing what they mean. And sometimes, they might be words I shouldn't say."

Gwen addressed Winston. "We're asking the Holy Ghost to put a guard on his mouth, claiming the prayer of Psalms one-forty-one, verse three."

As Winston was making a mental note to look up that Scripture passage, Barnabas took the initiative to verbalize the passage: "Set a guard, Oh Lord, over my mouth. Keep watch over the door of my lips."

The look he gave his mother was clearly that of a chastised child, seeking to get back into the good graces of an offended parent.

"And why is that?" she questioned sternly.

His shoulders sagged under the scrutiny of her interrogation and he let out a petulant breath. "Psalm nineteen-fourteen," he replied obediently. "Let the words of my mouth and the meditation of my heart be acceptable in Your sight, Oh Lord," he quoted.

"It amazes me that you can remember all those verses," Winston said, hoping to diffuse some discomfort.

"Well," he explained sheepishly, "Some of them are just in my head…" He used his hand to gesture around his scalp. "But some I'm having to learn new, so we can add the power of God's Word to my recovery."

"We're very proud." She finally gave her son the smile he was obviously craving, then picked up a knitting project.

Barnabas didn't return the smile.

"I need to remember more than Bible verses." His volume was softer, as if not wanting his mother to hear. "I need to remember my *life*." There was intense sadness in his voice.

"Don't embarrass your friend, Barnabas," she instructed quietly. "It's going to take time. God has already done so much."

She excused herself and for more than thirty minutes, he was alone with Barnabas.

"You said we talked about books. What's your favorite book?"

"It's actually a set of books: *The Chronicles of Narnia*, by C.S. Lewis. I love them and re-read the entire series at least once a year."

He got a thoughtful look. "I think Daddy might have read those to me when I was a kid. Something about a lion?"

"Right. One of the main characters is a lion named Aslan. He's the ruler of Narnia. The first book is called *The Lion, the Witch and the Wardrobe*. Wonderful imagery and allegory...and just a fun story."

Barnabas got excited. "I'll read them, so we can talk about them. Who knows, they might become my favorites too. I'm having to build a brand new list of favorites."

Winston also mentioned they both liked the TV show, *Lost*. He gave an overview of the show and then promised to get him copies of the DVDs.

When Gwen returned, Barnabas was beaming. "I have a new...old friend. Hopefully, one of many more to come."

He looked at Winston. "And I have a girlfriend, who's ready for me to get better so we can make some plans for the future. We call that progress."

Shocked was the most obvious word to describe what Winston felt.

A girlfriend? he repeated silently.

"I...Who is...I didn't know you had a girlfriend," he stammered.

"Neat, huh? She came to visit me a few days ago."

"I think that's enough for today," Gwen advised before Winston could get further details. "I'm sure Winston has things to do and you need to rest before physical therapy.

"Thanks for coming," Barnabas said with his trademark grin. "I hope this visit to the Twilight Zone wasn't too weird for you. Please come back before I go back to Birmingham."

They hugged and Winston promised to visit again in the near future. He was receiving another hug from Gwen when Barnabas asked, "By the way, what do you do?"

"I'm an attorney," he informed. "Remind me next time I visit, and I'll tell you some lawyer jokes."

They all laughed.

"I hope I don't need you as lawyer, but I will make sure I remember you as a friend"

"Well, why don't I give you my card, in case you need either?"

———————

"I'm glad he came by," Barnabas told his mother. "He's nice. I do hope he'll come again. I enjoyed talking with him. I wish I could remember him."

There was a resounding inner confirmation to his statement he didn't understand. Meeting Winston *felt* different than when Marti came to visit. *He* felt different with Winston. The visit with Marti had been awkward and uncomfortable. She was constantly touching him, which he didn't enjoy. They both struggled to keep the conversation going.

It was not that way with Winston. When they hugged, he relaxed and didn't want it to end. Talking with Winston was easy, too. And now that he was gone, Barnabas missed him, and wanted to remember their past together. He just wasn't sure why it seemed so important.

He said we went to dinner.

Barnabas concentrated on what that might look like, but nothing emerged. But he did wonder if they'd met at Oral Roberts University, though he wasn't sure why.

We had conversations about books and stuff.

He stilled his thoughts and tried to listen in on those possible distant discussions. He didn't recall any specifics, but had a warm feeling. Whatever they had done together, he knew they must have been close friends.

He forced his mind to retain the image of Winston. He focused on it, trying to mandate a memory of their past to become known. Suddenly, a vivid image of Winston popped into his mind. As clearly as he'd seen the young lawyer in his hospital room, he now could see him stark naked. Even a small birthmark below the navel could be seen. And almost as quickly, the vision vanished.

He was shocked, and more than a little confused. Inside, he knew immediately that he should be ashamed and repulsed by the memory-picture.

Something inside also told him he should be concerned by the fact that he wasn't.

———————

He has a girlfriend?

For the entire drive back to his office, Winston could not get that fact to stop pounding in his head.

Gwen had attempted to explain it to him as they walked toward the entrance. "Because of his memory loss, the choices he made to live a homosexual lifestyle have all been erased. We have a chance to restore him to a normal life, before he made those sinful choices."

"And how does she feel about being part of this…recovery?" He'd wanted to say "experiment," but thought better of it.

"She's a lovely girl. They were sweethearts all through high school. Jim thinks the torch she's carrying for our Barnabas just might be the light he needs to get back on the right path."

Glowing metaphor aside, he pushed for more. "Is she aware of…well, what his life was like here in Dallas? Before the injury?" He was being delicate.

She looked away, but not before he saw her blush. "Uh, we don't think it's best to talk about his sinful past. According to the Word of God, it's covered by the blood of Jesus. We believe that talking about it will invite the powers of darkness to try and regain their stronghold in his mind."

"But doesn't she deserve to know?"

"And she will, in time. Right now, we want to bring positive influences into his life to help him remember. Like you."

He relented, but only because they'd arrived at the massive, ornate front entrance, where she'd held one of the double doors open to facilitate his exit.

"Thank you again for inviting me to visit. I will definitely visit him again."

Driving back to work, he was trying to be logical. And exhibit some gratitude for the remarkable physical recovery Thumper was making. For days after the "accident," the doctors weren't sure if he would live. They warned that he might not walk and might not be able to talk. But now, though he looked frail, his recovery was nothing short of miraculous, which Gwen continued to emphasize.

As he reached his office and turned into the parking lot, he became aware of another emotion. It was well below the surface and had little room to assert because of all the other prominent, active feelings. But it was there and he knew exactly what it was, though he didn't want to admit it. He parked the car, turned off the engine, but sat quietly.

He has a girlfriend…and I'm jealous!

"Dammit," he muttered aloud, resting his forehead on the steering wheel.

Eighteen

"They printed your editorial."

"I know," Jonah said from Matt's bedroom where he was changing clothes after church. "They called to confirm all my information."

Jonah had written a thoughtful response to an article in the paper about an upcoming ex-gay conference being held in Dallas. He showed that the person who wrote the article—a prominent Christian counselor who'd written several books on the subject—had a predisposition that could not be ignored, much less taken seriously. Jonah challenged the writer's exaggerated claims about the "lifestyle" of gay men, then described numerous examples of ex-gay leaders who'd been exposed as hypocrites: caught in gay bars, soliciting street hustlers or seducing their clients. He refuted the link between gay men and pedophilia. Throughout the article, he detailed how Scripture had been misinterpreted. He also criticized the newspaper for using such a biased individual in any section other than the opinion page, or the comics.

Matt held up the newspaper and waved it vigorously. "I don't think you realize what I'm saying. They didn't put it in the 'letters to the editor' section. They put it as an editorial. Baby, it's huge. And this time, I'm not talking about your pee-pee."

Jonah walked over and looked. His editorial covered almost an entire side of the page.

"Well, that will certainly get some attention. Probably won't stop that damned conference, but at least it gives another side to the lies."

That evening, when Jonah got home, his two roommates were sitting in the living room of the house they shared. He'd had lived with Jack and Tyrone his entire time at CFNI. Jack was working on his advanced diploma in pastoral ministry and Ty was pursuing a diploma in youth ministry.

"How's it going?" he asked casually as he walked in. "How was church—"

"We need to talk," Jack said soberly.

Jonah looked back and forth at the two of them sitting on the sofa. He saw an open Bible on the coffee table. Next to it was the Sunday newspaper, folded to his editorial.

He sat down, but didn't allow them to speak. "I'm sure there's much that needs to be said, but not much that I haven't heard already…so let's see if I can move this along. Yes, I wrote it. Yes, I believe everything I wrote. And, in case there's any doubt, yes…I'm gay."

Tyrone placed a pillow on his lap and crossed his hands on top. Jonah wanted to make a comment about the Freudian symbolism of the action, but chose to remain quiet.

"You know we love you, brother," Jack affirmed with true sincerity. He paused and looked at Tyrone, as if to complete the thought. Ty remained silent.

"But?" Jonah left the question hanging with an exaggerated inflection.

"No 'but,'" Jack responded, shaking his head. "We love you. Period! We just want to understand, and help if we can. Is that why you decided not to continue with your advanced diploma?"

"Pretty much. I know I should have told you but I didn't know how, to be honest. This is something I'm just coming to terms with myself. I apologize that I didn't talk to you guys."

The two men looked at each other. Jonah saw a slight nod from Tyrone, like he wanted Jack to say something.

"Well…you know how it's gonna look…you and us, living together… here," Jack stammered.

I certainly didn't think this thing through at all, Jonah chided himself.

Of course they would see it in the paper. So would others in the school. How would it look to have an unrepentant homosexual living with them? They would be bound by Scripture to either guide him to repentance or separate from him.

"I'm truly sorry, guys," Jonah confessed with honest anguish. "I never wanted to put you in an awkward situation. I see now that I didn't give any thought to how this would impact you. I should have talked with you with first. Please forgive me."

Tyrone finally entered the conversation. "I don't understand, Jonah. You can't be…you know." He picked up his Bible. "Can we pray about this? I'm sure God will—"

Jonah held up his hand to stop what he knew was coming. "I *have* prayed about it, Ty. It's not like I woke up last week and suddenly realized I'm gay; I've been wrestling with this for years. This is who I am, man. It's how God made me and I'm at peace with it. Can you be, too?"

Tyrone put his Bible back down on the table with a loud thump. "God hates this sin. Calls it an abomination." His words now came with a noticeable hostility, with matching volume. "Vile, depraved, unnatural, wicked, detestable." He rattling them off slowly, as if some word from the spiritual thesaurus might change Jonah's mind.

Jonah waited, silently praying for a loving attitude.

"You are my brother in Christ, Ty and I love you, but a few weeks ago, a friend of mine was nearly beaten to death by someone who was yelling the same kind of things as he pounded on his face. He nearly died, and will *never* be the same. I know we disagree, but please don't let this one difference color our past or our friendship. You know me. We've lived together and we've prayed together many times—"

"I don't need some pervert telling me what to think," he sputtered.

Jack intervened: "Dude, you need to let it go."

"No!" he snarled. "It's wrong in the sight of God." He pointed a shaky finger at Jonah. "I will no longer welcome you here. I want you out!" And with that, he grabbed his Bible and stormed up the stairs.

When he was gone, Jack chuckled. "He wants you out, but now that you are, he's the drama queen."

Jonah was taken aback by Jack's attitude. The comment and the amused look his face came as complete surprise.

"He's right, though," Jonah conceded to Jack. "Not about me and God, but I could cause you guys problems with the school, or with other students. I'd never want that. I'll begin looking for a place to move."

"Hey, sorry about your friend. Were you…are you close?"

Jonah thought for a second, then decided on honesty. "He's my boyfriend's roommate."

Jack let out a breath, in the form of the word "Okay." Then he tapped on the newspaper. "It's really well written. I'm going to send it to my sister. She thinks everyone at CFNI is a homophobic bigot."

"Your sister?"

Jack smiled. "She's the pastor at a gay and lesbian church in Northern California. We've talked about this issue for years. We don't see eye to eye, but I know that it's never as black or white as some"—he cut his eyes upward, in the direction of the stairs—"would have us believe."

"We lived together all this time, and you've never mentioned your sister. I should be hurt."

"Hey, if you want to compare who's keeping the bigger secrets, we can talk about—"

"Never mind," he interjected before Jack could finish. "You win."

"I should have anticipated it."

Jonah and Matt were having dinner and discussing the incident with the roommates. "I wrote the letter with no forethought of the ramifications for these guys that I've lived with for two years. That was thoughtless."

"I'm sorry, sweetie," Matt consoled. "Try to think of the good it can do. That *was* the reason you wrote it in the first place."

"My boss also read it."

"Was she upset?"

"Not sure. She walked by my desk and said, 'Saw your article. Learn something new every day.' She didn't even slow down to give me a chance to speak."

They both laughed.

Later that week, Jonah got a call from a national nonprofit headquartered in Dallas.

"My name is Dale Donnley. I'm the membership manager at The Transformation Project. I wanted to call and let you know how much your editorial meant to me and others in our office."

"Thank you," he said with an enthusiastic relief. Because the editorial had included his full name and the city where he lived, he'd gotten several phone calls and letters after the article was published, but most were not kind.

"I'd also like to invite you to come by our offices," she continued. "Our executive director would like to meet you, and I'll introduce you to our staff. We'll even treat you to lunch."

He thought it was merely a polite gesture, so he gave her a noncommittal response. But when she pressed, assuring him it was a serious invitation, they set a date for the next week.

The visit was amazing. Dale greeted him when he arrived and took him on a tour of the small facilities, which was basically a gigantic room full of cubicles. Across one wall was a series of offices for the executive management team. She took him to each cubicle and every office and would allow the person to tell him about their role with the organization.

He learned that The Transformation Project worked nationally on several key areas, including hunger, homelessness, abuse and illiteracy. It was the umbrella organization for many groups throughout the country devoted to these issues.

"Hope I'm not being too personal, but are you gay?" he asked Dale once they were seated in her office. "Not that it matters," he added quickly, just in case. "But I heard you refer to your 'partner,' so I was curious."

Dale looked amused, then quickly glanced around to see who might be listening. She leaned in and quietly revealed: "I'm transgendered. Our director knows, and the HR manager, but most folks here have no clue. A few years ago, I was Dale...dude. Now I'm Dale—loving spouse to a wonderful man named George. Even though I'm fully transitioned, in Texas my partner and I can't be married. Yet."

Meeting a transgendered person was a new experience for him, and Jonah hoped that he'd have some time to talk with her in more detail. It was a subject he wanted to better understand.

There was a knock on the door, and a disembodied voice announced that lunch was ready.

"Listen," she cautioned as they stood to leave. "I'm sure you're going to get lots of questions, and some might seem like they're coming from a place of religious hostility, but please don't take offense. Our organization is moving in some new areas, and many are still in learning mode. But I can assure you, we are all open to change." She giggled at her own pun. "Most just don't change as much as I did."

Dale was right about the questions, which went on for more than an hour. He talked about his journey to reconcile his faith with his sexuality. Some wanted to know about his experience as a gay man, others focused on his ministerial perspective. There was a lengthy discussion of the church's current position on homosexuality as well as how the harsh, hateful rhetoric of fundamentalism hurts gay people. He used the attack of Thumper—without mentioning his name—as an example. He got emotional relating the story and noticed others were touched as well.

Around one-thirty, Danielle McKinney, the executive director, stood and thanked everyone for their participation.

"You are a remarkable young man," she told him after they were seated in her office. It was situated at the back corner of the bank of cubicles. The furnishings were nice, but clearly not extravagant. It was casual, a bit feminine and comfortable.

"I was hoping that your demeanor and presence would be as inspiring as your editorial, and you certainly did not disappoint. You are a powerful presenter and speaker."

He wasn't sure what to say, so he thanked her, which came with an involuntary blush at the gushing praise.

"You've learned some of what we do, but there's so much more to it. As you are clearly aware, the political climate in this country has changed drastically under this administration. I don't want to get on a soapbox, but we're certainly seeing the gap between the haves and have-nots become more pronounced. In the past few years, conservatism has turned harsh and exclusive. The 'we' versus 'them' mentality is more prominent than I've ever seen. Some of our organizations are struggling with how to do their jobs if it includes compromising what they see as their principles."

She pulled out a piece of paper from her desk drawer. "This is a letter I received a few weeks ago. One of our ministries has decided to shut down its food pantry. And their reason? One of the supporting churches adopted an inclusive policy for gays in their membership. In other words, they would rather stop feeding the hungry than be associated with an inclusive church."

Danielle gave several examples of problems being encountered throughout the country. Not all involved the issue of including gays; some were racial and one was gender-related, centering on women in the pastoral ministry.

"Participating in TTP is voluntary," she explained. "But once you affiliate, you must abide by our code of conduct. We don't want to force any group to violate their own values, but we have to do what we feel is morally and ethically right. As you might imagine, it's quite a dilemma."

He agreed, but didn't know how to ask how he fit into this "dilemma."

She smiled. "I know I'm rambling, but I want to impress on you not only the importance of this work, but the severity of the problems we are facing. In recent days, we are seeing more and more of our affiliates confronting the issues and problems of diversity. They come to us to learn how to deal with it, so we want to provide them with some tangible assistance. And that's why I've invited you here."

He instinctively sat up straighter and slid forward in his seat. Questions immediately presented in his mind, but all he said was, "Sounds intriguing."

She moved around the desk, taking the seat beside him.

"Our board has made a bold decision to embrace diversity. Not merely as words on a mission statement, but with an active implementation. We are creating a new initiative to encourage dialogue on the many aspects of this issue. But it's not just talk. It will be designed to work with our groups to confront the obstacles they may face when embracing diversity—from the initial idea through discussion with the leadership to the training of the staff...all the way to taking it to the streets. We want to give them tools to implement diversity and make it successful."

He suddenly got an idea of why he was there, and was honored. "I think it's a great idea. I'm sure that I could help several hours a week. We could design a website that housed the materials—"

Her face told him she was pleased, but then she placed her hand on his arm, stopping his discourse.

"I'm delighted that you see the potential, and that you are willing to help, but we need you to think a little...bigger. We don't want you to design a website, we're hoping you will help us design the program. I'd like you to consider talking with our Board of Directors about coming on staff with TTP."

"So this"—his arm gestured in the general direction of the door, but indicating much more—"this was a job interview?"

"Let's call it a pre-interview," she said playfully. "I wanted to meet you and watch your interaction with the staff. The way you handled yourself in there was impressive *and* moving. I think you would be a major asset to this organization." She scooted up in her chair. "And without sounding too prophetic, I believe you are going to make a huge difference in the lives of many people. Why not start that here…at TTP?"

He was stunned and didn't know what to say. His mind was racing, but what came out of his mouth was a garbled confirmation of his confusion: "I don't know what to say."

"Take a few days and think about it. If you're interested, let me know and we'll begin the process."

NINETEEN

"How's Thumper?"

Winston's hand was still raised from knocking the one time on the door, but Matt had opened the door and immediately fired off his question. Jonah slipped in front and extended his hand to the speechless guest.

"You must be Winston. I'm Jonah Caudle. Please forgive my boyfriend's interrogation."

Winston smiled and walked in. Both of them were staring at him. Once he was out of sightline, Matt used both hands to fan his face, as if he were suddenly sweating. Jonah silently mouthed the word "WOW!"

Winston was striking, though Matt's description could never do him justice. His dark black hair had the popular mussed look that appeared to be casual, but usually wasn't. He was wearing a pair of khaki slacks, loafers and—to the joy of both of them—a form-fitting green polo shirt that not only accented his hazel eyes, but clearly showed his narrow, tight waist and well-developed chest.

"I didn't know if you guys like wine, but I brought one of my favorite reds— Carménère. It's from Chile and goes great with steak." He looked at Matt. "I assume that's still the menu."

Matt took the bottle and pointed to the chair for Winston to be seated. "Thank you for the wine," he said. "I'll open it and let it breathe. Yes, we're having steaks, some grilled tomatoes and portabella mushrooms, baked potatoes, salad and homemade wheat bread."

"I got us a nice cheesecake from Eatzi's for dessert," Jonah remarked. "Since I don't cook, and their food is so awesome, I figured it would be one less thing for Mattie to make."

Matt kissed Jonah on the cheek. "But I also made your favorite—apple cobbler, so the cheesecake will have to wait."

Jonah and Matt sat down on the sofa. "So," Matt started, "now that all the niceties are taken care of and we're all comfortable...what can you tell us about Thumper?"

"One track mind," Jonah muttered.

Winston thought he would have been more uncomfortable. After all, he had only met Matt once, at the hospital a few days after Thumper's attack. That had not gone well. He'd never met Jonah. And the two were a gay couple.

His presence here—for a social visit, not an evangelistic mission—would not go over well with those in the *Circle* nor the folks at his church. But he'd promised Matt that when he had information about Thumper, he'd come over and give them an update.

Thumper's parents obviously wouldn't want them to know the location of the hospital; they had been clear on that detail. But he'd gone over it in his mind, and found no ethical reason not to give general details of Thumper's condition with his friends.

"As I told Matt, I did visit Thumper right after he got to the new facility and I saw him again yesterday. He's doing physical therapy several times a week and meeting with a counselor every day."

"When's he getting out?" Jonah inquired.

The next instant, Matt asked, "What does he remember?"

Winston looked at Matt, to answer him first. "The doctors are calling it retrograde amnesia, which means the memories affected are all prior to the attack."

"My friend at the hospital said the amnesia is fairly significant, blocking out the past ten years," Matt said, but there was clearly a question imbedded.

"It's not as bad as it could be. He has some past memories. He remembers events and incidents, but they're disconnected and out of sequence. And yes, most happened years ago."

He related that Thumper did not remember the attack. And even though he hated to mention it, he told them that as far as the doctors could tell, Thumper had no memory of his life in Dallas.

"So it's true," Matt mumbled, mostly to himself. "He doesn't remember me." He looked around sadly. "He doesn't remember any of us."

Winston understood what he was feeling. The only way to compare it was to grief. But it didn't involve the actual death of a loved one, but the loss of all the valued time shared together. He assumed it must be similar to what those who have loved ones with Alzheimer's feel.

"But he's going to be…okay?" Matt's voice cracked with emotion.

Define "okay," Winston wanted to say.

To them, he decided to be philosophical. "He has a long road ahead of him. But he's surrounded by people who care about him and who only want the best for him. There are many possibilities."

"He would love that," Matt observed. "Sounds like the ending of *Star Trek, Wrath of Khan*."

Winston also told them that once Thumper got out of the hospital—which should be soon—he'd be moving back to Birmingham with his parents.

"How often does someone get to truly start over fresh?" Jonah mused. "Thumper has that chance, so we can only leave it in God's hands. And though the Thumper we knew would probably balk at the idea, I say we pray and commit him into the loving care and guidance of our Heavenly Father."

The three of them joined hands and Jonah initiated the prayer. Winston followed, but Matt was too emotional to speak.

He was amazed that praying with this gay couple didn't feel forced or counterfeit; they genuinely loved Thumper and were sincerely seeking God's guidance. Together, as they asked God for support and requested healing for Thumper, he had the same sense of divine presence as when he prayed with his pastor or the guys in the *Circle*. That certainly didn't fit the image the teachers in the restoration program painted of those living "the gay lifestyle."

"I love it when I'm right," he bragged, though neither of them were listening.

Matt was putting coffee on the table to go with the dessert, while Jonah and Winston were in the living room, oblivious to him. They were deep in a theological discussion that was either over his head and out of the realm of his interest.

It had begun innocently at the dinner table. Winston mentioned seeing Jonah's editorial in the newspaper.

"Are you part of this ex-gay conference?" Jonah asked.

"Not personally, but the group that I'm involved with is participating."

"I'm learning that the Scriptures used to condemn homosexuality…and homosexuals," Jonah said nonchalantly, "are not as dogmatic as those who use them against us."

The discussion was on. To help in their interaction, Jonah got his Bible and Winston retrieved his from his car. They moved to the sofa, sat close and looked like two students cramming for an exam.

They put each verse under a theological microscope of word meaning, history, culture, context, tradition and modern understanding. They talked about everything from God's plan at creation—Adam and Eve—to the eternal destiny for the unrepentant homosexual.

He'd heard it all before; Jonah had been teaching a Bible study on the subject for the past several weeks at church. He alternated between trying to listen to the discussion and reading a magazine.

He managed to sit through a detailed conversation about whether the cities of Sodom and Gomorrah were truly destroyed because of homosexuality. His attention faded in and out while they dissected the word "abomination" from the book of Leviticus and its meaning for the modern gay man, particularly one who also claims to be a Christian. He finally chose to exit the room when Winston made the challenge: "There's no way you can tell me that the passage in Romans can be taken any other way than God's disposition toward homosexual activity."

So as they moved to the New Testament, he moved to the kitchen and prepared dessert.

"If you scholars can tear yourselves away from your ancient scrolls, I have hot cobbler and cold ice cream," he announced. When they didn't move, he got firmer. "At the table. Now!" he hollered, slapping his hands together for emphasis.

"What about the Bible's teaching on sex outside marriage?" Winston was asking as they walked to the table.

"Give us the right to get married and then we'll discuss it," Jonah popped back.

"We weren't arguing," Jonah insisted when Matt wanted to know who was winning the debate.

Winston agreed. "He's giving me a perspective I haven't heard before. Lots to consider…and to study later."

After Winston left, Matt wanted to get Jonah's view of the discussion.

"Having this kind of dialogue with a lawyer is daunting, to say the least. And the fact that he's involved with that ex-gay group makes it more difficult."

Matt looked puzzled. "They have him brainwashed?"

Jonah crinkled his nose and squinted his eyes. "More because he's got a vested interest in maintaining a particular theological framework. He's spent years trying to be straight. If what I shared with him is true, he'd have little basis for his can't-be-gay life. It all collapses like a house of cards hit by the Wind of God's Spirit, to use a Biblical analogy."

Because he'd never struggled with those issues, Matt always had trouble understanding the conflict that was so strong and painful for people like Winston or Thumper.

"Then what happens?"

"I've been reading lots of testimonies of those who've come through the process. It's different for each person, but once the truth begins to dig in, it's like a termite. Just a matter of time. Then, what you always thought to be true is suddenly…*not*. For me, it was a gradual revelation that I'd been wrong about what the Bible really teaches. But many talk about some event that causes it all to fall in place…or fall apart."

"Is there anything we can do?"

Jonah took Matt's hand. "If it does all collapse, he'll need friends around him to help him rebuild."

TWENTY

WINSTON WAS AT THE OFFICE, BUT he wasn't working. The conversation with Jonah would not stop repeating in his mind and he couldn't concentrate.

In the days since the dinner, he'd given it plenty of deliberation and study. He was not a theologian, but he'd done what he thought was a significant amount of research on the topic: read books, listened to speakers, attended conferences and talked to scores of people. They all had essentially the same belief that homosexuality was wrong, and the Bible left no doubt on the subject!

So why am I now having doubts?

Winston had always accepted the no-other-option explanations of the six Bible passages on the subject. It was comfortable. But Jonah presented some excellent arguments. And much to Winston's surprise, his explanations made sense.

In a style that wasn't dogmatic or confrontational, Jonah had taken these verses and shown it wasn't that black and white. Without denying the Truth of Scripture, and using traditionally accepted methods of biblical interpretation, he presented a different way of understanding the passages.

What now? Winston wondered.

He knew this new information was more than a mere adjustment to what he believed; this was major shift in his belief system. The implications were daunting and confusing. That reality had kept him up a couple of nights and persistently pounded his mind during the day.

If homosexuality as an orientation is not a sin, what does that mean...for me?

But in spite of these emerging uncertainties, he determined he would not abandon his years of progress. He'd worked hard to break his past cycle of destructive sexual behavior and learned valuable lessons about himself in the process. That was worth preserving. He also knew the shallow existence he'd lived before still held no attraction for him.

Attraction.

That word stuck in his head. Indeed, that was the operative word.

Though he had no interest in returning to a lifestyle of one-night stands and casual sex, he could not deny that the desires—the *attraction*—had never gone away.

Thumper popped into his mind as definitive confirmation.

Jonah had pointed out that distinction during their discussion. "Perhaps it's not about behavior—whether I have sex or not—but about my basic, essential and unchangeable orientation. I can control my actions and activities, but not my attraction. It's about who I am, not what I do…or *who* I do."

He glanced at the clock. It wasn't even three o'clock, but he decided to call it a day.

Maybe if I go to the gym, I'll feel better, he reasoned.

As he reached for the switch to turn off the light, the phone rang.

Almost made it.

When he answered, the voice on the other end of the line was muffled beyond comprehension. At first, he thought someone was pranking him—laughing so hard he couldn't understand what they were saying. But then he realized the caller was crying—uncontrollable sobs that didn't allow for coherent communication.

Because of his visibility as a member of the *Full Circle* leadership, he'd had calls like this before. It could be a young man who'd come to realize the gay lifestyle was not the life he wants, a man who just learned the devastating news of his HIV status, a *Circle* member who'd experienced a sexual failure or a parent who'd recently learned they have a gay son.

"Calm down," he gently instructed the unknown caller. "Take some deep breaths." He waited, but the sobbing continued, as well as the caller's attempt to speak. "Take your time," he told the distraught person.

"It's Glenda Ford," she finally managed to voice through still-present sniffles. "Robby's mother."

Robert "Robby" Ford was a regular, longtime member of the *Circle* ministry. His dad was the pastor of a local Nazarene Church. Winston took his own deep breath, preparing for what was to come, knowing it couldn't be good, given her emotional condition.

"What's wrong, Glenda?"

She blew her nose, and it sounded like she used the phone as a tissue. "I came home this morning—I was supposed to work later—but I wasn't feeling good…"

He could almost complete the story; it had happened too often. Boy brings another boy home, thinking no one will be there. But through a series of unforeseen, out-of-the-ordinary circumstances, they get caught.

"He's dead, Winston."

He suddenly tuned back into the story that had taken on a twist he'd not anticipated or could have imagined.

"Huh?"

More sobbing. He wasn't able to understand much of what she was saying; the words were garbled and lost in the emotion. But he did hear the lethal phrase "his father's shotgun" all too clearly.

He scrambled for some kind of rationality. "I'll be right over," he sputtered.

He'd been to the house on numerous occasions, including several dinners with the family. Pastor Ford had invited him to speak to the church's singles' group at a retreat last summer. Mrs. Ford liked him; she thought he was like a big brother to Robby, their only child.

By the time he got there, others had arrived, including Robby's father. "Thank you for coming," he said as Winston walked in. "His mother's lying down. The doctor was just here and gave her something so she could rest."

Winston first met Robby a few weeks after moving to Dallas, when he began attending the *Circle* meetings. Robby was already actively involved in the program, and in the past year, had stepped up his leadership role. He did mentoring with some of the new guys, led a weekly Bible Study at the center and frequently spoke to outside groups about his own change-experience.

Looking around the room, he saw Dan, the Executive Director of *Full Circle*, standing with several members of the ministry near a glass double-door that opened onto the patio. He walked over and nodded a greeting to the grieving group.

"Does anyone know the details?" he asked, hoping to get information about the funeral arrangements.

"He left a note and blew his brains out," one of the guys answered. His face was stained wet.

With the unintended change of topic, he pushed for more. "How do you know there was a note?"

"I heard the cops talking to Robby's mom. Wrote that he'd tried, but it didn't work. Told his folks he loved them and that he was sorry."

The young man looked at Dan. "I should have said something earlier."

Now the entire group was staring at the young man, waiting for further explanation.

"I've known Robby since kindergarten; we grew up in church together. He's like my best friend. He's the one who got me going to the *Circle*. That was before…"

He stopped and looked around the room cautiously. He lowered his volume. "Robby was having a rough time. He had…failures. Met some guy at the library and they hooked up a few times. He was always repentant, and promised not to do it again, but it didn't stick. I also know that he was messing around with a couple of the rookies."

"Rookie" was the term they used for guys entering the restoration program. It was more than someone who only attended the *Circle* meetings—usually called "Seekers." The weekly meetings were open to anyone; the *Full*

Circle program was more in-depth and required enrollment, and long-term commitment.

Winston suddenly couldn't breathe.

How did I not see this?

He'd talked with Robby a few days ago, at a leadership meeting. He replayed that meeting in his mind to determine if there had been any signals he should have picked up.

Robby's father interrupted his thoughts when he walked up and placed his hand on Dan's shoulder. "The service will be Friday. We'd like you to help us by finding some guys to be pallbearers. He loved the group so much."

"What are we doing, Dan?" Winston asked, consciously keeping his volume and his emotions in control. "What the hell are we doing?"

"I know you're upset, but we have to look at the bigger picture."

They were in the executive director's office. Winston had requested the meeting to vent some of what he was feeling in the weeks since Robby's funeral.

"What big picture?" he challenged. "I admit, I'm not seeing clearly these days."

Dan Larson was a big man. "Big and burly," as they would say. Before his conversion—while he was still in the gay lifestyle—his nickname was Horse, which he swore referred solely to his physical stature. Using the equine analogy, at nearly six foot two and probably three hundred pounds, he was a Clydesdale.

Dan's office looked like it could have been decorated by a blind factory worker. It was as if there had been a conscious decision to make it the anti-gay stereotype of no style and no frills.

Almost everything was functional, with little or no attention to décor. The cinder-block walls were painted an off-white shade of beige. The steel bookcases were industrial hand-me-downs, minus any paint treatment. In addition to various-sized cardboard boxes of supplies, they were filled with books, which at least added some color to the room. The single window was covered in a faded shade that maintained the vanilla motif. The only thing in the room that could be considered decorative was a group photos of the current leadership board, taped to the wall.

Dan walked around the desk and sat in a chair beside him. "We can't lose sight of all the good we've done here—"

"The *good* we've done?" he interrupted with increased intensity. "One of our leaders is dead because he couldn't live up to what we preach. We didn't provide him with a system of support, and now he's dead."

Those in leadership with the ministry were encouraged—or *expected*—to attend the weekly *Circle* meetings, but public confessions of failures or personal struggles were strongly discouraged.

"It might be confusing to those who are new to the program," they were regularly told in leadership training. "As leaders, we're a light for those coming out of the darkness. If you need help, we suggest you choose a more private avenue for accountability."

"It's a tragedy, that's for sure," Dan agreed with a sad shrug. "And he will spend eternity paying for that decision. But we must not let the actions of one person undermine our ongoing mission."

Winston snickered—completely out of place, given the context of the conversation. "That's where you're wrong, my friend. I've been doing some checking and it's not just one person. I've talked to other guys in the program, and most of them—when I convinced them to be totally honest with me—have the same struggles now they had when they entered the program. They might not act out, or they've learned to replace the feeling with some other activity, but the desires are still there. Many are on meds for depression, others use alcohol. But more than half are still sexually active. Is that what we consider success?"

"We both know healing is a process."

"I'm not talking about the process. I'm talking about the results. We brag about our success rate, telling people that seventy-five percent of those who complete our program are living a life of healthy sexual expression. I've blithely quoted that number on numerous occasions when I've spoken at conferences, to churches and even to reporters…but what does it mean? Is it accurate?"

Winston tossed a file folder on Dan's desk. He glanced down at it, but didn't touch it.

"I looked through our records. Our so-called success rate is based solely on those who *finish* the program. Three out of four who enter our program will finish, but do we ever follow up? What happens once they're out from under our scrutiny? Do they return to the gay lifestyle? Are the desires really gone? In truth, we have no way of knowing if it worked or not once they leave us, but we sure as hell count them in our success statistics."

"One person…one ministry can only do so much. I'm proud of how we help so many hurting men and women—"

"What about those who enter in the program, but don't complete it? I found that in the past five years, there have been almost three hundred who enrolled, but for whatever reason, they dropped out. What happens to them?

We certainly don't include them in our success statistics, because that would lower our numbers, right?

Winston kept talking over Dan's attempt to reply. "And then there's those who visit the *Circle*, but never come back. I'm thinking there must be hundreds of them every year. How is this success, Dan?"

"Where do you get the right to go through our files—"

With no attempt to hide his irritation, he interrupted. "I'm not only a member of the board, I'm legal counsel for the ministry. I have full access to all ministry records."

Dan stood and walked back to the chair behind his desk. "We can't make someone stay in the program. This kind of change requires commitment and personal accountability. It's takes years of work and discipline."

"That's a crock! Robbie was active for five years. He was here before I came in."

"You can't judge the entire program on the failure of one person. Look at yourself. You are a testimony of what this program can do."

This time, Winston laughed out loud. "You don't get it, do you? I'm not basing my concern on one person. I just showed you hundreds of reasons I'm concerned. And as for me being any kind of proof, that's more a testimony to personal fortitude and discipline. I've never had a sexual relapse and I'm articulate, but that doesn't mean I should be held up as the poster-boy for the program."

Dan vigorously shook his head. "That's unfair. You are a success *because* of the program. It's where you learned the spiritual exercises and received the tools to make good choices and stay in recovery. God is healing you… through the program."

"I hate to burst your bubble, but we need to take a hard look at our precious program. What we're doing is *not* working. It killed Robby. Others are having the same struggle. We can't take credit for success, but refuse to assume responsibility for failures. If we aren't helping them, then we damn-well better come up with something that does, or we *will* be held accountable for their deaths."

Dan's posture stiffened, and his tone took on a pronounced seriousness. "You seem to be having some doubts about God's work here. Is there something more to this, Winston? Is this why you didn't attend the restoration conference? Are you having second thoughts about your true sexual identity?"

Winston felt a deep sadness for this man he admired so much. "I *am* having second thoughts, Dan. And I *do* have serious doubts."

He took a deep breath and considered about how much he should disclose. "I'm having second thoughts about this program and whether it works. And more than that, I have doubts about whether it should."

The shock was evident. "You can't mean you support a homosexual lifestyle. Please tell me—"

Winston stood, interrupting the lecture he knew was coming. "I appreciate what you've done for me, Dan. I've learned so much and my life is better because of the lessons you've taught me. Though I love you as a brother in Christ, I can no longer support the mission of the group. I hope you can understand."

He extended his hand across the desk, but Dan defiantly refused the gesture, so Winston bowed slightly in his direction and left the office.

TWENTY-ONE

"HOW ARE YOU ADJUSTING TO LIFE outside a hospital?"

"It's okay."

The doctor put down his notebook and looked at Barnabas. "That didn't sound very convincing? Is anything wrong?"

"Everything's fine." His tone was flat and he made no attempt to add emotion he didn't feel.

After almost two months in the hospitals, first at Baylor and then at Rushdoony, Barnabas had been excited about going home. It was one of the few places he could remember, even though the memories were disjointed.

But the truth was, it had only been two weeks and he was feeling suffocated. His mom was always around. Every move he made caused her to come to his aid. If he groaned at a twinge in his nearly healed hip, it got her near-panicked attention.

Boredom was a constant issue, since he wasn't allowed to watch TV.

"We don't want to over-stimulate you while the doctor is working to restore your memories," his parents justified.

Radio was mostly off limits as well, except for religious stations.

They did let him read; indeed, the doctor encouraged it. He wasn't permitted to go to the library, and his parents picked out his reading list— mostly what his dad deemed "classic literature" or Christian fiction. But it not only broke up the monotony of his day, he could escape into the lives of the characters on the page or those chronicled in biographies. He read some books that he was sure he'd read before, but it didn't matter.

"It's like falling in love all over again...for the first time," he'd told Marti.

She really seemed to like that concept. When he shared it with her, she got chocked up and hugged him very tight. "I'm so glad to hear you say that," she'd said.

"I understand you and Marti went on a date last weekend?" The doctor's attempt at enthusiasm was annoying.

"We went to church," he corrected. "Hardly a date."

Though he refused to admit it to the doctor, he had enjoyed the day, if only because it was the first time he'd gotten out of the house since moving back to Birmingham.

The doctor jotted some notes. "But it's a good step, Barnabas. Rejoice in the progress."

The thought of Dr. D rejoicing was a visual he found funny. The only emotion the man seemed to convey was detachment; his only facial expression was a serious glance over the rims of the half-glasses perched on his nose. Thumper had secretly dubbed him "Doctor Dreary."

Randall Davidson was pleased with the progress the patient was making. During their time in the hospitals, they'd met daily and had some significant sessions. Now that Barnabas was home, they only had two sessions each week. Brother Jimmy had made arrangements to have him flown in so they could continue the treatment protocol.

Today, Barnabas was exhibiting some anxiety, which he attributed to the many external stimuli associated with moving back home. He had decided last week to increase the anti-anxiety medication and also prescribed a stronger sleeping pill.

"Why don't we stop for now and work on our relaxation." Without waiting, he reached over and turned on the sound machine. By now in the hypnosis segment of the treatment, Barnabas would hear the sound and almost instantly begin to relax into the suggestive state. But due to the new environment, the doctor had once again added a mild sedative to help induce hypnosis.

"Let's go back to the time you recently spent with Marti," he instructed, once it was evident that Barnabas was under hypnosis. "You enjoy spending time with her, don't you Barnabas? She is a pretty woman and you are attracted to her, aren't you?"

"We have a good time," he muttered.

He needs to admit to having feelings for the girl.

The doctor made some notes. "We talked before about how you would get turned on when you and Marti were making out, back when you both were younger. I know you still feel that way when you're with her. It's acceptable to have those feelings, Barnabas. It's perfectly normal. You have physical desires for Marti."

He seemed to give the concept some thought, so the doctor proceeded. "I want you to think back on a time when you can remember being sexually stimulated. Remember a time when you were physically turned on." He waited. "Can you remember a time for me?"

Almost immediately, the answer was obvious. The patient's breathing rate changed and his face flushed. He moved slowly and slightly in a provocative manner.

"Yea," he moaned as he adjusted the front of his jeans.

It was a bit uncomfortable, but the doctor knew it was necessary to accomplish the intended results.

"Those feelings are normal, Barnabas. Now, I want you to know that these feelings are caused by Marti. You are turned on because you are sexually attracted to her. Isn't that right, Barnabas?"

Moan.

"Keep those feelings, and now I want you to also picture Marti. She's wearing a skimpy swim suit that shows her nice figure. You are sexually aroused by her figure. You see her shapely figure and you have these feelings. Marti is the reason for these sexual desires."

"Oh, Marti. You make me so horny."

The doctor resisted correcting the harsh terminology. "That's right, Barnabas. You are a normal man and Marti, uh...stirs feelings in you. You desire to have sex with her."

"I still don't feel quite right about this."

Matt looked up from the half-emptied box. "Moving in together?"

Jonah leaned down and kissed him on the cheek. "Well, it is a bit rushed, but I was talking about his stuff." Jonah made a sweeping gesture with both arms.

He was referring to all the items still in Thumper's bedroom. Contrary to what Mrs. Rivers had told him at the hospital, no one ever came to pick up anything.

"We're just going to put it in boxes, stick in the closet, and deal with it all later," Matt instructed.

Once Thumper returned to Birmingham, Matt called the number he'd given to the police officer the night of Thumper's attack. No one answered, so he left a voice mail, identifying himself and asking what to do with Thumper's belongings. The next time he called, an electronic operator informed him that he had been blocked from calling that number. But not long afterwards, he received a brief note in the mail:

> *Doctor and Mrs. Rivers have determined they will not be needing their son's belongings. Please do with them as you see fit. Enclosed find a check to cover his portion of the rent and expenses.*

There was no signature, just the embossed title: Administrative Assistant to Dr. James Rivers.

Surprisingly, the check was extremely generous.

They'd decided to use Thumper's room and his furniture as a guest room; the closet, chest and wardrobe would be for storage and out-of-season clothes. They agreed to keep his car, and even contracted with the building for an additional parking space. All of his electronics would remain, though they did cancel the cable service in his room. Also staying were the bookcases and the many books that filled them.

"As for moving in together, it may be a bit sudden, but we know it's necessary. You can't continue to live with the guys, so quit stalling and get back to work."

"Hey, I'm already sweating from three trips."

Matt blew a kiss. "And as a reward for all your manual labor, I promise to help you shower off later. But until then, stop your whining and go get more boxes."

Winston had not realized how much of his life revolved around *Full Circle* ministry. Besides the weekly *Circle* meetings, he also had monthly board meetings, leadership meetings, trainings, conferences and workshops. In addition, he would regularly get together with some of the guys; they would go to movies, out to dinner or have game nights. But since he'd left the group, he found a significant amount of extra time in his schedule.

He tried to make the most of the new-found time surplus. He studied the material from *Evangelicals Concerned* that Jonah had given him about the Bible and homosexuality. He also took care of overdue projects around the condo. He did more cooking, experimenting with new recipes. However, there was one missing element his busyness could not fill. Without the people and activities from the ministry, his life was nearly void of human contact outside of work.

His years in counseling had taught him the danger of such isolation. Loneliness was one of the most powerful triggers; it could lead to acting out. So even though he was having doubts about many aspects of the restoration program, he was determined not to give in to shallow temptations.

Jonah and Matt were very supportive of his decision to leave the ministry. He and Jonah talked regularly on the phone, but Winston found that spending time with them—while always enjoyable—only magnified his sense of singleness.

He'd called the Rivers' house once to check on Thumper, but didn't actually speak with him. Gwen said he was doing much better since returning home, but was out with his girlfriend. That news also added to Winston's awareness of how much he missed Thumper.

An unexpected event injected some hope into his solitary schedule. It began with a voice mail message, left at his office while he was at lunch.

"Winston, this is Libby Lawrence. It was so good to see you yesterday at the Alliance meeting. We should get together for lunch one day this week. Maybe dinner and a drink. Give me a call."

Elizabeth Lawrence was the executive director and CEO of one of the largest women's cancer charities in the state. They'd met the previous year at the monthly Dallas Nonprofit Alliance breakfast. In the past, he would attend the meetings periodically, but since he needed to be around people, he'd decided that his involvement would offer some protection from the danger of his isolation. It also gave him the opportunity to pass out his business cards to the leaders of nonprofits and charities.

At yesterday's meeting, they'd stayed for nearly an hour after the meeting, sipping coffee and chatting about their lives. She was probably ten years older, but beautiful, attentive and easy to talk to. It was only after listening to the message did he realize that she'd been flirting with him.

He listened to the message again and made the near-instant decision that it was time to take a major step forward—one that he had not attempted in the seven years since he'd left the gay lifestyle and embarked on his healing journey. He called Libby and they decided to get together Friday night for dinner. He made certain they both used the word "date" as they planned the evening.

In the Rivers' house, Halloween was not celebrated. In any form. His dad refused to call it a *holiday* since that word originally implied a "holy" day and he saw nothing sacred about it. He would preach scathing sermons against the demonic elements in the observance, cite scores of Biblical passages, and give detailed predictions of the evil consequences of taking his warnings lightly. His spine-chilling examples rivaled those of a fireside ghost story at summer camp. During one of the discourses, Barnabas had vague memories of similar tirades when he was younger.

But while his dad would rail against "that October devil-day," Thanksgiving and Christmas were wonderful, elaborate events around their house. Thanksgiving involved more food than could be consumed by a small country. His mom insisted on cooking, but because of the huge number of people who attended, they also brought in additional help. It was tradition to invite all the church elders, along with their families to share the holiday meal. With wives, children, spouses of children and even a few grandchildren, that could mean as many as a hundred people.

On Thanksgiving day, as more and more guests arrived, Barnabas found that the large crowd made him anxious. He tried to be social, but finally ended up going to his room and closing the door. He was reading when his mom brought a plate of food—which he didn't want—and gently scolded him for missing the celebration.

"These are the people who prayed for you when we thought you wouldn't pull through," she pointed out with the usual emotion in her voice. "Some of them have known you since you were a child. They were so excited to see you."

Christmas festivities began immediately after Thanksgiving. In fact, while one group of hired help was cleaning up on Friday after the huge dinner, his mom was involved with another group, getting the Christmas decorations from storage.

The first week was dedicated to getting the house ready for the many parties during the month. Among the events, there would be another evening with the church leaders, a party for the youth of the church and even a reception for the widows and what his dad called "the unclaimed blessings"—his term for older women who'd never married.

The afternoon of the first event, his mom came to his room to see how he was feeling and to firmly let him know she was counting on him to be there. She emphasized how important it was to his father.

"I'll try," was his response.

She sat on the end of his bed. "I'm sure Martha is excited to see you. Just between you and me," she whispered with a tone of mock secrecy, "I know she bought a new dress for tonight."

He manufactured a look of pleasure. "I'm looking forward to seeing her, and I promise to try and stay for the whole party."

She stood to leave. "Oh, I bought a little gift for you to give to her."

When he frowned, she informed: "It's Christmas, dear. It's the appropriate thing to do."

Marti did look lovely, and he complimented her dress, per his mom's instructions. It got a positive response, just like his mom predicted. Marti beamed as she kissed him on the cheek. While she was close to his ear, she spoke in a soft voice, "I wish I could give you more this Christmas, but I'd have to take off this new dress, so that will have to wait." She giggled at her suggestive remark.

About a hour into the party, his dad's powerful voice got everyone's attention. "I want to thank you all for coming tonight. Gwen and I look forward to this time every year. Not only to celebrate the birth of our Savior, but to enjoy the gift of the friendships God has bestowed on us. You all are so very special to us."

Applause filled the room and the stout pastor did a slight bow and hugged his wife. When the noise of admiration stopped, he continued. "There is never a shortage of gifts that reflect the love of friends and family, but this year is especially poignant. We're humbled by a most wonderful gift from our loving heavenly Father. We prayed faithfully and diligently and God answered our heart-felt petition. Just as He promised."

Barnabas noticed that many people in the room were turning and looking in his direction. He graciously acknowledged their attention.

"I'm reminded of the wonderful story that Jesus told in Luke, chapter fifteen. Most call it 'The Prodigal Son,' but more accurately, it's the account of God's loving grace and restoration. Today, we rejoice that our son has been restored unto us. God has honored His Word and rewarded our faithfulness."

His dad took out a handkerchief and wiped what most would consider tears from his face, though Barnabas could see it was sweat. His mom moved next to Barnabas and put her arm around his waist.

"We're not going to kill a fatted calf," his dad told the crowd. "But tonight, we celebrate. Our son has returned to us. Praise Jesus!"

Applause erupted, along with shouts of praise. Many came over and hugged him. Suddenly the room seemed to increase in temperature, and then seemed to be moving in all directions at once. He was sweating more than his dad. His stomach reacted with a wave of nausea and he forced himself not to be sick in front of all these people.

"I need to get some air," he gasped, causing his mom to release her grip.

She looked at him with clear disappointment, but must have seen the reality of his distress. She took him by the arm and guided him through the crowd, telling people as they passed that he needed to get some rest. They moved through the kitchen, out the back door and into the cold December night, where he violently vomited over the patio railing.

Twenty-Two

HE DIDN'T KNOW THE PHONE NUMBER. More accurately, he didn't know if he knew the number. But as he was getting ready for Sunday School, it was suddenly there, in his mind. He had no idea why or who might be on the other end.

In recent weeks, it had happened sporadically: faces, images, places, sounds, smells. Unknown and nameless, but at the same time, somehow familiar. He had decided not to tell the doctor of this recent development, certain he would dismiss them as merely recollections from an old movie or TV show.

He wanted to take the phone onto the porch, but it was too cold, so he went into his dad's private study to make the call. It rang several times, then went to voice mail.

"Hello, this is Matt and Jonah. We can't take your call right now, so please leave a message. We'll get back to you as soon as possible. Of course, if you don't leave a message, it's not likely we'll call you back."

He didn't leave a message. His mom came in and wanted to know who was on the phone, so he hung up. Besides, the names given by the electronic voice held no meaning to him. He chalked it up to another of the many memory tricks.

But it didn't prevent him from becoming annoyed. And depressed.

"Can I borrow your blue turtleneck sweater?" Jonah asked as he walked into the bedroom.

"Come listen to this," Matt said, ignoring the request. He'd seen the light on the answering machine blinking and remembered hearing the phone while they were in the shower.

"That call we got earlier," he pointed to the phone as Jonah stood in the doorway, still draped only in a towel. "It's the strangest message."

Matt pushed the button and then waited. They heard a click, indicating the place where a caller would normally leave a message. But in this case, there was a momentary silence. Faint, in the background, a woman's voice could be heard: "Who are you talking to, dear?"

"No one, Momma," came the reply, slightly masked by noise, as the male caller apparently moved the phone to hang it up.

"Didn't that sound like Thumper?"

Jonah wrinkled his nose. "I guess. It was so quick."

"It was Thumper," Matt concluded.

"What does the Caller ID say?"

Matt's arms dropped to his side and his shoulders sagged. "Private number," he answered.

Before they left for church, he'd listened to the message at least five additional times. He was convinced it was Thumper. Jonah, not as certain, remained supportive.

Barnabas arrived on time, as always. Marti waved at Mrs. Rivers, who'd dropped him off, then kissed him on the cheek when he got inside her apartment.

Marti lived only a few blocks from the Rivers' home, so they'd agreed to his visit, but outlined in detail their expectations: if they left the apartment, the destination must be discussed with first, only preapproved movies could be rented, no alcohol and had a curfew of eleven o'clock. Marti didn't understand all the restrictions, but wasn't going to challenge them for fear she'd be forbidden from seeing him.

"How did your session go today?"

He frowned. "The usual. Lots of talking." He used the familiar hand-gesture to not only indicate the idea of talking, but to convey his disdain for the process. "Blah, blah, blah," he verbalized.

A few weeks ago, just after the new year, Barnabas' doctor had invited her to meet in the study at the Rivers' house, where he did the weekly sessions. Dr. D said he needed her help with Barnabas' recovery, then asked, "How do you think he's doing? You're with him when his guard is down. You're his girlfriend. Tell me about his mood, his emotions."

"He still seems a bit…dazed."

"That's the medication. They are designed to help his mood, since he continues to get frustrated with his memory loss. We increased his anti-anxiety meds after the problems he had during the holidays."

She wanted to tell the doctor that "mood" was not the problem. Whether it was the result of the accident or the drugs they were giving him, most of the time, it was like he didn't even have a personality. If emotion could flatline, Barnabas would be in full arrest.

Before she'd left, the doctor admonished her to keep on taking him to familiar places. She acknowledged that they had gone out numerous times, visiting their old high school, several local attractions, the park where he'd played soccer and some of his favorite restaurants. She also confirmed that his parents were always advised about where they went and what they did.

"I still can't believe my parents let me come over," Barnabas said to her as he laid his coat across the back of the sofa and walked into the living room. "What's the plan for the evening?"

"I thought we'd have dinner and watch a movie." Brother Jimmy had approved her movie selection—a PG remake of an old Disney comedy.

Marti watched as Barnabas looked at the bags on the counter separating her kitchen from the living room.

"Golden Rule," he read the name aloud. "That's the barbeque place, right?"

Golden Rule Barbeque had been in Birmingham since the 1800s. In high school, it was one of the places they would go as a couple, especially after church on Sundays.

"Do you remember it?" she asked.

"Nope, saw it while driving around with Mom last week. She mentioned that I used to like eating there." He added: "Smells great."

She was putting food on the plates when he reached over and took a piece of the meat. He started to eat it, but then moved it to her lips, waiting for her to take a bite. "Golden Rule," he said. "Do unto others as you would have them do unto you."

"Absolutely," she agreed, taking a small bite.

She leaned in and kissed him. As in high school, his kiss was tender and hesitant. But she would not let it stay that way. Not tonight. She put her hand on the back of his neck and held him close, slipping her tongue into his mouth. Much to her delight, the passion of his kiss increased.

There was a time when she would stop him. It wasn't any specific action or movement on his part; he always seemed more reticent about the progress of their make-out sessions. Back then, when passion took a secondary place to their imposed commitment of sexual purity, it was as if an internal, divinely programmed alarm would go off and she would know it was time to shut it down. Tonight, there would be no alarm. She'd made that decision when she learned he was returning home.

After they'd lost touch when he went to college, she tried to move on with her life. She dated during her own junior-college years and even had a couple of long-term relationships. She'd slept with a few of the guys, but always found herself thinking about Barnabas. No man could measure up to her fantasy of him, so the relationships always ended. Now, she understood why. Barnabas was the only man she'd ever loved. God had probably allowed the accident to happen so they would finally be together.

She moved her hands across his chest and was thrilled with his reaction.

When she brushed one of his nipples, he let out a moan. The fact that she could bring this kind of response from him only motivated her more. Continuing her touching, she also moved him toward the sofa. Once they were closer, she unbuttoned his shirt and exposed his upper body.

"We shouldn't. I want to respect—"

"It's okay," she assured.

His shirt fell to the floor and she moved her hands across his chest and down his stomach. Her touch was light, barely making contact with his skin. He leaned back, pushing his torso toward her, as if giving her permission to continue.

"I love you," she affirmed. "I have always loved you. This is a good thing, Barnabas. I am giving myself to you out of love."

To prove her point, she unbuttoned her own shirt and removed it, then did the same with her bra. He watched with unbroken attention. When he didn't move, she took his hand and placed it on her breast.

"That feels nice, baby. I can feel your love when you touch me like that."

When his other hand got involved with caressing her breast, she unbuckled his belt and then his pants. She pushed them down and allowed her fingers to run under the elastic band of his underwear. He was enjoying the attention and his male member proved it.

"Why don't we go to my bedroom?"

Without waiting for a response, she took him by the hand and led the way. He stepped out of his pants and followed.

She completed her own disrobing and stood, allowing him to look at her.

"I want to do this," she repeated over and over while helping him undress and get into her bed. "I want you to make love to me."

Though she had never been this aggressive in her past sexual experiences, she reached over and grasped him gently. She liked that her touch made it harden in her hand. She moved her hand up and down, hearing how her touch brought him such pleasure.

"Oh...God...yes. Stroke my dick," he instructed.

She'd heard that some men liked to talk dirty during lovemaking, so she decided to join in. "I think we should put that hard...dick...inside me." She almost laughed, hearing herself say the vulgar word.

But he obeyed, rolling over on top of her and sliding into her, first with gentle movements. As he increased his thrusts, it quickly brought her to a passion she'd never imagined.

"Oh yes, Barnabas. It feels so good."

His movement gave her the indication that he was close to climax. She looked up at him and his eyes were partially shut.

"Fuck, yeah. Take that cock. I'm gonna give it to ya' 'til you shoot."

She stiffened up, shocked at the degree of profanity.

He pumped faster, then shouted as he came inside her. "Jesus Holy Fucking Christ."

"Barnabas!"

He opened his eyes, a look of terror in his face. "Fuck...I mean...Marti, I am so sorry. I didn't mean for this to happen," he sobbed as he rolled off her.

She put her arms around him. "Honey, it's alright. I'm glad this happened. We're both adults and we made this choice. Please don't be upset."

Though she tried to talk him out of it, he left almost immediately after getting dressed, saying that he'd walk the short distance to his parents' house.

"Look what came in the mail," Jonah said as Matt prepared dinner.

Matt walked into the room, wiping his hands on the apron. "I'm guessing it's not the Food Network, wanting to give me my own show."

"It's the offer letter from TTP." He waved it in Matt's direction, seeing the immediate interest.

For the past few months, Jonah had been in negotiations with The Transformation Project, a national nonprofit based in Dallas. After his initial meeting in October with the executive director, several weeks passed before he was invited to meet a small group of board members. They discussed general ideas for the newly created position and even asked for his input on how the job description might be framed. He left the meeting convinced the job offer would be forthcoming. However, what he learned was an important lesson about nonprofits: decision-making can be slow.

"About damn time." Matt bounced into the room and sat next to him on the sofa.

In November, Jonah met with the entire Board of Directors. Once again, the job and job description were discussed. They wanted to know about his qualifications, his experience and his goals for the position, as well as what he believed he could bring to the organization.

He thought a few of the board members were abrupt, based on the rapid-fire grilling about his sexuality, his faith, the teachings of Scripture and the current political climate. He knew that the scope of some questions would usually be considered illegal—especially the politics and religion—but since the job would confront these issues, he'd been told in advance to expect this line of questioning.

The meeting lasted nearly three hours, and when he left, he was not only unsure if he would be offered the job, he was uncertain if he wanted it.

Danielle, the executive director, must have sensed his frustration and called him later in the week. "You did great!" she encouraged. "I've heard from several board members how impressed they were. We're all excited."

Following that conversation, it was a couple of weeks before he received an e-mail from the executive director's administrative assistant:

> *Ms. McKinney wanted to let you know that no decision has been made on the position. You are still our only candidate, but with the holidays, it's been difficult to get everyone together. You will be hearing from us after the first of the year.*

It had taken more than three months from the initial meeting to receiving the offer letter.

"Wow," Matt exclaimed as he read the letter. "That's a good salary package, especially for a nonprofit."

"They want me to start in three weeks. I'll have to give my notice to SnynapTech immediately."

Matt hugged him. "And we have to go out and buy you some new clothes. You're an executive now—Director of Diversity Outreach for The Transformation Project."

Barnabas picked at his food while Marti tried to engage him in small talk. It was difficult to even look at her; he was troubled by what they had done their last time together. Privately, he had vowed to avoid her so it wouldn't happen again. But she was a force of nature. A *sneaky* force of nature! She'd called his mom and they had arranged tonight's dinner at her apartment.

As they were eating, she demurely asked how he was feeling about their "encounter." That was the word she used.

"I wasn't planning for...uh, that to happen," he stammered, staring at the food on his plate and moving a carrots back and forth with his fork. "We promised to wait until we were married."

"I know that you are the only person—the right person—for me." She moved closer to him. "One day, we'll get a marriage license and have a wedding, but right now, in my mind...we're already married."

He didn't know what to say, and she didn't give him time to think of anything. She moved him into the living room. Her hand touched his thigh, but instantly moved up until she was stoking him through his jeans.

"That feels so good," he told her.

"I know, baby. I want to make you feel good."

She worked to remove his pants, then raised her skirt and pushed down her panties. She straddled him on the sofa and lowered herself onto him, taking him in slowly.

"That's the way," she coaxed as she leaned her face close to his ear.

Her voice faded. He could feel her going up and down on him, but there was also a sensation of dizziness. He was floating. Then, a sudden memory-flash: a series of images like watching a movie in his mind.

He saw himself having passionate sex. His naked body was thrusting and he was talking. The talk was dirty, like what had happened the first time he'd made love to Marti. But this wasn't Marti and they weren't in her bedroom, though he could faintly hear her voice: "That's it, Honey. That feels wonderful, baby. It's so right and it's so good."

So good, he thought. *Take that dick.*

Suddenly, a face came into focus. A man's face. He could see the man's firm, sweaty muscular body, responding beneath his own. The unnamed man was enjoying what they were doing; it showed on his face and in his coarse instruction: *Fuck me. Slam it in me. Gimme that dick.*

The images were so vivid and the experience felt so real.

"Oh, Jesus!" he screamed.

"Yes, baby. Yes," she moaned, obviously climaxing too.

And like a dream fleeing in the morning hours, the images and faces faded. The voice of the apparition that once begged in passion now echoed away.

Though he struggled to remember precise details of the now-submerged vision, raw feelings remained on the surface: a confusing combination of fear, intrigue…and desire.

PART 3:

For our struggle is not against flesh and blood

TWENTY-THREE

"How have you been feeling this week? Your mom's worried that you have no appetite."

After five months as a patient of "Doctor Dreary," a couple of things had become clear to Barnabas. One, he was tired of talking about his life and his feelings. When memories were mostly non-existent, or as shattered as Humpty Dumpty, it was a waste of time. And without the anchor of memories, feelings were detached and unpredictable.

The recent encounters with Marti, and especially the sexual memory-flash with the nameless man, had messed with his feelings even more. He was confused, but decided to add that experience to the growing list of things he wouldn't discuss in the sessions. He instinctively knew that not only would the doctor disapprove, his parents would be told. And with them, disapproval would be the least of the reactions he'd have to endure.

"How are things with your parents?" He sounded like he was reading off his notebook. "I know they have been traveling recently."

Several weeks earlier, during family dinner, his dad advised them that he needed to resume his travel schedule. "God's work is beckoning. But it will only be a few days out of the month," he assured. "Your mother will stay here with you."

That arrangement didn't last long. The second trip, his dad indicated that they both needed to go. "We have a nurse who'll come in to give you the medications and Jolanda will be here to cook for you. Do you think you'll be okay?"

Barnabas hid his exhilaration. Once they were gone, he'd been able to sneak away several times. He went to movies he was sure they'd object to him seeing and got several books he knew they wouldn't want him to read. He also watched lots of forbidden TV in the evenings. Being free of his parents for the short periods of time had magnified his desire to be on his own.

"I need my own place," he announced to the doctor with rehearsed determination. "I'm twenty-four years old and shouldn't be living with my parents."

"Yes, your mother told me about that conversation," came the response. "She said it upset some of the people at your birthday party."

"Party? I only knew one person, and that was Marti. The rest were from Daddy's church. Besides, she asked what I wanted for my birthday and I told her."

The doctor never looked up. "She said the discussion got a bit heated."

156

"In her definition, anytime I disagree with them, it's heated."

"They have your best interests at heart, Barnabas. We all do." He was looking over the narrow spectacles, waiting for a reply.

"So I've heard," he retorted, not hiding his scorn.

Dr. Davidson laid the notebook on the table beside his chair and turned on the white noise machine. "Well, it does seem as though you have some strong feelings about this. Why don't we do our relaxation exercises?"

Another thing that Barnabas had learned over the past few months was that these so-called "relaxation sessions" involved more than just relaxing. He'd first noticed it by accident, when he happened to glance at his watch as the doctor turned on the sound machine. As he was leaving the study later, he looked at the clock in the living room, and nearly an hour had passed. After that, he paid closer attention.

"I want you to close your eyes. Listen to the sound of the waves and let your mind drift…"

Barnabas closed his eyes, but contrary to the instructions, forced his mind to concentrate. One of his favorite ways to tune out the doctor was to recall—in as much detail as possible—scenes from one of the books he was reading. Today, it was *Robinson Crusoe*.

He knew it didn't always work, but he was getting better at resisting. And what he was learning about the doctor's intentions only increased his resolve to resist!

"I'm pregnant."

Marti's declaration was sudden, causing both Barnabas and his mom to stop eating. The three of them were having dinner prior to going to Wednesday night Bible study. His mom gasped audibly, while he shouted, "What?"

"I'm six weeks along," she said with a sly smile. "Just found out today."

"I am shocked, and very disappointed," his mother scolded, glaring at Marti.

Marti instantly appeared remorseful. "I don't blame you," she whimpered. "I knew it was wrong when we did it, but he wanted to…uh, you know…and I was trying to be supportive of his recovery."

She was talking about him like he wasn't there. As if he had not been present when she seduced him. More than once. He was about to correct her story, but his mom was faster.

"Your father is going to blow his top when he hears this," she chastised, using her finger to point at him, in case he didn't know who she was addressing. "We raised you better than that."

157

He put down his fork, making a definite and intentional noise. "First off, she's not giving you an accurate picture of what happened, and please don't talk to me like I'm sixteen years old."

A pronounced pout was now evident on Marti's face. "I resent what you are implying, Barnabas. You and I both know—"

"You should leave," he snapped at her.

Marti looked at his mother for some kind of signal. Then he stood and wailed. "Get the hell out of here. *Now!*"

His mom intervened. "Barnabas, sit down." She looked over at the still-horrified Marti. "Perhaps you should leave, dear. We will deal with this when cooler heads prevail."

Once Marti was gone, he sat back down and waited for the inevitable conversation. But his mom began clearing off the plates as if nothing had happened, beyond the exit of a dinner guest.

"She's not telling the entire truth," he protested. "It wasn't like that."

She stopped on the way out of the dining room. "It doesn't matter what it was *like*, Barnabas. It matters that what you've done has consequences. You have created a life. The question now is not who's wrong, but what's right."

She pushed open the door to the kitchen, then hesitated, but didn't turn around. "I will speak to your father and Doctor D. We will handle this, Barnabas." As the kitchen door closed, he heard her add: "As always."

Twenty-Four

"WINSTON..." THE VOICE ON THE MESSAGE was muffled, as if the caller was mumbling. "...this is Barnabas. Barnabas Rivers."

Winston had been out of town for the weekend at a legal conference in Austin, and missed the call when it came in late the previous evening—eleven twenty-five, according to the time stamp. He was stopping by the condo to drop off his suitcase before heading to the office.

"I need to talk to you. Winston, I need..." More garbled mumbling, and then the call ended.

The tone of voice alarmed him.

Was it desperation? Depression? Is he drunk?

He looked up the Rivers' number and returned the call. The line was busy. He scrolled through his address book and called Gwen's cell phone.

She answered on the second ring. "Winston, it's so wonderful to hear from you, dear. It's been too long."

"Are you in Birmingham? I tried you at home."

"No, we're in Anaheim for a crusade. Just having our breakfast, looking out over the beach. Jimmy is speaking tonight. Did you need something?"

He didn't want to alarm her unnecessarily. "I was checking on Thum— uh, Barnabas. How's he doing?"

"He's progressing, the doctor says. Still a long way to go, but God has it all in His wonderful control. Praise Jesus, we speak it and it's done."

"Glad to hear he's doing better. I tried to call him...you know, just to chat, but the line was busy. When will you guys be back in Birmingham?"

"We're here until Thursday, then we fly to Portland to begin a Revival meeting on Sunday. I'm hoping we'll go home after that, but you know Jimmy."

"If he's able to stay by himself, I assume that means he's getting stronger?"

"Jimmy needed to get back on the road, and he doesn't like to travel without me. Says that Barnabas is big enough to start taking some responsibility." She laughed nervously. "Our housekeeper is there to feed him, and lay out his medications. He eats like a bird, though. She has our number if he needs anything."

The small talk ended quickly and he tried the Rivers' home number again. The line was still busy. He wasn't sure why, but he felt an intense anxiety. He knew what had to be done. When he got to the office, he told Sasha to cancel his appointments for the next few days. She was stunned, but he explained that he had to help a friend. She gave an understanding look, and promised to take care of it. She got him booked on a flight to Birmingham for that evening.

He worked for a few hours, and tried unsuccessfully to get Thumper on the phone. Around four, he hurried home, packed some clothes and drove to the airport.

He couldn't relax on the flight, which took less than two hours. By the time he arrived, claimed his luggage and picked up the rental car, it was after ten o'clock. He was hungry, but sensed the need to go directly to see Thumper.

He felt guilty that he'd deceived Gwen to get their address—telling her that he wanted to send a card to encourage Barnabas—but he wasn't sure she would have given it to him otherwise. Throughout their conversation, she seemed evasive…even defensive…about her son's condition.

It took about thirty minutes to get from the airport to the eastern section of the city where the Rivers lived. When he arrived, he knocked softly on the door and listened for any noise. He knocked again, harder this time.

A frail-looking version of Thumper finally opened the front door.

Has he lost more weight? Winston wondered.

The pullover shirt he was wearing had enough extra room to allow another entire person to crawl in. The tint from the yellow porch light cast a jaundiced hue to his sunken cheeks and eyes. He stood briefly and stared, with a perplexed look on his face.

"Winston?" Thumper leaned out, staring even harder.

"Yes, Barnabas. You called me. Remember?"

Please God, let him remember.

Without acknowledging, Thumper turned and walked back into the house. Winston followed, closing the door behind him. When he got into the living room, Thumper was already seated. The room was nearly dark; the only light was coming from the kitchen.

"Do you want something to drink? I'm not allowed to have alcohol, but there's bottled water and some of Momma's sweet tea." His words were thick, like a drunk talking in their sleep.

"Did I get you out of bed? I can come back tomorrow."

"Nights are the worst," he mumbled, but not directly to Winston. "I'm usually better in the mornings. The pills make me so groggy."

How does Gwen see this as progress? he wondered.

The man sitting in front of him was not well. And certainly not better.

Barnabas needed to get some sleep, so Winston helped him to bed. As he turned off the lights in the living room, noticed numerous prescription bottles on the kitchen counter. He quickly counted six bottles with Barnabas' name on them.

Before he left, he scanned the room, found the phone and replaced the receiver Barnabas had apparently left off the hook.

He checked into a nearby motel, then the next morning showed up with coffee and Krispy Kreme doughnuts. As promised, mornings were better.

"Thank you for coming. I do remember calling you the other night. Yesterday was a seriously bad day. I took a sleeping pill, and I might have taken another one, too. On top of my new anti-anxiety meds and....well, I get a bit loopy."

"What did you want to talk with me about? Do your parents know about all the medication you are taking? Why was yesterday such a bad day?" He hoped the rapid-fire questions wouldn't overwhelm Thumper.

"You were so nice to me at the hospital. I've thought of you often since then. You gave me your card and told me to call if I needed a friend...or a lawyer. I think I need both right now. I honestly didn't expect you to come all the way here, but I'm really glad you did."

"I am your friend, Thum—, uh Barnabas."

"It's okay, you can call me Thumper. I do remember that name."

Winston was intrigued. "What else do you remember?"

Thumper sipped his coffee. "Flashes, mostly. Something will jump in my head, and then it's gone. Like seeing you in an Oral Roberts University sweatshirt. Did we meet there?"

"No, but the first time we met, I believe I was wearing one." He said the shirt was from a conference he'd attended at the school. "How do these *flashes* happen?"

He thought for a second. "Hard to describe. When I was a kid, I had this camera that took instant pictures. You'd click, then the camera would spit out this paper and as you watched it, the picture would gradually fade in. It's like that...in reverse. I see an image, and then it just fades away."

"That must be annoying."

"It's annoying that I can remember the camera, and even how it worked, but my life is a blank. People around me wonder why I get so aggravated, but they don't have a clue. You know that feeling when there's a word on the tip of your tongue, but you can't remember it? Or you leave the house, knowing you're forgetting something? Well, that's my life...all the time."

He took a bite of a doughnut. "It's more than just the loss of my memories, though. I miss a life that I don't remember, but I'm sure was better than what I have now. I assume I had friends in my old life..." He looked to Winston for confirmation.

"Of course you did...you do, Thumper."

His eyes closed partially, as if thinking. A tight-lipped, almost-smile formed. "I miss my friends, and I don't even know who they are. It makes no sense, but it's like a big hole in my heart. It's crazy. I feel something for people I can't even remember and I feel nothing for those I do know."

"What do you mean?"

"Everyone here tell me that Marti is my girlfriend, and she tells me that we're deeply in love. But I don't feel it. Honestly, I don't even like being around her."

"What does the doctor—"

"Fuck the doctor!" he interrupted with intensity. "No matter what I tell him about the flashes, he denies that it's a real memory. Keeps saying it's a movie I saw or a book I read. Then he schedules another treatment or gives me more pills."

Winston struggled to understand. Thumper sounded so paranoid. "Do *you* think you're getting better?"

Thumper seemed to be staring at some undefined place behind Winston.

"There are times I think I'm going crazy. There are days—like the past few—that I barely get out of bed. But other times, it's not so bad. When I go a couple of days between sessions, I can remember stuff. When I skip taking the meds…like when my parents are traveling, it's better. But now the doctor has started these new treatments, and it muddles up my thoughts…and my moods."

Winston was getting more concerned. "What new treatments?"

Thumper glanced around, like someone might be listening. "I've tried to find out more, but the doctor talks to me like I'm a child. Tells me to trust him. Says that they only want what's best for me. 'They' being him and my parents."

Thumper paused and looked directly at him. "But I don't trust him, Winston. And I know it's terrible, but I don't trust them either. Something's not right. I know for a fact that the relaxation treatments he's been doing are nothing more than hypnosis."

That wasn't too surprising. Winston knew that hypnosis could be a good way to unlock past memories.

"How do you know you're being hypnotized?"

Thumper detailed the sequence of events—how he'd first detected the time lapse. "I noticed it once, then started paying attention. When it happened again, I got suspicious and began actively resisting the hypnosis."

Thumper also related some of what he would hear in the sessions. "When I'm supposed to be hypnotized, he tells me I'm sexually attracted to Marti. He goes on and on about how I'm aroused by her. Not asking me. Telling me.

When I can't remember something, he makes shit up and tells me 'this is how it happened.' Winston, he's re-writing my past, not helping me restore it."

The hair on the back of Winston's neck tingled, like he was watching a crucial scene in a mystery movie.

"A couple of weeks ago, he started me on some new medication. It was right after we found out that Marti was pregnant—"

"What?" Winston exclaimed, a bit too loud. "And you're the father?"

A sad nod. He quickly detailed the events of the sexual experiences with Marti.

"After we found out, she met with my doctor and then suddenly, I have this new medication. When I ask what it's for, he says it's to help with the anxiety of the pregnancy. And the same ol' bullshit about trusting him. The pills make me feel horrible…"

"Are you anxious or depressed about the pregnancy?"

"More like getting kicked in the balls," he said, then apologized. Winston waved it off.

"She did this to me—seduced me—then blamed me. My parents are demanding that I 'do the right thing.' Now the three of them are planning a wedding for the spring. I alternate between despair, panic and indifference. I'm fucked up, Winston."

Before he could respond, Thumper continued. "Then, the doctor tells me we're going to start these new procedures. Says it's to help with my memory. Again, I ask him about the treatments, but he gives me his usual garbage. Last week, when I'm waiting for the third treatment, I overheard the nurse talking to the lab guy. She says I'm going to have another ECT. I snuck out earlier this week—while my folks were in Anaheim—and did some research at the library. I learned what ECT is and it's scary as hell, Winston."

ECT? Winston knew what that was from law school. Electroconvulsive therapy—known to most people as "shock treatment." It was used to treat severe depression in patients who didn't improve with traditional medications. The side effects of ECT were not better memories, but confusion and forgetfulness. In order to administer it, a doctor needed a signed Informed Consent document showing the patient had approved the treatment.

This was sounding less like the paranoid rantings of someone with memory problems.

"Did you agree to these ECTs, Thumper? Think carefully. Did you sign anything giving the doctor permission to do this procedure?" He noticed his voice had a slight edge of anger. Or was it fear?

"I don't think so."

Winston wrinkled his face. "I'm gonna need a little more than that, Kiddo. You need to be certain."

This time, Thumper gave it some thought.

"There's lots of stuff in my past that's gone, but I do remember things over the last few weeks. I didn't sign anything. One day, at our session, Doctor Dreary—that's what I call him—informed me that I needed this new treatment. It was part of the *protocol*. God, he loves that word. Told me that he would talk to my parents about it. He promised it would help. I do know that he has me scheduled for at least six more, 'cause they gave me a schedule of appointments."

Winston took a few minutes to let it all sink in. This amounted to an allegation of medical malpractice. Perhaps worse. His legal training dictated logic and rational decisions. Such accusations were serious and required an equally serious response. Research and investigation would need to be done to determine the validity of Thumper's account. This was a time for thoughtful, measured, calculated action. Find a local attorney who specializes in this area, conduct a thorough investigation...

"I think we should get you out of here," were the words he heard himself saying.

There was a stunned look on Thumper's face.

"Let's pack some clothes."

Thumper was frozen, watching Winston as he moved at a pace that would rival a comic book hero. "Where we gonna go? I don't have any money."

Winston's mind was racing. He'd made the decision to cast logic aside because his gut was telling him something was seriously wrong. He sensed that Thumper was in danger, but had no way to justify why he felt that way.

God, help me, he prayed.

"You'll come to Dallas with me. Do you have a suitcase? We need to get you the hell out of here."

Twenty-Five

THUMPER CLOSED HIS EYES AND ALLOWED the deep drone of the airplane engines to drown out all the conversation going on in his head.

This is crazy, he told himself when he agreed to leave with Winston.

But somehow, he also knew that he could trust Winston. And he couldn't say that about anyone else in his life right now.

"Be sure to grab all your medications," Winston had instructed as they packed. They hadn't found a suitcase, so Winston went to a neighborhood Wal-Mart and purchased two—one that would be checked and one for carry on. By the time they'd finished, they were barely able to make the last flight out of Birmingham.

"You okay?" he heard Winston ask from the seat next to him.

He grinned. "My parents are going to fucking freak out."

The lady sitting across the aisle heard the profanity and gave a disapproving look.

Winston patted him on the forearm. "Let me worry about…" He stopped and then laughed out loud. "Yep, the shit's gonna hit the fan shortly."

"The couch pulls out to make a bed. It's pretty comfortable; I slept on it once when my parents came for a visit."

Winston could certainly afford a larger apartment, but his pragmatism couldn't justify it. He wasn't home much and didn't want to clean a larger place. He liked the size—one bedroom studio, with a custom, extra large bathroom and stunning balcony view of the Trinity River. His parents had encouraged him to buy bigger—at least an extra bedroom for when they visited. But in the three years he'd lived there, they had only visited twice, and only once did they stay with him; the other time, they opted for the nearby, upscale Anatole Hotel.

The large master bedroom was separated from the living area by a Shoji screen door. The full bath could only be accessed from his bedroom, but there was a powder room in the living area, next to the small, well-equipped galley kitchen.

It was almost midnight when they arrived from Birmingham and they were both exhausted. He insisted that Thumper take the sleeping pill. "Until we know more about the medications, let's be safe. Besides, you need to rest."

Thumper slipped off his shirt and Winston was able to see how scrawny he was. There was no definition to the chest that had been so evident before. The muscles in his abs were visible, but were sunken. His ribs were visible and prominent.

"I just don't have an appetite," Thumper said, as if answering the unasked question in Winston's concerned look.

"Is it okay if I tell you something?" Thumper called out from the living room while Winston was getting ready for bed. He finished brushing his teeth and walked out of the bedroom. Thumper was settled in the sofa bed, with the covers drawn up to his bare stomach. He looked very serious.

"It's kinda a secret." Thumper said softly, as if someone else might be listening.

Winston took a seat in a chair facing the fold-out bed. "Hey, I stole you from your parents' house and I'm hiding you in my condo, so I guess we have no secrets." He liked that it made Thumper smile.

"I have come to know that I'm a homosexual," he stated matter-of-factly. "I hope that doesn't offend or shock you."

"How did you...what gives you...what makes you think that?"

"Again, it's one of those strange unexplainables in my life. Having sex with Marti didn't, you know...feel right. I don't remember ever being with a man, but I know I have. and I know it's what I want."

He told Winston about the brief, but intense memory-flash that occurred while having sex with Marti. He also shared that once his parents resumed their ministry travels, he'd been able to visit the library and had done lots of reading on the subject.

Winston had more questions. A great deal of confusion to clear up. But it would all have to wait. Thumper had fallen asleep.

Early the next morning, Winston got up quietly around seven and tip-toed past the sleeping houseguest into the kitchen to make coffee. He was lost in the process when he heard a sound behind him. There was Thumper, standing in the doorway.

"Didn't mean to wake," Winston apologized.

"Wasn't you," Thumper voiced through a yawn. "Been napping off and on for a couple of hours. Waking up in an unfamiliar place is not new to me. You got any cereal? I'm hungry."

"I think we should get some pancakes. With lots of butter and syrup. We need to fatten you up, Kiddo."

"Now you sound like Momma," he chuckled. "But that does sound great. I'll shower and then we can go."

"After we eat, I have a couple of stops for us. If you're up to it."

"I'm all yours," Thumper said as he walked toward the bathroom.

Winston consciously refused any rogue responses to that statement.

"You okay?" Jonah asked when he walked in the apartment. He'd left work immediately after he listened to the serious-sounding voice mail from Matt: "I need you to come home. I'm leaving my office now, please meet me at the apartment." That was the entire message. Cryptic, with enough emotion to make Jonah shudder.

There were tears in Matt's eye, but his face exuded happiness. "Thumper's on his way over here."

"What?" He was dumbfounded. "How?"

Matt told Jonah that he'd gotten a call from Winston, saying that Thumper was with him. They were eating breakfast, making a stop at Winston's office, and then they were coming to the apartment.

"They should be here by ten."

"Incredible. That must mean he's got his memory back."

"No," he said with a serious tone. "Winston wants us to play it casual. Warned us not to be shocked when we see him and that he'd tell us everything when they got here."

But though they'd tried to prepare, *shock* was exactly what they displayed when the door opened. Jonah's face gave him away, but it was Matt who was the most obvious. "Oh my hell!"

Thumper looked up at Winston. "Told you this shirt was not my color!"

Matt blushed and haltingly gave them both a hug.

"Winston says I used to live here," Thumper said once they were all seated. He was looking around with inquisitive eyes.

"Does it look familiar?" Matt asked.

"Do you remember...us?" Jonah followed up.

Thumper graciously told them no.

"Y'all are...a couple?" He seemed intrigued by the concept.

Matt and Jonah both nodded.

"A gay couple," he commented to Winston, as if he'd never seen one before. Looking back at Jonah and Matt, he added: "I'm gay, too. But I guess you already knew that."

Both Jonah and Matt snickered involuntarily.

"It seems you're getting some of your essential memories back," Jonah said, working to suppress open laughter.

For several minutes, Matt and Jonah talked about their lives, individually and as a couple. Matt provided Thumper with details about being roommates, including how they'd met—emphasizing the classes they'd had together, but leaving out the sexual dimensions of their relationship. Matt also showed Thumper his old bedroom, which was basically unchanged.

After about an hour of talking, it was apparent that Thumper was tired. His attention span was shorter and he occasionally zoned out.

"Would you like to take a nap?" Winston suggested.

"I don't want to be rude." He looked apologetically at Jonah and Matt. "But the meds just drain me."

"Hey, it's your bed," Matt reminded. "Make yourself at home."

By the time he'd closed the bedroom door, Thumper was asleep. Winston walked back into the living room, where Jonah and Matt were patiently waiting.

"What the fuck is going on?" Matt demanded as soon as Winston sat back down. "He looks like shit on a bad day."

He took a minute to consider his answer. "I'm not sure what I can tell you. I'm not officially his attorney, but he did ask for my help, so there's possibly an issue of attorney-client confidentiality involved, which means—"

"Please talk to us, Winston," Matt requested. "It's not like we'd ever do anything to hurt what you're doing to help him."

He took a deep breath and started talking, beginning with the strange phone call. He told about his trip to Birmingham and how he found Thumper.

"I believe there might be some...*irregularities* with his medical treatment." He provided more details, including his snap decision to bring Thumper back to Dallas.

"What does that mean?" Jonah questioned.

"Too early to tell. I called a friend of mine who specializes in medical malpractice. I gave him the names of all the meds that I brought with us from Birmingham, and he's going to check for me."

"What can we do?" Matt asked.

"Well, I didn't just bring him here for a reunion. I need—"

"A babysitter?" Matt completed. "We're your girls."

Jonah rolled his eyes, but let Winston know they'd be glad to help.

He thanked them as he walked toward the door. Jonah gave him a big hug. "You're doing the right thing, brother. We'll be praying for you."

"I'm going to need that. Once I get back to my office, I have to call his parents and let them know what I've done."

"Wow," Jonah exclaimed. "I'm not sure how to pray for someone who's about to get the wrath of God called down on him."

Once Winston left, Jonah quietly checked on Thumper. "He's out like a light," he reported as he joined Matt on the sofa.

"I guess they were wrong," Matt said in his snarky tone. "You *can* be too thin."

They talked for a while about Thumper. They'd both noticed that he walked with a slight limp. His arm was bruised, which he told them was from the IV given at the last shock treatment. Their conversation wasn't only about his physical appearance, but also the revelations about Thumper's life since the accident. The treatments. The girlfriend. The pregnancy.

For a few minutes, they sat quietly. Matt laid his head on Jonah's shoulder and just enjoyed the closeness.

"Winston won't be back for a couple of hours. You gettin' hungry?"

Jonah sat up and turned to face him. "Speaking of Winston. You did pick up on that, didn't you?" He arched his eyebrows to reinforce the question.

"It couldn't have been more obvious if he had a t-shirt that read 'I heart Thumper.'"

"Yep. That's going to throw a big ol' bag of gummy bears into his carefully constructed ex-gay theology."

"You did what?" The man was so loud that Winston had to hold the phone away from his ear. "This is how you treat our friendship?"

He could almost see the red face of the preacher as he yelled like it was one of his hell-fire sermons.

"Thumper is also my friend, sir. I felt he needed my help…and my protection."

"Protection?" Still no variation in the volume from the other end of the call. "You make it sound like we're trying to harm our son."

He remained calm. "I would never question your motives, sir. I just know that some of the medications he's taking and some of the treatments seem a bit suspect."

"What makes you think you know more than his doctor?"

Arguing was pointless. "There appear to be problems and I'm investigating them. He asked for my help and that's what I'm doing. I will be preparing a report and you'll have a copy in a few days."

He could hear talking in the background. "And you can expect to hear from my lawyers."

The line went dead.

The sounds of Dr. Rivers' screams were gone, but it was certainly not quiet in Winston's head. Some of the confidence of his decision to help Thumper was being challenged. Most of all, his motive for the decisions were under assault.

Why did I do it? came the internal interrogation.

I'm a lawyer. This is what I do.

The explanation was sterile, but he had to admit the reality of the simple logic.

He's my friend and needed my help.

That one felt comfortable. Regardless of what other explanations might surface, he knew there was definite truth in the statement.

I owe it to him.

He acknowledged the significant guilt after their final meeting, before Thumper was attacked, so he was able to take some comfort in trying to help him now.

But even after accepting all of those rational reasons, there was still no way to silence the persistent and increasingly-hard-to-ignore realization.

I'm doing it because I'm in love with him!

After he picked up Thumper, Winston made a stop at Target to get some extra toiletries for Thumper, and then the grocery store for supplies. When they arrived back at the condo—even before he could get all the lights turned on—Thumper surprised him with a question: "Do you know a lot of gay people?"

"In my line of work, I meet an assortment of people. Like Matt and Jonah," he offered as proof.

"I met them while you were in the hospital here. Actually, I ran into Matt at the emergency room and later he introduced me to Jonah. I'd get updates from your parents and let them know how you were doing."

He realized the explanation was long and rambling, but the conversation's direction made him nervous.

"But you're not gay." It wasn't a question. "I mean, I heard you talking on the phone to your girlfriend the other night, so…" He finished the statement with a shrug.

Before he could frame an response, Thumper continued. "Makes sense, 'cause you're friends with my folks and they don't like gay people. Momma thinks a lot of you, so I figure you…well, you know." Then he laughed. "Of course, that was before you kidnapped me. I figure you won't get invited to Thanksgiving dinner now."

He grinned, even though the concept of kidnapping challenged his legal integrity, not to mention scared the shit out of him.

"I'm glad you don't have a problem with gay people, especially since I'm staying here with you."

"Our friendship was not based on you being gay," Winston said, knowing that was true enough for this discussion. "It's a bit more...complicated."

He walked into the kitchen and fixed a drink: bourbon and Seven-Up.

"Your parents have many misconceptions about gay people. They have a strict, traditional understanding of the Bible which I no longer believe is correct. That colors their perception and their ability to accept..."

Internally, there was a debate on which word to end the sentence: *Them or us?*

"They have problems accepting gay people," he concluded, taking a drink of his cocktail.

"Can I tell you something? It's a little embarrassing."

"For you or for me?" Winston quipped.

"I think I might have had...uh, feelings for you back before the accident."

He poured more Bourbon into his drink and chugged half of it.

"What makes you think that?"

"I knew the first time you visited me in the hospital that I liked you. And I knew it was different than what I felt when I met Marti. A while later, I think I had one of my memory-flashes and I sorta saw you...without any clothes. I couldn't imagine when or how I would have seen you...like that, so I figured it might have been some kind of wet dream."

"Are you sure? Sure it was me?"

Thumper closed his right eye, as if thinking. His nose and forehead wrinkled. "Only if you have a birthmark right underneath your belly button." He used his finger to point to the area on his own body.

Winston's face turned a deep red, clearly confirming the accuracy of the detail. "I think I can solve that mystery. We ran into each other one day at the gym. I was coming out of the shower. We'd recently met and it was a bit awkward. At least for me. I'm sure that's what you're remembering."

Thumper's entire face lit up. "Well, I'm glad it wasn't a dream. Knowing it was actually your body is kinda hot."

Winston laughed, loud and long. "You remind me of someone I once knew."

"Who?"

He drank the last of the cocktail in one gulp.

"You!"

TWENTY-SIX

MATT WAS JUST GETTING IN FROM working out when the phone rang. It was Saturday, but the Call Center was open seven days a week, so he often had to work weekends. When he answered, a familiar voice greeted him.

"Hey, it's Thumper."

It had been a couple of weeks since Winston brought Thumper back to Dallas. Or "rescued him," as Matt called it. They came to the apartment that first day, but due to everyone's busy schedule, he'd not seen Thumper since that day.

Hearing Thumper on the phone, Matt felt an instant sense of joy. For a moment, the tragic events of the past months vanished and he was talking to his best friend. It was like the amnesia itself had been forgotten.

"I hope this is not a bad time to call." There was a polite formality to his statement.

"Not at all," Matt replied enthusiastically. "I've been wanting to talk with you, but things have been crazy around here. Jonah was out of town for nearly a week speaking at a conference in Chicago and I've been helping with training for our new call center in Fort Worth. Winston also told me that you've been feeling a bit under the weather, so I wanted to give you some space to re-adjust."

"Yeah, I've been going to this doctor who's working with me to get off all the medications that idiot had me taking. The first week was a bitch: mood swings, headaches, tired all the time. But it's getting better now. How are you guys doing?"

"Jonah's at a fundraiser for work and I was about to wash clothes and clean the apartment. It's the glamorous life of a domestic goddess."

There was a moment of silence on the other end of the call.

"I was kinda wondering if it'd be possible for us to get together and… you know, catch up."

"Absolutely," Matt agreed with unbridled eagerness. "You guys wanna come over later?"

"I don't want to impose on your Saturday, but if it's okay, I'd really like it to be just you and me."

The request caught him off guard. "Is everything okay? Are you having second thoughts about coming to Dallas?"

Thumper laughed. "No, it's not that at all. You mentioned that you and I lived together, and I'd like you to talk to me about those times. Would that be okay?"

"Sounds great. I'll come pick you up. Give me fifteen minutes."

"Thanks for meeting with me," Thumper said as they drove away from the condo complex. "It's always nice to get out of the house."

"Anything special you want to do?"

"Sightseeing. Show me all the places I used to visit and tell me all about them."

"Absolutely. I'll be Julie, your cruise director." He cackled at his own joke, until he looked over and saw Thumper's blank expression. "Never mind."

For several hours, they drove around the city. It was a warm, beautiful spring day, so Matt dropped the top on his VW Beetle. First, they visited the college campus where they'd graduated. Next, he stopped at Page Turner Bookstore where Thumper had worked.

When Sharon, the owner, saw him, she screeched, ran out of her office and grabbed him like a long-lost relative. Matt had talked with her several times during Thumper's hospitalization, keeping her updated on his condition.

"I have missed you, " she said through streaming tears. "It's just not the same since you...uh, with you not here. When you comin' back to work?" she asked, with apparent sincerity.

Thumper politely declined, telling her he wasn't physically able to stand for long periods of time. "Plus, I think my lack of memory might be a problem with the customers," he pointed out.

"Listen, you could have amnesia, with a full lobotomy and still know more than some of the folks I have working here."

Before they left, she gave him a hardback copy of *To Kill a Mockingbird* and a one hundred dollar gift certificate. "You told me that this was your favorite book. I hope when you read it again, you'll still love it."

From the bookstore, they drove to the strip—the gay section of Dallas. Matt was a bit hesitant, but also knew there was no way to show Thumper his past without including it in the tour. But he made certain to avoid the parking lot where he'd been attacked.

"Did I come here often?"

There was an endearing irony to Thumper's question, and Matt tried not to show his amusement. He gave the simple, most obvious answer, then added: "You were popular."

They parked the car and went into one of the shops on the strip because Thumper wanted a shirt with a rainbow on it.

"It's a symbol of being gay," he stated when he made the request.

"You hungry?" Matt asked as they walked back to the car after spending almost an hour walking the strip and visiting the various shops.

"Always. I'm trying to put some weight back on, and since I've gotten off most of the medication, I stay hungry. But you'll have to pick the place. I can't remember the best places to eat these days," he joked.

"I was thinking we'd go back to the apartment. I'll make us something and we'll have more privacy."

Once they arrived, Thumper sat down at the dining room table as Matt made preparations for lunch. Again, there was a sense of familiarity that made Matt happy.

They chatted casually while he gathered the ingredients for lunch. Thumper was excited about the DVDs he was watching: everything from TV shows like *Friends*, to documentaries.

"I go to the library almost every day to get more. It gives me something to do while Winston's at work."

He was particularly animated when he talked about a set of DVDs he was watching from The History Channel.

"You're welcome to borrow any of my DVDs. Especially the musicals. History is important, but it's imperative that we get you acclimated to the gay world again."

"My parent's let me watch *The Sound of Music*. Does that count?"

"Not until you can sing all the words to *Edelweiss* by heart."

"I have so much to catch up on," Thumper said, now with a melancholy edge. "What memories I have are years ago and very random. I'm like Rip Van Winkle when it comes to recent events."

"I reckon most people can't imagine what it's really like to lose your memory. It's obviously nothing like we see in the movies."

"When I was living at home, my mom and I'd watch *Wheel of Fortune* after dinner. My life is kinda like trying to solve one of those puzzles. Some of the parts are visible. But there are lots of blank spaces. And I'm racking my brain tryin' to fill in the missing pieces so it all makes sense."

He saw that Matt was staring at him, worried and concerned.

"I'd like to buy a vowel, please," he said with a smile that Matt suspected was more of an attempt to lighten the mood than a real indicator of what Thumper was feeling.

"We're here for you, I want to know that. We'll help you fill in the blanks as much as we can."

He went back to the kitchen and brought back a pitcher of iced tea. "Not to be fussy, but does Winston know you're here?"

"Of course. He's like a mother hen. So worried that I'm going to get lost when I walk to the library or to the grocery store. He's at some board meeting today and was okay with me going out, since you were driving."

"Well, I'm glad you called me. It was fun to be your tour guide and chauffeur."

"I'm studying to take my driver's test. Winston thought it might be best for me to re-take it, even though my current license is technically still valid."

"You're car is still here," Matt informed from the kitchen. "We drive it occasionally to keep it running. We didn't know when…" His voice trailed off.

"I understand," Thumper replied. "And thanks for taking care of it for me. You were…you are a good friend."

His eyes welled up, so he kept his back to Thumper, not wanting to upset him. "I've missed you so much."

"I'm sorry I don't remember you. I hope it doesn't hurt your feelings."

He walked to kitchen doorway. "You shouldn't apologize. It's not your fault. I can't imagine what it must be like for you, but I'll admit, it's not easy. You were such a big part of my life and to think all of that is gone now."

"But *you* remember, so it's never gone. And you'll be able to tell me all about it."

Matt walked over and hugged him. "I'll tell you whatever you want to know."

"You and I…we were…you know, involved at one time." It was more of a statement than a question.

Matt gave a startled look, then laughed and shook his head in disbelief. "You may not have your memories, but you still have the gift to see someone's private thoughts."

Thumper appeared confused.

"One of your many talents was knowing stuff that you shouldn't be able to know. It was cute and intriguing…and annoying as hell. But yes, we were… uhm, involved. We met, had a very short affair, then became best friends. How did you know?"

"Not sure, just a hunch."

Matt sat down and for several minutes related the details of how they met and the transition to becoming roommates. He had to define the term "fuck buddy." Thumper also suspected his history with Jonah, so again, Matt was honest.

"I was a slut. Tragic that I can't remember all the fun and all the sex I must have had. Now, I'm like a virgin, with the desire to be with a man, but no memory of what it's like. God's twisted sense of humor, I reckon." He finished with a quick chuckle.

Matt walked back to kitchen and began pulling more ingredients from the refrigerator.

"So, how are things going? I'm sure Winston is being the consummate and gracious host."

"He's the best. Lately, he's been real busy with the lawsuits." He updated him on the basic details.

"He's always busy. Brings work home every evening, so it can get a bit lonely."

"You guys sound like an old married couple," Matt remarked.

"I wish! He's proof that that I'm gay and that my sex drive is returning."

The statement demanded a further explanation, and Matt jerked up suddenly, hitting his head on the open freezer door. "Do you have feelings for him?"

Thumper's head cocked to the side and his face showed he was giving it serious thought.

"I sometimes think the amnesia messed with my feelings too. Since I have no memory of the past, it's not easy to get a handle on actual feelings about people or events, past or present. Don't get me wrong. I do have emotions. I get angry, and frustrated. I get overwhelmed at times and sometimes when I'm reading a book or watching TV, I get a lump in my throat. But it's all jumbled up."

Matt gave a half-hearted nod. "So your feelings for Winston...?" He intentionally waited for Thumper to respond.

"I think it's more like desire. Or *lust*, as Daddy would call it. I sometimes wonder what it'd be like to touch him. Or have him touch me. To be naked with him. I've thought about how it would feel to kiss him. And once..." His face turned red.

"It's okay. You don't remember, but we tell each other everything."

He took in a slow, deep breath. "I had this dream, and we were together. I could feel him...you know...enter inside me. It was so wonderful that I actually had an orgasm."

Matt could not hide his complete surprise. "What?"

Thumper turned red again. "I'm sorry. Was that inappropriate to say? I've been doing some reading about...uh, gay sex, and I thought—"

In a comforting tone, Matt assured him everything was fine. "It's just that you—the *previous* you—would never consider allowing someone to...uhm... do that to you. You prided yourself on being a total...you know, top. Trust me, I tried once and you were adamant. Said you preferred giving the pleasure."

At the time, Matt had asserted that it was more of a control issue than anything to do with pleasure. But privately, he'd always suspected it was connected to Thumper's internal struggles with being gay. He believed that in Thumper's mind, being penetrated was "more gay" than the alternative.

"I can't imagine why I would think that. In my dream, it was amazing."

He appeared to be giving the concept some thought. "Of course, when I woke up, I was sick at my stomach. Probably not ready for the real thing yet."

"You've been reading about sex?"

He wrinkled his nose and had a furtive grin. "Winston thought I needed some information, especially about safe sex…just in case. He brought me one book. It was pretty clinical and—"

"Boring?" Matt suggested from the kitchen.

"*Very* boring. So I went to the library near his house and got a few more. Some are a bit more graphic." He reached in his backpacked and pulled out a book.

Matt walked over and glanced through the book—*The Gay Man's Guide to Great Sex*—which was less a book *about* sex, and more like a step-by-step how-to instructional manual, complete with explicit pictures.

"Oh my," he marveled as he thumbed through the pages. "I guess I need to go to the library more often."

He gave it back to Thumper. "Are you? Having sex?"

"For now, it's all I can do to read about it. If I get too horny…well, that leads to nausea."

Matt was confused, and concerned. "Why do you get sick?"

"It's strange, but when I think about having sex with a man it makes me sick." He shrugged. "Guess my broken brain is not ready to deal with me being gay yet."

The explanation didn't ring true, and Matt make a mental note to talk with Winston. "Have you considered going to a therapist? I'm sure they could help?"

The grimace on Thumper's face gave his answer.

Matt placed the food on the table and sat down.

"Do they think you'll ever regain your memory?"

"Not likely. I still get glimpses of images, but I never know if they're my memories, something that was implanted or a scene from a movie I saw years ago."

"That sucks! I hope that asshole who did this to you will be put in jail for many years."

"More than likely he'll lose his license to practice medicine—"

"Oh, I didn't mean him. I was talking about the sonnabitch who attacked you."

The look on Thumper's face would be difficult to describe. There was definite confusion, along with surprise. But there was also an obvious fear and anxiety.

"Attacked?" he repeated softly. "Is that how this happened to me?"

Oh shit, Matt thought.

"What did your parents tell you?" he asked quickly, before giving away more details.

"They always called it an accident, so I just assumed it was a car accident. I asked them once. They said it was best to see if the memories came back. But that might explain…"

He looked like he was trying to remember something. "I have these nightmares, but it's never anything or anyone specific. I wake up terrified that someone is trying to hurt me."

Matt moved around the table and sat by him, placing his hand on his friend's.

"Will you tell me what really happened? You said we tell each other everything. I want…I need to know."

Lunch was delayed as he related the story of the attack. Off and on during the story, Thumper would interrupt with questions.

"So you met the guy who did this to me?" His tone was more inquisitive than harsh.

He related the encounter with Earl, and told Thumper about Milton. He included the details of Milton's mental illness.

"What happened to him?"

Matt forced himself to control the rage. Every time he thought about it, he would get so angry. "He never stood trial. His attorney got the judge to agree that he was mentally unstable at the time of the attack. Your parents even pushed that it not go to trial."

"Not surprising," Thumper smirked. "They wouldn't want anyone to know *why* I was attacked."

"Winston did some checking. He was sentenced to a secure mental health facility for a short time. Once he was back on his medication and stable, they released him. Now he only has to check in for regular evaluation to make sure he's still taking his medications. It's a crock of shit."

"What about the other guy?"

"Earl was given community service, since he wasn't actually involved in hurting you, and he did try to help you. Before the attack, you did your famous mind trick on him and forced him to face that he was gay. But he was so racked with guilt, he enrolled in one of those programs to heal himself of his homosexuality, kinda like the one that Winston—"

Another surprised look appeared on Thumper's face.

Dammit, Matt scolded himself again.

Thumper grinned. "Don't worry about it. Once again, you've helped make some things clear for me."

While they were eating, Thumper talked about what he did during the day while Winston was at work. "I'm learning about computers. Winston hired a tutor to come in twice a week to teach me. It's lots of fun and very interesting. I also watch a lot of TV. I saw all the *Star Wars* movies. They were awesome. At night, we're watching past episodes of *Lost*, 'cause Winston said I used to like that show."

"Oh God, yes. You talked about it all the time. I tried to watch it with you, but it confused the hell out of me."

He also talked about some of the books he'd been reading. "I'm half way through *Gone With the Wind*," he reported.

"You know all the books in that bedroom are yours? Feel free to take any of them with you."

"I'm not sure how many would fit under the sofa bed at Winston's place."

He stopped talking for a few moment, causing Matt to look up from eating dessert.

"Speaking of the bedroom, I kinda need a favor. Winston's house is nice, but it's only one bedroom. Even though it's only been a few weeks, I feel like I'm in the way. He's so gracious, but is there any way...I mean, would it be possible—"

"Like I told you before, the furniture is yours anyway. I'm sure Jonah wouldn't have a problem if you wanted to move back in here."

Thumper was overjoyed. He jumped up and grabbed Matt in a big embrace. "That's awesome. Thanks, Mattie."

He pulled away immediately. "You called me Mattie." His voice was trembling. "That's what you called...what you used to call me...before..." His eyes were wet with emotion.

Thumper pulled Matt back into the embrace. "See, that means that even though I can't remember our past, somewhere, it's alive inside me."

"I definitely think you need to call and tell him."

Matt had told Jonah about the meeting with Thumper, including how he let it slip about the attack.

When Winston answered his cell phone, Matt stammered. "Winston, it's Matt. And Jonah," he added, taking courage in including his partner.

"Hey, guys. Good to hear from you. I have it on my list to call you. I wanted to thank you for spending time with Thumper today. He was positively giddy when he called me. He even told me that you're going back to school to get your...and this was his term...PCA."

"Close," Matt corrected with a chuckle. "I'm going to classes to prepare for my Certified Public Accountant exam. I don't want to work for the cable company all my life, so I better make some plans."

"That's cool. I'll gladly let you do my taxes," Winston offered.

"I'm very proud of him." Jonah praised from the extension. "He also plans to get his certification in financial planning, so he can make us all rich beyond our wildest dreams."

"Winston, while Thumper was here, he told me he wants to move back into his room. Thinks he's crowding you. We're okay with it, but wanted to talk with you."

He laughed out loud. "Well, he's not crowding me, but I was going to talk to you guys about the same thing. He's sleeping on a sofa bed, with no place to put his clothes. I thought he needed more space. I appreciate you doing that. How 'bout we plan to move him over there Saturday? Afterwards, I'll buy us all some dinner."

Matt thought Winston might be ending the call, so he jumped in. "There's one more thing. I wanted to give you a heads-up. I kinda spilled the beans about what happened to him… uhm, about the attack."

There was a silence on the other end and it made him nervous.

"I'm really sorry, Winston."

"It's not your fault. You didn't know and I should have mentioned it earlier. I've debated for weeks about whether to tell him. I didn't want to put more stress on him. He's doing so well and I would not want to do anything that might hinder his progress."

"He's doing better because of you, Winston," Matt declared. "You are so good for him. He couldn't stop talking about you today."

Matt thought he heard a slight sniffle.

"I'm the grateful one. Helping Thumper is important to me. Meeting him, and you guys is the best thing to happen to me in a long time. I've learned so much."

"I hope you know, we love you," Jonah said. "Not just for what you're doing for Thumper, but just because. I'm glad God brought you into our lives."

TWENTY-SEVEN

HE FLIPPED THROUGH THE GROWING PAPER heap on his desk. Renee, his paralegal, laid several file folders and large brown envelopes on the edge of the desk and waited—either to make certain he saw her place them there or to be sure they didn't fall off the mountainous stack.

"Please tell me that at least one of those files is from the doctor," Winston grumbled.

"It's supposed to be here today," she said in a tone that displayed her own distress. "They *promised* to messenger it over."

They'd been waiting weeks for all the files from Dr. Davidson. The lawyers had trickled them in slowly, so Winston had focused his attention on the records they'd subpoenaed from the two hospitals and the clinic where the ECTs were administered. Almost daily, Renee was on the phone, wanting to know when the materials would arrive.

"You don't think he's trying to alter the records, do you?"

Winston looked up. It wasn't like he hadn't thought of that possibility, but since he had the other records, that action would merely add more charges to the lawsuit.

"I think his lawyers are advising him to stall, until they can come up with a strategy."

Dr. Davidson was claiming he had "implied" permission from the parents for any and all treatment decisions. However, from the statement they'd already received from the Rivers, they had no knowledge of the shock treatments. In March, Winston filed a medical malpractice lawsuit against Dr. Davidson.

In addition, the few records they had gotten from the doctor detailed the alarming facts about the treatments inflicted on Thumper—the hypnosis, the implanted memories and the drugs—which added weight to lawsuit. For good measure, he named the clinic where the ECTs had been administered in the suit as well. He'd also filed a suit against both hospitals for their role in allowing Dr. Davidson to practice.

Now, two months later, they were knee-deep in paperwork.

Winston was more than stunned at the sheer amount of drugs given to Thumper. Not only anti-anxiety, but also heavy sleeping prescriptions. In addition, one drug was designed to decrease sexual desire and performance— the same drug used on pedophiles and serial rapists; it had been prescribed after the doctor found out about Thumper and Marti having sex.

Based on Matt's observation, Winston checked and learned that the doctor had used aversion therapy—a radical form of behavior modification—to try and suppress Thumper's homosexual desires.

Aversion therapy utilized negative reinforcement, such as a bad taste, foul smells or pain, to create a negative connection with an undesirable behavior. The person undergoing this kind of treatment learned to associate an unpleasant or painful consequence with doing something, such as drinking alcohol or overeating.

Apparently Doctor Davidson had instilled the idea that same-sex thoughts, attraction or actions would bring sickness. Thumper would often get violently ill when discussing his re-emerging sexual desires.

It had taken several weeks, and assistance from another attorney, but he'd also been able to get through all the government paperwork and get Thumper on Social Security disability. It wasn't much, based on his age and prior earnings, but it provided a small monthly income.

"I did hear from the Rivers' attorney," Renee informed. "And the attorney for their insurance company."

Thumper had been fine with all the medical lawsuits, but surprised everyone one evening when he announced that he also wanted to sue his parents.

"Really?" Jonah had questioned.

Thumper got serious. "I've given it some thought, and I think they should be held accountable for their part in what happened to me. Daddy always liked that word—*accountable*. Do you think we have grounds?"

"Absolutely," Winston answered. "I can think of several legal reasons we could use."

"Well, it's something I want to do…for moral and ethical reasons, too."

"Guess I'm not the only one who's not getting invited to Thanksgiving dinner," Winston said with a laugh.

That brought a smile. "Just one more thing for me to be thankful for, I reckon."

As soon as Thumper brought it up, Winston began mapping out a strategy for the lawsuit. Because they had agreed to the controversial treatment—the hypnosis, the drugs and probably the implanted memories—that amounted to complicity in the medical malpractice suit. They could also be charged as negligent for the damage that was caused in Thumper's treatments, especially the shock therapy.

"If I had my way," Winston confided to Jonah over lunch. "I'd include child endangerment to the charges. They turned their son over to that quack doctor for treatments, knowing it was an unproven, experimental procedure, and he was harmed as a result."

When Jonah related the story about Milton listening to tapes by Thumper's father just before the attack, Winston grumbled that he wanted to add child abuse to the charges.

"We want you to come back home. You need your treatments, so you can get better."

Thumper could hear the concern in his mother's voice. It was the first time since leaving Birmingham that he'd talked with her.

"I'm doing fine, Momma. And I'm not supposed to be talking to you or Daddy. The lawsuits—"

"I don't care about that, son. God will work all that out between you and your father. I want you to come home so we can get you the help you need."

He resolved to stay calm. "This isn't just between me and Daddy, don't you understand? You were involved, too. What that doctor did...what y'all did to me...was wrong."

He stopped, knowing his anger was coming through. "I'm better here than I was when I was home, Momma. I've moved back to my apartment, living with my friends."

The breath she released might have been intended as an apprehensive sigh, but it came across more as a frustrated huff.

"They're taking good care of me, Momma. And being here is giving me lots of time to think about who I am and what I want."

"I don't even know what that means." She now sounded exasperated. "You're my son, that's who you are."

He intentionally snickered loud enough for her to hear. "We both know there's more to who I am than you are willing to admit...or accept. You're ashamed that I'm gay, so you and that damned doctor tried to fix me. Well, it didn't work and now I have to rebuild my life."

"So you decided to punish us with this lawsuit?"

He decided not to answer, so he waited.

She sniffled. He wasn't sure if it was real or one of her manipulative tactics.

"We only want what's best for you, Barnabas. God spoke to your father about the doctor and the treatment."

Jonah walked in the apartment and Thumper mouthed that he was talking to his mom. Jonah's eyes widened in surprise. Thumper gave an exaggerated shrug.

"If God doesn't like who I am, that's between me and God," he said to his mom. "I don't need Daddy to tell me what God told him about me. Frankly, I don't give a damn what either of them think of me."

Jonah walked into the bedroom, shaking his head in obvious amusement.

His mother tried to speak, but Thumper didn't allow it. "The treatment that God instructed Daddy to approve…" His words now came with open sarcasm. "Those treatments screwed with my mind and what few memories I had left. That doctor did bad stuff to me, Momma. He did it without my consent…or yours. God was not involved in this deception. But you were. And so was Daddy."

She wouldn't give up. "We tried to reclaim your life from Satan's hold. To give you back a life that God would approve and use for His glory."

"I don't want the life y'all tried to force on me."

"What about Marti? And the baby? You need to do the right thing and—"

"Marriage would not be the right thing for me or for Marti…and it won't make me straight."

Looking back at the circumstances, he'd come to suspect that Marti had intentionally gotten pregnant. But as his mom had pointed out, the consequences were real. He and Marti were finally talking, making plans for the birth of the baby. It was uncomfortable at first, but they both agreed it was best for their child.

"I accept my responsibility for the pregnancy, but a sham wedding is not the solution. I know this: by being honest about who I am, I'll be a better father to my child."

When the call ended, Jonah walked back out into the room.

"I know Winston doesn't want me to talk to them." Thumper said quickly. "But I've been avoiding her calls for weeks, and thought at least this might appease her."

"It's fine," Jonah assured, promising not to tell Winston. "You said some pretty strong things. Are you okay?"

He leaned back on the sofa and stared up at the ceiling. "I have no job, and I assume, no skills. I'm pretty much living off my friends. I have an education that I can't even remember. In a few months, I'll be a father. It's all a bit overwhelming right now."

Jonah sat down in the chair facing the couch. "We don't see it as living off us, Thumper. We are here to help. That's what friends do. The rest will come in time. You need to have a little—"

"Faith?" he interjected.

"I was going to say 'patience,' but faith is good, too. I know that God is going to work all this out."

Thumper frowned. "I'm not sure. Since the accident…uh, the *attack*, the few memories I do have are from when I was a kid. I remember Sunday

School, learning the Bible, singing in the choir, the youth group. But it feels so distant and detached. I have more questions and doubts than anything else."

"I'm learning that God is always so much bigger than our preconceptions," Jonah offered in a reassuring way. "And God is secure enough to handle our doubt…and is much more patient with our questions than those who think they have all the answers."

TWENTY-EIGHT

IN LATE MAY, A FEW MONTHS after filing the suit against Thumper's parents, Winston was contacted by a reporter. The fact that a son was suing his parents initially got his attention, but once the reporter did some research, the other elements caused him to follow up. Winston determined that some publicity might be good for the cases, so he scheduled time for Thumper to talk with the reporter.

A week later, a huge article appeared in the *Dallas Morning News*. It contained the facts of Thumper's attack and medical information about retrograde amnesia. There was an overview of the Rivers' TV and church ministry, including the basics of Pentecostal beliefs, especially concerning homosexuality. His parents had refused to talk with the reporter, but a spokesperson for the church gave a standard-issue, professionally written statement, acknowledging their eternal love and concern for their "beloved son."

Most of the article was Thumper telling his story. He related intricate details about the treatments he endured with Dr. Davidson, calling him by name several times. He also specifically mentioned both hospitals and the ECT clinic, per Winston's coaching.

Thumper also talked about his frustrations at not being able to remember, even relating the shock when he first looked at his own reflection in the mirror. "I knew it was me, because…well, there I was. But it was also like staring at someone who looks familiar, but you just can't place where you know them."

At times, he was poignant. "Most people my age remember exactly where they were on Nine-Eleven, but I didn't know about the planes crashing into the Twin Towers. I couldn't believe it when I watched the news footage in a documentary. I vaguely remember George Bush, but it was the other guy—the old one."

The reporter concluded the story with the question "What have you learned in this entire ordeal?"

"Learning is a daily occurrence for me these days," Thumper was quoted. "When you have no past, you cherish the now for the future memories it will provide. Mostly, I'm learning the meaning of family, and it's not about biology or birth certificates. Those who love, support and protect you…that's family."

Also within the story was a short profile of Winston, even though he didn't talk with the reporter. It was not negative, but mentioned that while

Winston's law practice focused primarily on religious nonprofits, he was handling this case because of his friendship with Thumper.

The backlash was immediate.

When the first client informed him they were seeking new counsel, he was surprised, but not suspicious. The executive director of a large Assembly of God missionary organization was very polite and just said they "felt led by the Lord" to look at someone different. After working with Christian groups for several years, he'd learned not to question mystical explanations.

Within a week, he'd lost an additional three long-standing clients, and the retainers that go with them. He assumed it was related to the story in the newspaper, so he pressed two of the exiting clients for a more detailed—and honest—explanation.

"I have nothing against you as a person," the pastor of one of the largest Baptist churches in the city told him. "But after the story came out in the paper, we heard that you're having some moral problems in your own life and we can't risk any negative exposure, even by association."

Eventually, he learned that Dan Larson, the executive director of *Full Circle Ministries*, was telling ministry donors—many of whom were also Winston's clients—about the resignation from the board. Dan included that Winston was questioning the validity of the group's mission, then alleged there was typically a direct link between those who left the group and then re-entered the gay lifestyle. He used Thumper's case as evidence.

"He is promoting this young man's gay agenda and endorsing his rebellion against Biblical truth," Dan wrote in the e-mail. "I suspect there might be more carnal motives involved here."

In spite of Winston's assurances that neither his departure from the group nor his association with Thumper's case involved any kind of sexual immorality, he was unable to convince any of the clients to remain with him.

On Friday after the article appeared, he got a call from Libby, the woman he'd been dating. "Well this certainly confirms my suspicions," she stated bluntly.

He understood her veiled reference and denied the implications, but to no avail.

"Obviously the fact that I don't have a dick is a deal breaker," she said snidely and hung up.

He also received numerous messages from his connections within the Christian community. Most expressed concern with his involvement in "this kind" of case, offering unsolicited Scriptural evidence of the sin of his participation.

Some were downright mean, making serious assumptions and accusations about his sexual behavior and predictions of his eternal destiny. He got a couple of calls from guys in the *Circle* who were upset about his "moral lapse and collaboration with the forces of darkness." Since both of them used the same exact phrase, he figured they'd heard it from Dan.

He spent the afternoon in self-chastisement, re-examining his motives in taking the case and speculating on the impact it was going to have on his life. By late in the day, he knew what he had to do, so he called Thumper to say they needed to talk.

"I'm thinking it might be a good time to transfer your case to a different attorney," he informed once they were seated at the apartment.

Thumper's face displayed his response: disappointment, hurt and even fear. "But I don't want someone else," he said, his voice carrying all the same emotions.

Winston braced himself and tried to appear chipper. "I only want what's best for you, Kiddo. This is not my area of expertise."

Matt, who was sitting with Thumper, leaned in. "Is something...is everything okay with his case?"

Winston tried to casually wave him off. "Absolutely. But I've gotten us this far, and I think someone with better skills in this area might be needed to finish it."

Thumper reluctantly agreed. "I trust you, Winston. You've done so much for me and I'm so grateful. If you think this is best, set it up."

Winston promised to come up with a suitable replacement recommendation and take care of all the transfer arrangements. As he was leaving, Matt followed him to the foyer outside the apartment.

"What's actually going on here? Is there something you're not telling him?"

Winston stopped and for a second, debated his response. "You read the newspaper article. I'm a nonprofit attorney and this is not typical of my practice. I'm trying to do the right thing here, Matt."

"Right for him...or for you?"

He was getting annoyed, but knew it had nothing to do with Matt's interrogation. "I only want what's best for him."

Matt's tone softened. "That's obvious to everyone except dead people, Winston. Which is why I don't want you to back off. We both know that no other lawyer will treat this case like you do...because you care for him."

"And that's also the problem," he countered. "Because I care, I can't be objective when it comes to him."

"Is this about the article in the newspaper? Are you getting flack?"

Winston acknowledged the impact, but insisted that transferring the case made sense.

"So we let the bigots determine our choices? I can't believe you'd give in to their crap, especially since one of those kind of people did this to Thumper."

Winston struggled to remain firm in his decision. "I think it would be best for all concerned if—"

"Please don't do this to him again," Matt begged. "The last time you pulled out of his life, it wrecked him. He may not remember it, but I sure as hell do."

As he replayed the emotions of those days following his angry encounter with Thumper, especially the guilt and regret after his attack, all the pretense of professionalism fell away. He fought back the tears. "I don't want to hurt him. Please believe that."

"I can't believe he's deserting Thumper." Matt was complaining to Jonah after dinner. Thumper was in his bedroom, watching a movie. He had volunteered to clean up so they'd have an opportunity to talk privately about the situation.

"What if he's right? Maybe someone else would be better. It doesn't mean he's going to vanish from his…from *our* lives."

"You didn't see him. He's usually so calm and confident, but this afternoon, he was rattled. Very out of character."

Jonah gave it some thought. "We talked about the possibility of a struggle as he comes to terms with his sexuality. Remember? Perhaps that's what going on. Make sense, doesn't it?"

Matt did remember the conversation. It didn't help what he was feeling right now.

"It reminds me of my namesake, the prophet Jonah. God had a mission for him, but instead, Jonah got on a ship going in the opposite direction. We're told that God created a storm which caused the men on the ship to throw him overboard, where he was swallowed by a fish, which the story said God had also prepared."

"What has that got to do with the lawsuits?" Matt asked, a bit frustrated.

"Sometimes, God has to create a storm of circumstances to get us moving in the right direction. I mean, look at everything that's going on in his life. A friend commits suicide because he can't change from gay to straight, which is one of Winston's primary life-goals. He's had major holes punched in his theology and decides to leave the comfort of his ex-gay group. Suddenly, he's in the local newspaper and rumors about him are rampant, causing him to lose clients and some of his reputation. On top of it all, he's developed romantic feelings for Thumper, which confirms he's spent many years of his life in a program that doesn't work. In his mind, he's in danger of losing his career, his practice, his friends…maybe even his faith. Everything important to him is crumbling. It's like the 'perfect storm' of circumstances. He's bound to be in some serious pain. Maybe he's trying to get back some control."

"What can we do?" Matt wondered aloud, now feeling bad about his judgmental attitude.

"Mainly, we pray for him. Beyond that, we let him know that we're his friends."

"I brought a peace offering," Jonah said as he stuck his head in the office door. "Also known as lunch." He held up the large bag from a local deli.

Winston looked up from his desk, obviously pleased to see him. "That's very kind." He motioned for Jonah to come. He walked in and placed the deli bag on the desk.

"I heard things got a little…*intense* the other day. So I called your receptionist yesterday and found out you didn't have any appointments, and thought you might like to talk. Or we can just eat.

"Are you okay?" he asked once he was seated.

"I've been better."

"Matt feels terrible about what he said to you."

Winston unwrapped the turkey sandwich. "He's looking out for his best friend. Like he always does. I took no offense. He's a good man." He looked over the desk at Jonah. "You're a lucky guy."

"I hope you know that we both love you very much. If you need to back off this case, we will support you."

"I admit it, I'm afraid," Winston confessed. "And I panicked. When that article came out, it felt like my life came crashing down. The executive director of *Full Circle Ministry* is using it to spread rumors about me. I've been getting lots of nasty calls and letters." He related the gist of the messages.

"I'm not trying to bail on Thumper, but this is going to seriously impact my practice, which is made up predominantly with religious organizations that are fairly conservative. If backing off this case can help both of us, then maybe it's a good thing."

"You've got a lot changes going on in your life, that's for sure," Jonah said compassionately. "From leaving the ex-gay group to your decision to help Thumper. I'm sure it's a lot to handle."

Winston took a drink of iced tea. "I'm actually grateful for some of what

I learned in the program, like how to recognize my destructive pattern of acting out with casual, indiscriminate sex. But, I've certainly rejected most of the dogma that I was taught. I can look at it now and see the manipulative tactics the group uses: the guilt, the control, the condemnation."

"I wish we could get Earl to see that," Jonah remarked. Once he reminded Winston of Earl's decision to enroll in a live-in program in Denver, he continued. "He called me a few weeks ago, totally devastated. Apparently, he met some guy there and they had a hot-and-heavy affair. The guy felt guilty and confessed to the group, which got Earl kicked out. He's so bitter and angry now that he's questioning his entire faith and whoring around like it's a catch-up contest."

"I blame the rigidity of those kinds of programs," Winston said, nodding his head. "They tell us it's either-or: either we are in recovery or we're living in sin. There's no middle ground—like reconciling our sexual orientation as a Christian. Folks like my friend Robbie fail...see no way out...and they kill themself. Can't believe I was part of that." The grief was evident on his face and in his voice.

"I hope I'm not being too forward here, but help me understand. Do you still see yourself as ex-gay or straight? Are you...gay?"

"I'm more in paradigm transition," was the simple reply.

When it became apparent that Jonah didn't understand, he went into more detail. "Before I got involved with the program, I was hedonistic, self-absorbed and completely out of control. When I look back, I don't like who I was. Once I embraced my faith in Christ, I worked for years to redefine myself and so much of my energy and efforts were focused on my 'not gay' identity. So I know who I was as a gay man without my faith and I know who I was when I was in the program. What I have to figure out is: apart from the program, and without the trappings of my past sexual addiction... who am I now?"

"I can't imagine what you must be feeling, but please know that I'm here for you."

Winston put down the almost-finished sandwich. "I appreciate that, brother. You've done so much already. I no longer reject the idea that a person can be gay and Christian. I see how you've been able to balance both in your life, and it's a testimony. But what if I don't want to be gay?"

"No one can make that kind of decision for you, but I encourage you not to make a decision based on fear or in reaction to rumors. That's certainly no way to live. What does your heart tell you?"

Winston let out a grunt. "I wish I knew. My heart is as mixed up as my brain lately. For the past few months, I'd been dating this beautiful and interesting woman. We have so much in common and had some wonderful conversations. Recently though, I realized that what I most enjoy is just having someone to spend time with. Since leaving the ministry and my home church, I've been fairly isolated. And lonely. I like her company but I don't necessarily like *her*, if that makes sense. She made it clear that she wants to take our relationship to the physical level, but personal convictions aside, I'm not attracted to her. I'm not sure what that means exactly."

"How did your...uh, girlfriend handle the recent news about your involvement in Thumper's case?"

Winston laughed. "I was dumped." He recounted the conversation with Jonah.

"Well, that's mean."

"But that seems to be the prevailing attitude of my friends. Since the article came out, I can only think of two calls that were positive, and one of those was you. Even my pastor—who I figure is now my former pastor—was pretty judgmental. I guess that's why I reacted and felt the need to make the decision about Thumper's case. I'll call and let him know that I've reconsidered."

"Can I ask a question? Again, if I'm being too personal—"

With a smile on his face, Winston swung both arms out to his side. "Why stop now? Take your best shot."

"Before his accident, did you have...uh, feelings for Thumper?"

"When I met Thumper, I had a solid facade that had worked for years, fooling others as well as myself. Thumper was the first person to see right through it and force me to face the reality that my life was not as secure as I pretended." Winston chuckled. "Yes, I had feelings for him: anger, annoyance, frustration and total fear."

They both laughed.

"Were you and Thumper ever...you know...more than *just* friends?"

"No," was the only answer Winston gave, without looking up from the table.

"Did you want it to be...more?"

Winston seemed to be thinking.

"Of course, I couldn't and wouldn't admit it at the time, but yes, I was instantly...uh, enamored with Thumper. Over time, it grew beyond harmless flirtation. Tried to break it off with him because I knew the feelings were there, but refused to confront them. Then he was attacked and I felt so guilty about the way it ended." There was a long pause, accompanied with the measured release of a sigh. "I sometimes wonder what would have happened if I could have been honest with myself, and with him."

Jonah reached across the desk and placed his hand on Winston. "It's all about timing, my friend. As the book of Ecclesiastes teaches us, 'To everything, there is a season.' You weren't ready. Just like when I first met

Thumper, I wasn't ready, but later, God brought me and Matt together. Everything in its own time and season."

———————————————

After the story appeared in the Dallas newspaper, it was picked up by the Associated Press newswire, and within a few weeks, was carried by newspapers all over the country. Suddenly, Thumper was getting phone calls, asking for interviews. In a single week, he was featured on every station in the Dallas area.

As interest in Thumper grew, more media contacted him. The focus of stories about him would vary, depending on the publication and their audience. Many simply covered his amnesia and what it's like now. One liberal religious publication used his story as a platform to criticize the fundamentalists who fostered a culture that led the mentally sick young man to attack him. They were also scathing in their depiction of his parents for condoning the severe treatment program.

The *Advocate*, the country's largest gay and lesbian news magazine, did an interview with him. He appeared on the cover, with the caption "The End of the Nature v. Nurture Debate?" Thumper was suddenly the poster child for the debate on the origin and curability of homosexuality.

Of course, not all the people who contacted him were positive or supportive. There were prank calls, scores of late-night hang up calls and even some threats. He had to have his phone number changed several times.

Many who followed his parents' ministry were scathing in their condemnation of both his "sinful lifestyle" and his open criticism of his father. Almost daily he received long, Scripture-filled letters, calling him to repentance or warning him of his ultimate destiny in hell.

One Christian magazine—whose primary audience was Pentecostal and charismatic Christians—did a story about his parents and their valiant effort to "redeem their son from the snare of homosexuality." The magazine bemoaned the negative impact the story was having on the Rivers' ministry and noted that several TV stations had dropped all the River's broadcasts and even included a picture of gay-rights activists who had picketed in front of the church. Throughout the article, Thumper was portrayed as a self-serving opportunist. It was even hinted that he didn't have amnesia, but was using the diagnosis to get money from his parents' ministry in order to promote the gay agenda.

The biggest surprise came a few weeks after his appearance on *The Today Show*, when he got a phone call from a New York celebrity management company. When the young woman introduced herself—Clarissa Tibbadeaux—

Thumper admitted that he didn't even know what a celebrity management company does.

"We want to represent you," she replied with perky confidence. "First, we want to sell the rights to your story. We've talked to a couple of publishers and there's lots of interest. We think it would be a bestseller book. Maybe even a movie deal. We'll ensure that you get top dollar."

He'd laughed and told her, "I don't even remember my story, so how do we make it into a book?"

Though she pressed him for a decision, he promised to have his attorney call her to discuss it further. In the end, she was right about the interest in his story, and the money; he was offered a substantial advance by a national publisher.

"What are you going to do with the money?" Matt asked when the four of them were having dinner.

"I've already sent two thousand dollars to Marti to help with the expenses getting ready for the baby." Then he grinned big. "Beyond that…like they say on TV, we're going to Disneyland."

TWENTY-NINE

IT WAS THEIR LAST FULL DAY in California before flying back to Texas. Though his friends originally figured Thumper was kidding when he said they were going to Disneyland, he'd insisted they all join him on the five-day trip. He paid for the plane tickets and a large hotel suite.

It was Sunday, and Matt and Jonah were attending a church service in Laguna Beach with some of the guys they'd met at an *Evangelicals Concerned* event earlier in the summer. Jonah had first learned about the ministry of gay and lesbian Christians when he was researching the issues of the Bible and homosexuality. They invited Thumper, but he declined. Winston then suggested they all meet up for lunch after the church service.

After breakfast, Winston and Thumper spent the morning browsing the shops and galleries of Laguna Beach. Thumper bought a gaudy Hawaiian-style shirt and several souvenirs.

"This is like my first vacation, so I need something to, you know... remember it."

When he saw Winston admiring a lion sculpture carved out of wood, he walked over. "Looks like Aslan, from '*Narnia*, doesn't it?"

Winston grinned. "It does, actually."

"I read those books, by the way. *The Chronicles of Narnia.* You told me they were your favorite, so as soon as I got home from the hospital, I had Mom buy them for me."

Winston cocked his head. "You remember that?"

"Absolutely. Read them twice. They are amazing."

Thumper ran his finger over the smooth back of the lion. "This would look great in your apartment," he noted. "By the picture window, on that small table."

He could see that Winston liked the idea, so he bought it as a gift, over lots of ignored objections.

After dropping off the bags in the car, they decided to walk on the beach. It was heading toward noon, so the area was beginning to get crowded.

"I love the sound of the ocean," Winston remarked as they walked. He'd taken off his shirt to soak in some of the July sun.

The sight of Winston's well-sculpted body made Thumper horny, which in turn, made him queasy. So he focused on the sound of the waves to help him relax, much like he'd done in his sessions with "Doctor Dreary." Ironic, since it was those sessions that were now causing the nausea.

Bastard, he thought.

"Uh, I know about the problems you've been having because of my case," Thumper muttered, kicking the water with his feet. "They think that you and I are—"

"It's not your fault," Winston interrupted, as if anticipating what he wanted to say. "You did not cause this."

"You've lost clients because of me. People are saying bad things about you. Because of me. It *is* my fault."

He wanted to cry and it must have showed, because Winston pulled him close into a tight hug. Winston's warm breath drifted across his ear and down his neck. It felt great, but caused an embarrassing effect he knew could not be hidden in his shorts. He turned his head a little and looked up. Winston slowly moved his face downward to kiss him. A sudden rush of emotion went through Thumper, like a shiver of feelings. And just as suddenly, he got sick and threw up on the nearby rocks.

They immediately left the beach and went to the restaurant where they'd arranged to meet Jonah and Matt. Winston was embarrassed and annoyed at his actions and concerned about the impact on Thumper. He walked to a nearby convenience store and got something to help with the nausea.

"Is everything okay," Jonah asked when they walked up to the table and saw Thumper taking the pink pills.

"We were talking about some of the crap that's been happening to me since the article came out," Winston related. "Then he got a little queasy." He hoped his white-lie account would protect both of them from the embarrassment of a more truthful explanation.

Matt apologized for telling Thumper about the negative reactions from the newspaper article.

"Like I told him," Winston pointed to Thumper, "This is not your fault. It's Dan Larson. He's telling people that I'm back 'in the lifestyle.'" He used air quotes to highlight the phrase. "And since I'm handling Thumper's case, he also suggested that I'm sleeping with him."

"It's not true," Thumper informed, as if there was any doubt. Then he looked over at Winston and winked. "Sad, but not true."

The overt flirt made Winston blush.

"Talk about the worst punch line ever to a lawyer joke: I have a lawyer who won't screw his client."

"Has the drop in clients stopped?" Matt asked.

Winston took a sip of his lemonade. "I lost most of my major religious clients. It definitely is having a huge financial impact. Good thing I have…

or had…a savings account. But I've picked up several nonprofit organizations from the publicity generated by Thumper's case. They aren't big clients, but I'm satisfied."

"What are you going to do about this Dan-person who's spreading the rumors?" Jonah questioned.

"I'm honestly not sure. 'Turn the other cheek' only goes so far."

"Gotta love Christians." Thumper's statement carried a marked animosity.

"You do know that not all Christians are like that, don't you?" Winston pointed out.

Thumper gave it some thought, with an accompanying frown. "I know y'all aren't like that. But I've also learned there are too many who are, and most of them don't even think y'all can be Christian. I have no interest in the kind of religion practiced by my parents and those like them. My personal faith experience is gone with my memories. God is a vague concept to me."

"I'm so sorry, Thumper," Matt said, reaching across and squeezing his hand. "I'm always so flabbergasted at what this amnesia stole from you. And how strong you are in dealing with it."

"Hey, I'm doing good. And that's because of you…and Jonah…and Winston. You guys are my family. And for now, y'all are my faith, too."

Without thinking, Winston reached over to pat Thumper on the arm, in a show of concern. But he actually missed and placed his hand on Thumper's bare leg. The touch caused an barely-perceptible gasp from Thumper. For a brief moment, Winston didn't move his hand, enjoying the feel of Thumper's skin.

The experience would have been better had there been more privacy; Matt and Jonah were sitting across the table. Matt was frozen in mid-bite and Jonah had to poke his boyfriend in the ribs to distract the stare.

Winston removed his hand and exhaled a loud, deep breath. "Better stop that. Don't want to add fuel to the rumors."

Thumper said he wasn't feeling well and excused himself.

THIRTY

"My name is Alan, and I'm a new creation in Christ."

Winston stood in the hall, out of sight of those in the room and listened. He knew the routine and almost instinctively repeated the expected response with the rest of the group: "Praise God for His work of restoration!"

The *Circle* met once a week in a large meeting room at the ministry's facilities, a few blocks south of Dallas' medical district. The room was decorated—if it was accurate to even use that word—for function. There was an entire wall of whiteboards that were used for training new leaders, as well as the ongoing workshops conducted for those in the restoration program. Another wall had several cork boards, replete with pertinent announcements, advertisements from supporting businesses, personal items for sale and colorful flyers advertising local events—all pre-approved prior to posting. Metal racks contained an assortment of religious literature, evangelism tracts, and brochures about the *Full Circle Ministry*. There was a table of books for sale, covering topics that concentrated on the issues surrounding sexual brokenness, including theological treatments of the sin of homosexuality, biographies of those sharing how they had successfully changed their sexual desires and the usual assortment of Bibles.

The *Circle* meetings were essentially the same each week. The group leader would welcome everyone, followed by prayer requests, a short devotional from the Bible and a lesson from the program curriculum. Then anyone could share about their experience the previous week, which was called the "accountability time." It could be about personal successes, victories over their evil impulses, insights into a program lesson or questions for the group. However, most of the time was usually focused on those who had experienced a failure during the week—almost always a lapse in sexual behavior.

Winston stepped into the room and loudly cleared his throat. Alan, who was about to launch into his discourse, stopped in mid-breath.

"Sorry to interrupt." He looked around the circle. "Please forgive the intrusion, guys, but I need to speak with Dan—"

"This is not the time nor place for this," Dan bellowed. "You are disrupting our meeting."

He moved into the room, but stayed outside the circle of chairs.

"I get that, Dan. But I've left you six messages. Six! If I didn't know better, I'd think you're avoiding me."

There was usually at least one new person visiting for the first time, sometimes out of personal curiosity, but most often because of parental or pastoral pressure. The weekly Circle meeting was the only regular activity that anyone could attend; the other meetings and workshops required enrollment in the program and the first month's tuition in advance. Though occasionally they held open workshops on topics related to the issue of homosexuality and the Christian, including seminars for local ministers.

The group was visibly uncomfortable with the two-way conversation going on around them. Several squirmed in their seats, a few talked among themselves. Most looked to Dan for some kind of direction.

"Who is he?" Alan asked Dan.

Winston didn't recognize Alan either and figured he must be new to the group.

"He used to be part of the ministry, but he went back into the lifestyle."

The answer came from Joseph Weston, who served on the leadership council and had been involved in the group for many years. He was another of the ministry's success stories—once a well-known drag queen, now married to a former lesbian from the women's group.

Winston stepped between two chairs and entered the circle.

"I know that's what you've been told, Joseph. Dan would like you to believe it, but it's not the truth."

"Why are you here?" Dan questioned.

"When I left the program and the board, it was because I could no longer support the mission of the organization. You and I discussed it. In the privacy of your office. Once I resigned, I didn't talk to anyone about our conversation and I didn't go around bad-mouthing you or the ministry. What do I get in return? You lie to my clients, telling them I've abandoned my Christian faith, and even falsely accuse me of having an affair with a client. Why do you feel the need to discredit me to validate this ministry?"

Dan huffed and crossed his arms on his chest. "I have no idea—"

"Don't compound the lying, Dan. They told me what you said; one of them even showed me the e-mail you sent her. I want you to stop spreading untrue rumors about me. And please stop picking on my client. He's suffered enough at the hands of Christians. So I'm appealing to you as a brother in Christ—"

"Oh, that's rich," Joseph hissed, with both hands on his hips. "You want him to be a brother in Christ, while you're defending that unrepentant homosexual—"

He took a step toward Joseph, causing him to freeze in silence.

Listen to me, you prissy, pretentious little queen.

That's what he wanted to say. Instead, he stood silently in the middle of the group for a few moments. Then, he closed his eyes and took a deep breath.

"My name is Winston. I am a new creation in Christ."

There was a spattering of those who started to repeat the rote response of affirmation, but it trailed off quickly into an uncomfortable silence.

Winston opened his eyes and looked directly at Dan. "I am a new creation in Christ…and I'm gay."

Several in the group gasped and Joseph flopped down on the metal chair in his always dramatic fashion.

"I'm a Christian because I made a choice to trust Christ," Winston continued. "But I'm gay because that's the way God made me. They are both a gift from God, and I will not deny either."

Dan now had a smug look on his face. Winston sadly shook his head as he moved to leave the circle, but stopped and turned again to the group.

"Don't be deceived, brothers," he said through a sincere smile. "Just because I'm not having sex"—he paused to emphasize that point, again looking at Dan—"doesn't change my sexual orientation. That's only behavior. And even though I'm not in this group doesn't mean God has abandoned me or that I have abandoned God."

As he walked out the door, he heard Alan. "Is that true?"

He was more nervous now than when he faced down the *Circle*.

Why? he wondered. *They are my best friends.*

After he left the meeting, he called Jonah to see if he could come by to talk.

"Is everything okay?" Matt asked as soon as they all sat down in the living room.

"Are you having second thoughts about my lawsuits again?" Thumper had a worried look.

Jonah laughed. "Welcome to tonight's episode of *I've Got a Secret*." He looked at Winston. "You certainly know how to build anticipation. Sorry for the third degree. The floor is yours."

Winston took a deep breath and launched into the story of his visit to the *Circle* meeting. He told them the details, including the confrontation with Joseph and the reaction of Dan.

"I felt it was important to deal with Dan," he concluded. "I was not intending to disrupt the meeting. Just thought it would get his attention so we could talk."

"You did the right thing," Jonah encouraged. "And you did it in your usual smooth, lawyer manner."

"Wish I could have been there to see their faces," Matt said.

Winston thanked them. "There's more. In the end, before I left, I confessed to the group…I was finally able to admit…I'm gay," he said through a tremor in his voice.

The table was silent, as if waiting for more. "I'm guessing this is not much of a surprise to you guys."

"Well, it's not quite as startling as finding out about Liberace," Matt joked. "But the important thing is that we love you."

"How are you doing?" Jonah asked.

Winston thought for a second. "I think it's going to be a major adjustment. I've spent so much time, energy and effort not being gay. Or more precisely, being not-gay. I'll need to unlearn and rethink. I don't even know how to relax and just feel what I feel. To be honest, it scares the shit out of me. Does that make sense?"

"It does to me," Jonah said. "As Christians who are gay, we're told what we feel is wrong and that we must fight those desires. We can never allow ourselves to truly give in, for fear of what might happen. Like rejection by our family, our churches. Not to mention that eternal damnation thing. It can take a toll."

"Emotionally, I'm a mess. But spiritually, I'm doing okay. And I owe much of that to you guys. Your lives are proof that so much of what I believed was false."

"Trust me, it will all fall into place," Jonah offered. "It did for me and I know you'll be fine in no time."

"Just know that we're here for you," Matt assured.

"Dan's probably already on the phone to our mutual contacts," he said, staring at his folded hands.

Thumper, who'd been uncharacteristically quiet, spoke up. "Well everyone knows: it ain't gossip if it's done as a prayer request."

Winston reached over and took Thumper's hand. "I hope you know how much I appreciate what you've done for me."

There was a surprised look on his face. "Me?"

He placed his hand on Thumper's face, but withdrew it quickly; he didn't want to cause any nausea reactions.

"You don't remember, but when you came into my life, it was the beginning of my journey into truth. Of living authentically. I am thankful for that."

"Well, as the Good Book tells us, 'You shall know the truth, and the truth will make you free.'" He reached up and touched where Winston's hand had been. "Now, if I can help you *feel* those homosexual feelings…you just let me know."

"Quoting the Bible and making a lewd proposition," Matt teased. "That's the Thumper we know and love."

THIRTY-ONE

"Do WE SAY ANYTHING?" MATT ASKED.

"Have you talked to Winston?" was Jonah's response.

They were standing in the kitchen, refreshing their drinks. Thumper and Winston were in the living room—with the movie paused—waiting for them to return.

"What if he doesn't even remember and then we bring it up?"

Jonah agreed it was a good point. "But what if he does? I'd hate for him to go through it alone...or to think we forgot."

Matt walked to the kitchen door and stuck his head out into the small dining area, looking around the corner to the living room. "Winston, could you...we could use your help in here, please."

"I heard all the whispering," Winston said as he walked to the kitchen door. "If you guys need some alone time, I can certainly take Thumper to a movie. He never seems to tire of watching—"

"Do you know what next week is?" Matt asked.

Winston crossed his arms and leaned against the kitchen pantry door. "If you knew how many times I've typed that date in all the legal filings, you wouldn't have to ask. I wish I didn't."

Jonah looked at Winston. "Does Thumper remember?"

"Do I remember what?" The question came from around the corner.

"Dammit," Jonah muttered.

"If you're going to keep secrets from me, y'all might want to avoid a room with no door and a pass-through window."

Thumper stood in the doorway and looked at them, waiting for an answer.

Winston took the lead. "Sunday is August sixth. It's the one-year anniversary of your...accident."

A thoughtful look came over Thumper, but he remained silent.

"We weren't sure if you'd want to talk about it," Jonah said in a gentle tone. "We didn't want to bring up any bad memories."

"A year," he mused softly. "And I still have no memory of any of it. I kinda remember stuff after I woke up, but actual days and months are fuzzy until after I moved back home to Birmingham."

Matt walked over and hugged him. "Are you okay, sweetie?"

"Is there anything we can do?" Winston asked. "We'll do whatever you want to do."

Suddenly, Matt started giggling. He held Thumper, both of them shaking with laughter. Matt looked at Winston. "He said you could take off your shirt and give him a lap dance. That would make him feel better."

Winston gave a grunt and turned toward the living room. "I can tell you're real broken up."

Thumper grabbed him by the arm. Winston turned and Thumper moved in close. Matt honestly thought Winston was going to lean down and kiss him.

"I do appreciate that you," Thumper said, not taking his eyes off Winston. "That all of you are concerned about me. I know how fortunate I am. From what I've heard about the attack, I should be dead, or a vegetable. It's not that I don't have feelings about what happened to me, but the actual day is not the issue. Does that make sense?"

They all mumbled a response. Matt kissed him on the cheek. "We'd never want to do anything that would hurt you," he explained.

"I love that I have such good friends. You guys are the best." He winked and smiled at Winston. "Ready to get back to our musical movie marathon? I'm betting in the end, Dolly Levy gets her man."

Winston gave him a sweet return-smile and the two of them walked back into the living room.

"It's like watching a sick, cosmic soap opera," Matt complained softly to Jonah when they were alone again. "They have feelings for each other, but they aren't together. Something's always keeping them apart. That's just wrong."

"Give 'em time, babe. Think about it: Thumper has no past, and is trying to rebuild his present. Winston has spent years trying to overcome his past, and now, he's unsure about his present. They both have lots to overcome."

"It would also be unethical."

They turned to see Winston standing in the doorway.

"Thumper wanted another Sprite." He held up an empty soda can, as if his presence needed an explanation.

"I'm his attorney, so a relationship of that kind would be highly inappropriate."

"We're just a couple of hopeless romantics," Jonah apologized.

Winston walked past them and grabbed a can from the refrigerator. "And well-meaning matchmakers, with such bad timing."

Matt sniffed. "Well, I always believe in a happy ending."

"Remind me never to watch *The Notebook* with you," Winston said with a grin as he headed back to the living room.

In September, Winston learned Thumper's parents wanted to settle their case before it went to court.

"I suspect it has to do with all the publicity," Winston told the guys. "It can't be good for their ministry that Thumper is in the newspapers, on TV and in magazines talking about what they did to him."

Several weeks later, a check arrived, and shortly afterwards Thumper received a short note from his mom letting him know they had resigned the church, were leaving the TV ministry and moving to a Christian retirement community in Orlando. No forwarding address was included.

Much to the horror of Jonah, Matt wanted to know how much money Thumper had received. He shared that he'd gotten a settlement of slightly less than sixty thousand dollars.

Winston quickly added that the money didn't actually come from Thumper's parents, but his father's ministerial malpractice insurance company.

"What are you going to do with it?" Jonah asked.

"Some of it's going into a trust for the baby. Winston is helping me set it up. Most will be invested, and I'll want your help to manage it." He looked directly at Matt, who was still working on his CPA.

"I'm going to give a chunk of it to some deserving gay and lesbian organization, mainly to piss off my parents. And I'm sure I have lots of outstanding legal fees that need to be paid as well. Especially after all the clients he's lost because of my cases."

He grinned at Winston. "Unless you want to take some of it out...in trade?"

"Plus, we still have the other cases," Winston said, ignoring Thumper's lewd offer. "I figure all of them are going to want to get out of the media spotlight quickly, too. Good thing for us that doctor was arrogant enough to keep meticulous notes and detailed recordings documenting everything. They aren't going to want those made public."

"Do you think they'll let it go to court?" Jonah asked.

"I'm confident they'll all want to settle rather than go to trial before a sympathetic jury. From a medical standpoint, we aren't looking for punitive damage, which could happen with a jury. But we are insisting that Doctor Davidson admit culpability. According to the suit, all the defendants must agree to an amount of money that's commensurate with the financial loss suffered by the plaintiff. We're talking about past financial loss and future earnings."

"Don't you just love it when he talks all...*lawyerly*? He's like a younger, sexy version of Atticus Finch."

Winston's face glowed a slight shade of pink. "I have got to read that book."

"For me," Thumper said to Matt, "it isn't about the money. I wanted my parents and their followers to understand what happened to me. It's about making sure they accepted their responsibility for what happened to me."

"In the case of the doctor," Winston continued. "We can't demand that his medical license be revoked, but we are insisting that it be reviewed. We're certain that all the publicity will guarantee that no one else has to endure what happened to my client."

"Thumper, your mother called earlier."

He'd walked in from a yoga class and was surprised at the announcement. He checked his cell phone. "She didn't call me. Do you know what she wanted?"

Matt walked into the living room from the bedroom. "She figured you wouldn't take her call, so she called me. We actually had a pleasant conversation."

"Is everything okay?" he asked tentatively, noting Matt's strange expression.

Matt suddenly smiled, then his chin began to quiver. "You have a daughter, Thumper. She was born this morning, at nine thirty-five. Six pounds, four ounces and sixteen inches long."

Suddenly, he couldn't breathe. "I'm a father," he said softly, as he sat down on the sofa.

Matt squealed and flopped down beside him. "More importantly, I'm an aunt."

Thumper picked up the phone and called his mom. It would be only the second time they'd spoken since he'd come back to Dallas. The conversation was awkward, but cordial.

He learned the baby would be named Loren Michelle Deaton.

"They are going to call her Lori, which I don't understand," she lamented. "I think Michelle is such a lovely name. It was my mother's name, you know."

He did know, but chose to let her talk.

"Your father is doing well, in case you wanted to know."

He didn't, but again stayed silent.

"He's been visiting the nursing home on the property and does a weekly sermon for the old folks there. He misses you very much."

Doubtful, he thought.

"I know Martha doesn't have medical insurance," she said in her passive-aggressive way. "We are helping out, of course."

She'd managed to hit his guilt button—which apparently functioned without the aid of memory. So for reasons he couldn't understand, he felt compelled to tell her about the money he'd already sent and the trust he'd set up for his daughter; he didn't include the detail that he was using their settlement money. And though he had not discussed it with Winston or Matt, he told her that he would be sending a check immediately to help with the medical bills.

He also didn't mention that for the past few months, he had diligently worked to rebuild a cordial relationship with Marti. He'd helped her get into a bigger apartment and paid for most of the furniture for the baby's room. He also sent a generous monthly child support check.

She sniffled and said she was proud of him.

And he believed her.

THIRTY-TWO

THE HOLIDAYS IN DALLAS WITH HIS friends were much different than what Thumper had experienced the previous year in Birmingham. Halloween, he learned, was one of the biggest events on the gay social calendar. Matt brought out photos of past years; all of Thumper's costumes involved a few tight fitting clothes and lots of visible skin.

They all dressed up and went to the annual Street Party on the strip, one of the biggest Halloween events in the country. Jonah and Matt were Bert and Ernie. Thumper opted for the obvious: Rip van Winkle. Winston, after much coaxing by Thumper and Matt, was "hot" as a fireman, complete with the hat, a hose, suspenders and no shirt.

Thumper snickered as he imagined what his father would think of the overt sexuality and decadence witnessed at the event: near-naked men, drag queens, lewd outfits, leashes that didn't involve pets and enough drinking to embarrass Bourbon Street.

"He'd have enough material to fuel his hell-fire-damnation sermons for years," Thumper concluded.

Thanksgiving was much more subdued. Matt and Jonah prepared a turkey and invited several folks from church to lunch. Thumper joined Winston working at a local homeless shelter—one of his clients—by helping prepare and serve a traditional meal. For dinner, the four of them all went to the Black-Eyed Pea on Cedar Springs Road for their own meal together. Afterwards, they had a few drinks and even got Winston on the dance floor at Village Station, one of the most popular gay dance clubs in Dallas.

Thumper was surprised at the moodiness he felt as Christmas approached. He couldn't point to any one reason, but a perfunctory Christmas card from his parents—his mom signed for both of them—was probably a factor. Winston had gone home to Atlanta to visit his parents, and he figured that was also part of it.

Matt and Jonah went out of their way to include him in their celebrations, and even invited him to several church-sponsored events. He declined.

"It may be Jesus' birthday," he said to Matt, "but I don't enjoy being around His groupies."

Around noon on Christmas day, they were surprised when Winston showed up.

"My folks are leaving on a cruise tomorrow, so I'd arranged to come back early."

Thumper's dark mood lifted and he enjoyed the rest of the day. That evening, they all exchanged gifts. The guys had gone in together and bought Thumper an entire box of DVDs—what Matt called the "definitive gay cinema" collection.

Thumper brought Matt and Jonah season tickets to the Dallas Summer Musicals, because he knew that Matt loved *Les Miz* and they both wanted to see *Mamma Mia*.

He struggled with what to get Winston, but found a first edition, autographed copy of *To Kill a Mockingbird*.

On the card he wrote: *To my Atticus Finch. Thanks for believing in me. It matters!*

Seeing the look on his face was worth the money he'd spent.

"Can I tell them my news?"

Winston laughed. "You're the one who wanted to wait. But the paperwork is all done, so yes, you can tell them."

Thumper saw the look on Matt's face. "I'm not pregnant, if that's what you're thinking." He looked at Winston, then back at Matt. "Not that I wouldn't welcome the—"

"I'm helping him with incorporation papers," Winston jumped in. "He's forming his own foundation."

"What will you…your foundation do?" Jonah asked enthusiastically. "What's it called?"

"I want to help organizations who are confronting the issue of religious abuse," Thumper said with great pride and excitement. "I've been doing some research, and it's a huge problem. Not only for gays and lesbians forced into repair programs, but boys being molested by priests, women forced to have sex with pastors, children beaten into submission by fundamentalist parents. I think with my notoriety—especially when the book comes out in the spring—we could bring some attention to the issue."

"He wanted to call it *Crossing the Rivers* as a slam to his parents," Winston said. "I was able to talk him out of it."

Thumper laughed. "They're leaving the TV ministry, but I figure they wouldn't let me use *Rivers of Life,* even though it's my last name, too…so I decided on *Rivers of Babylon*. It's from a song of captivity in Psalms: 'By the rivers of Babylon, we sat down and wept when we remembered Zion.' I think so many people look to their religion as a source of strength and joy, but it ends up being a place of bondage and tears."

"I like it," Jonah said.

Of course, Matt wanted to know how it would be funded.

"Always the accountant," Jonah remarked, causing Matt to stick out his tongue at him.

"I'm putting up the initial money to get it going," Thumper answered.

"More will go in if...when I win the other cases. I'll also designate any money from the book royalties as well. Should be enough to get us up and running, Winston thinks."

"But we're setting it up as a charitable foundation," Winston explained. "That way, we can also raise money."

"I'm getting more invitations to speak to groups, which will be opportunities to talk about religious abuse and my fee will go to the Foundation."

He let Matt know that he wanted him to oversee the foundation's financial operation.

The following week, everyone was stunned when Thumper mentioned he didn't want to go out to the bars on New Year's Eve. "The noise and lights just give me a headache, and I don't like close-quarter crowds. I think I'm gonna stay in and read or watch some TV."

Matt and Jonah laughed. "Well, we'd wanted to stay in, too. We don't do bars these days. That goes double on party nights like New Year's eve."

They commissioned Matt to pick out a marathon of movies with New Year's themes. They watched *Poseidon Adventure*, *Sunset Boulevard*, and *When Harry Met Sally*.

Winston fell asleep resting on his shoulder during the last movie. That was the highlight of the evening for Thumper.

It was the second week of January, and Thumper and Matt had spent the day together shopping for winter clothes. While they were at the mall, Winston called Thumper's cell and said he needed to come by later.

"Probably more legal papers to sign," Thumper had suggested to Matt. "He constantly has me signing something."

As soon as Winston arrived, he waved a thick brown envelope. "Got this from Doctor Davidson's attorney."

He paused, allowing everyone to wait. His trained face gave no indication of what was to come. Then he completed the thought: "They agreed to everything."

Thumper sat down on the sofa, a stunned look on his face.

"What does that mean?" Matt asked.

Winston looked down at Thumper. "Well, for one thing, it means he won. Once he signs these papers, accepting their settlement offer, it's over. A check should be here in a few weeks." He flipped the document around to let Matt and Jonah see the amount.

"Holy shit," Matt squealed. "That should pay the rent for a few hundred years."

"Most of it goes into the Foundation," Thumper said.

"A few weeks ago, they offered much more," Winston informed. "They wanted us to allow the Doctor Davidson to skate on admitting his responsibility. We refused. The two hospitals pressured him to make it go away. He has already resigned from the practice and his privileges have been revoked by both hospitals."

"And the other cases?" Jonah asked.

"It'll be like dominoes now—since the doctor caved, the hospitals and clinic will quickly settle as well. I figure by spring, it'll all be finalized."

Matt jumped up and squealed, clapping his hands together. He and Jonah hugged each other, and then they both hugged Thumper.

Jonah looked back and forth at Thumper and Winston. "What now?"

"No theme parks," Matt commanded. "I love Mickey Mouse as much as the next queen, but I can't take any time off from my classes right now."

"Let's go out to dinner," Thumper proposed as he stood, looking at Winston.

"Yes, let's celebrate." Matt bounced up and down.

"More than a celebration." Thumper was still looking directly at Winston. "A date." He waited for the statement to sink in.

Jonah and Matt were abruptly still and silent. They were all watching Winston, who'd been flipping through the settlement papers. He suddenly looked up to see everyone staring at him.

"You know that can't happen. As your attorney—"

Thumper held up his hand to stop the obvious objection. "That was not directed to my lawyer. Like you said, it's all over. Your legal work is done and Winston DuMont, Esquire is officially relieved of duties as my attorney.

"So, *Mister* Winston DuMont, gorgeous man of my wet dreams, would you like to go out to dinner with me? My treat."

For a few seconds, no one seemed to be breathing, waiting on his response. Winston looked down at the papers, then slid them back into the envelope and tossed them on the coffee table.

"I hope you don't think this is going to reduce my legal fees."

Matt let out a high-pitched squeal.

"We'll wait downstairs." Jonah pulled the reluctant Matt through the door with him.

"I'm not convinced this is a good idea," Winston cautioned once the guys were out of the room. "I'm finally coming to terms with my sexuality. You are still healing, and can't even remember your past, so I'm essentially the first person you've ever dated. I find it all a little...disconcerting."

For a moment, he was afraid Winston was going to call it off.

"But in case you haven't noticed, I'm crazy about you. Have been since… well, before you can remember. I think it's worth the effort."

Thumper let out the breath he'd been holding.

"I want to learn all about you," he informed. "Even if you've already told me. Let's begin with the first time you ever had sex with a guy…"

Winston laughed. "Well, I don't like talking about my sexual past."

Thumper looked up and whispered, "Fair enough. So how 'bout we discuss the *next* guy you're having sex with."

Winston put his arms around Thumper and pulled him close. "I guarantee, it will be *unforgettable*."

He leaned down and kissed him. Thumper instinctively knew that kissing this man was something he'd wanted for a long time—even beyond the gap in his memory.

It was even worth enduring the surge of nausea he experienced afterwards.

THIRTY-THREE

"So, HAVE YOU TWO HAD SEX yet?" Matt's question came as an abrupt change of topic. Jonah cackled and Winston almost choked on his water.

"It's a fair question," Matt said to the obvious objection Thumper was about to voice. "You've been officially dating for several weeks now."

"Besides, you asked us the same thing just after we started dating," Jonah added, looking at Thumper. "Embarrassed the hell out of me. On purpose!"

"We kinda figured it happened last week, on your birthday," Matt said to Thumper. "Beats the hell out of birthday candles, and much more fun to blow."

Winston cleared his throat. "We've decided to take that part a bit slow. For all intents and purposes, this will be his first time...with a man. That's a lot of pressure," he included with a glance at Thumper.

Thumper rubbed his hand across Winston's inner thigh. "I'm sure you'll do fine."

"No sex?" Matt exclaimed. "There was a time when Thumper would dump a guy if he thought sex was not in the immediate future."

"Interesting," Winston mused. "About how long would I have before he lost interest and moved on to a sure thing? Couple of days?"

It was Jonah who answered. "More like a couple of drinks."

"It's not the right time...yet," Thumper pointed out to the hopeful Matt. "I've been working with Doctor Sherry on the nausea issues, and—"

"And I'm dealing with the insecurity of knowing my boyfriend gets sick at the thought of having sex with me," Winston threw in with a chuckle.

Dr. Sherry Langford was wonderful and was helping Thumper deal with the negative side effects of Dr. Davidson's bogus treatment. He started going to her twice a week right after the first of the year.

There was no doubt that he needed help, but the previous experience made him reluctant. *Terrified* would be more accurate. But the birth of his daughter and beginning his relationship with Winston gave him renewed motivation; the loving insistence of his friends was also a factor.

Sherry—who preferred the personal designation over the more formal title of Dr. Langford—was as opposite of Dr. Davidson as possible. She was candid, expressive and intensely funny. At times, she could even be bawdy.

"We've done a good bit of preliminary work," she said during their fourth session. "But I want to know if there's something specific you'd like us to deal with? Is there anything—?"

"Sex," he blurted out.

She looked up from her notes. "I assume that's not a proposition," she quipped with a playful glean in her eyes. "That costs extra."

"My boyfriend and I…well…we decided to take the physical part slowly, but sometimes, when we make out and I…uh, you know…get turned on…I get sick and throw up. Other times, it's not as hard…uhm, I mean, difficult."

"Uh huh," she muttered, and wrote something in notebook. "That's a residual effect of that damned aversion therapy." Then she glanced up at him and grinned. "After all, I've seen your boyfriend, and no one could get sick thinking about having sex with him."

For the next few weeks, they worked on the problem. Surprisingly, she used more hypnosis in the process. He was skeptical that he could relax enough—or trust someone enough—to let himself be hypnotized again. But using the sex manuals and masturbation as a laboratory to test his response, he noticed a distinct difference within a few weeks. He couldn't wait to tell Dr. Sherry about his progress. And when he thought about telling Winston the good news, it actually assisted in one of his "climactic" experiments.

While it was true they'd not had sex yet, it had been a topic of conversation on several occasions. On the drive back to his apartment following a movie, Thumper decided to bring up the subject again.

"Speaking of sex," he said, completely out of context to the conversation they were having about the movie they'd seen. "Doctor Sherry and I feel I'm ready to…you know…take it to the next level."

He waited for what he hoped would be a let's-do-it-now response. He huffed when it became apparent Winston either wasn't listening or didn't care.

"Guess what I got today?" Winston asked quietly, as he turned the car on to Thumper's street.

"A new hearing aid?"

"I heard you just fine. I got the results of my HIV test. Since I haven't had sex in eight years, the results are as I'd expect. But I thought you might like to know before we consummate this relationship."

Thumper swatted Winston. "So you do want to have sex with me?"

He pulled into the parking lot, and looked directly at Thumper. "Of course, you doofus. Probably since the first day I met you, though I wouldn't have admitted it. But we both needed to be ready. I didn't want to rush you and I would never want to add to your pain."

"I guess I should get a test, too. Right?"

"I already made you an appointment with the clinic. Monday morning at nine. I promised to pay them if they'd open the office on Sunday, but they weren't as eager as I am to get this done."

The fact that Winston was eager to have sex made him incredibly horny, and not the least bit sick.

Matt didn't believe they would wait. "My money is on the produce section at Kroger's," he joked to Winston. "I figure you'll grab a long squash, libido will kick in and you'll take him right there on a make-shift bed of Charmin."

"I see you two still tell each other *every*thing," Winston noted with mock exasperation.

But they had waited. And once Thumper's HIV test results came back, the conversation turned more serious.

"In spite of the fact that Matt and Jonah are betting we'll just get naked and go at it like two teenagers on prom night, I'm not interested in a quickie," Winston declared as they were leaving the clinic.

On Friday, Winston sent a huge bouquet of flowers, along with a hand-written card, inviting him to dinner the following evening. Thumper immediately picked up the phone and called Matt at work.

"I don't know what to wear, Mattie."

"I know you have amnesia, sweetie, but surely you remember that sex is done with*out* clothes."

"We need to go shopping. I want the right outfit when I show up."

"Let's see. Where's the best place to buy tear-away clothing?"

What they ended up buying—after hours of trying on many outfits—was a new pair of jeans that didn't look new at all, and a tight, form-fitting knit shirt, with a contrasting over-shirt.

"It's casual," Matt pointed out. "But take the cotton shirt off, show off your physique, and he'll know you mean business."

THIRTY-FOUR

THUMPER SHOWED UP AT THE CONDO a few minutes early. As usual, Winston looked stunning. His black hair was close-cut, with enough on the top to allow for that spiky, disheveled look. The navy pullover shirt he was wearing brought out the blue tones of his hazel eyes, and the fit showed off his physique.

"Right on time." Winston leaned down and kissed Thumper. "I hope you don't mind, but I invited Matt and Jonah to join us for dinner—" He couldn't even finish the line. Thumper's reaction—a combination of surprise and disappointment—reduced him to uncontrollable laughter.

"Being a dick could prevent you from getting one later," Thumper warned as he walked in.

Everything in the condo set the mood for the evening: soft music, low light, candles and a fire in the fireplace. It was a nice, warm contrast to the chilly weather outside.

Winston wrapped his arms around him and held him close. Thumper couldn't believe this was actually going to happen. He'd been antsy all day. Even an intensive workout had done little to help him relax. He could feel Winston's heartbeat and his own breathing rate increased in response.

"I think if you held me like this all the time, the nightmares would go away," he said.

"If I thought that were true, I'd never let you go."

When Winston made the decision to end eight years of celibacy and pursue this romantic relationship, he'd expected more guilt from his years of ex-gay programming, but it had not surfaced. In his heart, he knew how he felt about Thumper and was certain this was right.

For what seemed like minutes, they stood in the embrace.

Thumper moved his head from against Winston's chest and looked up. "Are you…okay? I mean, are you…do you still—"

The question caused Winston to pull away, but still hold Thumper at arm's length. "If I told you I was terrified, would that spoil the moment?"

"Thank God. I'm so nervous, too."

"Then we'll focus on other things. You hungry? I've been cooking all afternoon." Winston walked toward the kitchen. "I pulled out an old favorite of mine: plum-glazed Cornish game hens, with a baked potato casserole and a spinach salad."

"It smells incredible. But you didn't have to go to all this trouble. From what I've heard, I'm pretty easy. I'd sleep with you for the promise of a Pop Tart in the morning."

In the three months they'd been dating, Winston had made a point to steer clear of situations where things might get too "heated up." Most of that time, Thumper had been in therapy to overcome his imposed aversion to gay sex, so Winston didn't want anything to happen that might cause a nausea reaction or hinder the recovery.

Their dates included movies, restaurants, a concert by the local gay men's chorus and lots of time with Jonah and Matt. They avoided too much alone time at his condo or Thumper's apartment to prevent temptation—and raging hormones—from weakening their determination.

"I've found that a hard dick will soften resolve," Winston had told Jonah one afternoon during lunch. "Besides, I want our first time to be romantic and memorable."

When they first sat down to dinner, their conversation became stilted, like some forced episode of *Ozzie and Harriet*. But as the meal progressed and they relaxed, Winston opened up about topics they'd never explored. He told stories about growing up in Atlanta and about his life in New York. He talked about law school, his short modeling career and even included some details of his sexual escapades.

"Whew," Thumper gasped. "That story is making me a bit…warm." He took off the cotton over-shirt.

Winston gave a short whistle at the sight of the tight shirt on his firm torso. "Nice! The trips to the gym are *so* paying off."

Thumper batted his eyelids. He leaned on the table and propped his chin with his hands. "I'm glad you noticed."

Winston slid his chair closer and put his hand on the back of Thumper's neck. He kissed him softly, allowing his hands to move down the front of the taut shirt.

"Do you know that you once bragged to me about how good you were at sex?" Winston remarked in a near-whisper. "That was the first time since entering the restoration program that I was seriously tempted."

A perplexed look, then a frown, came on his face. "Let's hope the skills come back to me you know, like riding a bike. That's assuming I ever knew how to ride a bike," he finished with a shrug.

Winston took Thumper's hand and they moved to his bedroom. They stood at the foot of the bed as he lifted up Thumper's shirt. He slowly, gently moved his hand across Thumper's chest. The first time he'd touched his chest was at the gym, when he walked out of the shower to find Thumper staring at him.

Thumper was still thinner than that day in the gym, but the regular workout routine was visibly effective. Winston's fingers followed the mounds of his chest, moved around his nipples, toying with the baby-fine patch of red hair around each of them. He could hear how his touch was affecting Thumper's breathing.

Winston was not rushing this experience. As his finger moved gradually down Thumper's stomach, the muscles tightened, highlighting the definition of his abs. His hand reached the line where bare skin vanished beneath the jeans. He slowly slid his hand under the fabric, and felt the shiver it evoked.

Thumper enjoyed the slow attention being given to his body, but was a bit impatient. He was ready to see and touch the body that often appeared to him as a memory-flash. He removed Winston's shirt, then moved back to get a better view. "My turn," he informed with a nervous laugh.

He proceeded to slowly remove all Winston's clothing, stopping only for the occasional "Oh My God!" exclamation. As he pushed down the slacks, thinking he would immediately go for the bulge visible through the underwear, he saw the birthmark that had been visible in his flashbacks. He touched it, then rubbed all around it, loving Winston's response.

Once they were both completely undressed, Winston again pulled him close. The feel of skin to skin, body parts touching body parts, was exhilarating. They crawled into bed, then moved up and down each other's body, kissing with passion and vocal acknowledgments of pleasure and intimacy.

"You'd let me know if this is causing you any…*discomfort* wouldn't you?" Winston asked.

Thumper put his lips on Winston's stomach and tasted the skin with his tongue, then answered. "I've waited a long time for this. Essentially, I've waited all my life…at least the life I can remember. I'm ready for this to happen…with you!"

However, in spite of his confident statement, there was some apprehension. He'd read books on the subject and had dreams about the experience— though he could never have imagined how wonderful it would be. But while the manuals gave facts and information—even pictures, they didn't cover protocol. He wasn't even sure if he was doing it right. They'd talked about having sex, but nothing about what they liked.

Not that I'd know what I like with a man.

"You okay down there?"

"Huh?" Thumper mumbled.

"You stopped what you were doing—which I was really enjoying, by the way—and had this far-off look."

Thumper moved up and laid his head on Winston's shoulder. "You liked it? I keep wondering if I'm…you know, doing this right. That I'm…satisfying you."

Winston propped up on his elbow so he could look at Thumper.

"I'm a bit out of practice myself, and I can't speak for the judges, but I thought you were doing a great job."

Winston gently pushed him on his back and crawled on top, straddling his waist. He slowly kissed down Thumper's body. The noise that escaped Thumper's clenched teeth was easy to interpret.

"Holy shit, that feels amazing. If you keep doing that, something's going to explode," Thumper panted.

"That's the goal, isn't it?"

"Not yet. I'm not ready for this to be over." His voice was heavy with strained breathing.

"Trust me, we're far from over," he replied.

In a few minutes, he moved up next to Thumper. "I want to be inside you." he said softly, watching carefully for any cue to a negative reaction.

"I was hoping you'd say that!"

They were both still a bit breathless, lying quietly on the bed—Winston's front cuddling against Thumper's back. It was nearly two in the morning, but neither of them seemed interested in sleeping at this point.

His own eight years of sexual inactivity brought an intensity that was difficult to contain, but it was nothing compared to Thumper's almost unquenchable desire. All inhibitions faded as their mutual pent-up energies were finally given expression. Their lovemaking had alternated between slow, methodical exploration of one another's body to near-frenzied fervor. Then they would change positions and experience additional forms of pleasure.

After the last time—he'd lost count—they showered, which only led to yet another passionate session. Now they were enjoying the intimate interlude.

"I love you," he said, nuzzling Thumper's neck.

He'd resisted the impulse to say it while they were making love, and now felt an immediate twinge of regret. "You told me once that you didn't believe in love, so I hope that doesn't freak you out."

Thumper rolled over and looked over at him.

"I'm not trying to put pressure on you, Kiddo. It's not like because I said it to you, you have to say it back to me. But I went too long unable to admit how I feel, then I almost lost you without you knowing how I feel, so I needed you to know now."

"I don't know what I meant back then, but I think that the person I used to be...well, from what I've learned, I'm different. I've changed."

He slowly rubbed his finger down Winston's sweat-damp stomach.

"I didn't have a past when you rescued me and brought me back here. You've helped me begin rebuilding my life. Everything about you...and us... and tonight is more than I ever could have excepted or anticipated."

Winston leaned in and kissed him tenderly.

"I know I have more healing to do and so much to re-learn, but I cannot imagine my future without you."

He saw that Winston's eyes were watery with emotion.

I love you, too!"

EPILOGUE

Thumper sat quietly on the sofa, listening to the muted sounds of the fountain in the backyard. It was after one in the morning and he'd had a nightmare, waking with an overwhelming sense of anxiety, covered in sweat and trembling uncontrollably. So he got up and went into the living room rather than fighting with sleep.

He no longer lived with Jonah and Matt. In August, he'd used some of his final settlement money to buy an older three-bedroom bungalow on the East side of Dallas, in an area known as the "M" streets, named for the various streets in the areas with that alphabetic moniker: Mockingbird, Merrimac, McCommas. Ironically, he signed the final mortgage papers on August sixth, the two-year anniversary of his attack.

"Can't get away from it," he said philosophically. "That date signifies new beginnings for me."

The house was big, but definitely a "fixer-upper." Matt reminded him that after all the settlements, Thumper could now afford a finished mansion in one of the upscale—or "ritzy," as Matt called it—neighborhoods. But he liked the area and enjoyed the renovation process, which he felt paralleled the rebuilding of his own life.

"But living in a construction area," he'd confessed to Matt, "is even messier than being one."

His first priority had been enlarging the smallest of the upstairs bedrooms. His own life had a wonderful addition: his daughter, Lori. So in keeping with the symbolism, he made room in his house for her. She was still too young to travel the distance from Orlando to Dallas alone, but now he was ready.

The large attic had been converted into a master bedroom, with an additional bathroom. The outdated kitchen needed a complete overhaul, so that was the current, ongoing project.

He would also be converting the other upstairs bedroom into an office to serve as the headquarters for his *Rivers of Babylon Foundation*. That project was scheduled to begin as soon as the kitchen was finished. Also on the "To Do" list, the downstairs bedroom would become a library and reading den.

He walked out on the new sunroom, taking a seat on an oversized lounge chair.

In spite of ongoing therapy, he would still periodically wake from a horrifying dream he couldn't remember, with an overshadowing dread he couldn't forget. The most he could recall, even with hypnosis, was walking alone in darkness, and then fear would envelop him like a malevolent fog.

Dr. Sherry pointed out it was obviously a lingering effect of the attack. "You can't remember the specifics of what happened to you," she speculated. "But your mind apparently retains the terror of being attacked. When you're asleep, you relive the events. But without any details, it's only the fear and panic you must have felt that night."

He leaned back in the chair, closed his eyes and let out a tight breath. "I'm ready for the fear to go away," he whispered, in what could only be called a prayer. Solemn, sincere and desperate.

In a few minutes—not quite asleep and not totally awake—he had a flashback. Suddenly, he remembered a time when he was young—probably eight or nine—and sitting on a pew next to his mom in the church where he'd grown up. For a brief moment, he could hear his father's booming voice, preaching from the pulpit. "When we first see the world, it's covered in darkness. When we first hear God, He says, 'Let there be light.' Light overpowers the darkness and light is stronger than our fear."

Let there be light.

Those words from a forgotten past were now echoing in his consciousness.

Let there be light.

In that instant, it was clear what he needed to do.

"You okay?" came a question from behind him.

He turned and looked back into the house. "Couldn't sleep."

"Another nightmare?"

Thumper nodded as he stood and walked back into the den.

Winston came up behind and wrapped his arms around Thumper's shoulders. He snuggled in, feeling Winston's bare chest on his back. He relaxed.

"What are you doing up?"

Winston kissed him on the neck. "I don't sleep well when you're not in bed."

"You slept alone for years," he teased with a huff, "but after three months—"

"We've been living here almost five months," Winston corrected. "What can I say, you're addictive."

Thumper turned his head to give a more unobstructed access to his neck. "Let's hope they don't develop a twelve-step cure." He moaned as the neck-kissing continued.

"Want to talk about it?"

He leaned his head back into Winston's chest. "Same ol' shit. I'm tired of being afraid and not knowing what makes me afraid. But I think I have a solution."

Winston moved around and stood in front of him, waiting for more. He wasn't sure how his partner would respond, but he took a deep breath.

"I want to meet the man who attacked me."

The look on Winston's face said it all. Before he could reply—or react—Thumper launched into the logic of his plan. "I think if I see him, it might help me put a face to the fear and then maybe put an end to the night terrors. Nothing can be as bad as just being afraid."

They sat down on the sofa. He talked about the memory-flash of his father's sermon. Winston had many concerns and questions, but eventually agreed, with the stipulation—he used that lawyer word—that they meet with Dr. Sherry and share it all with her. This decision gave Thumper some hope.

"How funny…and ironic…is it that a possible solution would come from my Dad?"

"What if it came from God?" Winston suggested. "Maybe God was speaking to you."

Thumper rolled his eyes. "Yeah, well neither of them are high on my speed-dial list these days."

When he saw the look of concerned sadness on Winston's face, he added: "But I'm always open to revelation and repentance on the matter."

"You should get some rest," Winston urged after several minutes of quiet. "You have to be at the airport early."

He looked at the clock over the mantle. "In about five hours. But I have everything packed, and a car will be picking me up. Wish you were going this time."

"Me too. But I'm doing a board training later in the morning. I'll be here when you get home, though."

Thumper liked these short jaunts. He was heading to Austin, the state capitol, and would be talking about hate crimes to a gathering of political leaders, do a book signing at a local gay and lesbian bookstore and would then fly back in the late afternoon. They were having dinner at Matt and Jonah's new condo in North Dallas.

The book about his experience, *What I Know Now* had been released in late spring of the previous year and continued to sell well nationally. It never made the bestsellers list, but the publishers were extremely pleased with the steady sales.

When the book came out, Matt arranged to hold a huge Release Party and book signing at Page Turner bookstore, where Thumper had worked before the attack. Sharon, the owner, had been so supportive during his recover, it was something he wanted to do for her.

During the successful event, Sharon once again joked about him returning to work. "If this national celebrity limelight ever gets boring, you can always come back to the exciting life of retail sales."

Once the book was published, his public appearances and speaking engagements increased. At least once a month, he would speak at an event somewhere in the country; he was especially popular with gay and lesbian organizations. As planned, the events gave him the opportunity to talk about religious abuse and the work of his foundation. Next month, he was going to an event for educators in Atlanta and Winston was going with him. They would spend a few days with Winston's parents.

"And when you get home, I'll help you pack all over again," Winston reminded.

Thumper was excited about their upcoming trip. They were leaving in two days for a two-week vacation. From Dallas, they would fly to Fort Lauderdale, where they were booked for nine days in an upscale resort that catered exclusively to gay men.

"But since I don't intend to wear much, I ain't takin' much," he noted. "I *will* need an entire bag just for sunscreen, though. Redheads don't fare well in the Florida sun. But that won't stop me from laying by the pool to watch all the hot guys watching my hot guy!"

"What makes you think they'll be looking at me?"

Thumper let his eyes move up and down Winston's body. "Have you seen you? Have you ever looked in a mirror?"

From Fort Lauderdale, they would fly to Birmingham to spend a few days with his daughter. Thumper had rented a hotel suite and Marti would be bringing baby Lori. Since he refused to have any contact with his parents, this arrangement made certain he wouldn't accidently see them if they came to visit Marti and the baby at the apartment.

He was pleased with the progress he'd made in establishing a genuine friendship with Marti. She didn't seem to hold any resentment towards him for leaving Birmingham after learning of her pregnancy and had graciously dealt with the news of his sexual orientation.

"I'm kinda relieved," she said after he came out to her. "I always thought it was me. That you just weren't that attracted to me. It just steams me that I lost you to a guy who's prettier than I am!"

He loved that Winston was so supportive of having Lori and Marti as part of their lives. Since Lori's birth, they'd visited Birmingham several times.

"Ready to go back to bed? You need to get some rest."

"I'm not that sleepy."

Winston moved closer, wrapping his arms around Thumper. "I'm betting we could find a way to help you…*relax*."

He looked up into Winston's hazel eyes. "As the Good Lord promised, 'Ask and you shall receive.'"

Author's afterthoughts

Though I did extensive research, I'm not a doctor, a mental health professional or a lawyer. So as a writer, I'll fall back on a 'literary license' defense for any inconsistencies in those areas.

Unfortunately, the work of ex-gay/reparative groups is too real. While some of the people involved may have a sincere desire to help, the movement is <u>dangerous</u>, as I show in the story. I've consciously tried not to exaggerate their beliefs or their processes. I was being factual when I showed that much of what they report as "success" is seriously skewed by faulty record-keeping. I was involved in this movement for years and served as executive director of an organization, so I speak from experience.

The actual treatment protocol in this book is *mostly* my imagination at work. However, instances of "implanted memories" have been documented, though the practice is condemned by legitimate mental health professionals. Aversion therapy is real, and has been employed for years, but its use for the treatment of homosexuality is a violation of the professional guidelines of both the American Psychological Association and American Psychiatric Association. Regardless, it's a known fact that many reparative programs have used it for the (mis)treatment of homosexuals.

I will admit to a preconception in this story: the unchangeable nature of sexual orientation. I believe it's as much a part of our inherent genetic structure as eye color or whether we're right-handed or left-handed. Behavior can be modified using stringent methodologies and intimidation, but actual orientation remains. Science is leaning in that direction, though it is far from a proven concept at this point. But that doesn't change my conviction, which comes across unapologetically in my book.

Finally, I've been a Christian since college. I cherish the truth of the Bible as God's Word and I consider myself an Evangelical, though others who claim that moniker might not agree, much less welcome me into their ranks. I've been an avid Bible student and teacher for 35 years, with 20+ years in the active ministry, most as a Pastor. So I know the Scripture, including those used to condemn homosexuality and homosexuals. As one of my characters learns, it's not as black and white as some might purport.